THE VAMPIRE AND THE SCORPION

BOOK ONE OF THE BLOOD AND VENOM SAGA

K. E. BEALE

CONTENTS

AUTHOR'S NOTE
And Content Warnings

The Vampire and the Scorpion contains on-the-page graphic, bloody violence, injury detail, explicit sex scenes, needles/ phlebotomy, kidnap, and substance abuse. It also contains suggestions or references to child abuse, sexual exploitation, rape, domestic violence, and suicide. As the first book in the series, future instalments may deal with other triggering themes. Reader discretion advised.

Though this can be enjoyed as a stand-alone, straight, romance novel, it's the first in an ongoing series that explores polyamorous, LGBT+ (MMF) relationships, full of misdirection, heartbreak, and drama along the way.

The story is written in British English, so for my American friends, please enjoy our spelling variations of words such as 'realise', 'colour', and 'practise', as well as some of our quirky idioms and slang.

ONE

Bitterness is unattractive, and I didn't bleach my hair only to ruin my image with a sour expression. I took a deep breath to calm my thundering heart. After all, no one would take me seriously if I lost my temper—again.

"I'm not sure I'm the best person suited for this role," I said with all the professionalism of someone in a job interview. It certainly felt like an interview, the way Greg sat opposite me, blue eyes locked on mine, clasped hands resting on the table, lackeys Matt and Chloe sitting either side. He even *looked* like an interviewer, not a trace of stubble upon his pale face, dressed in a white shirt and thin, black tie. Yes, he was one of those weirdos that wore a tie when dressed casually. We couldn't have contrasted more, with me in faded, ripped jeans, and oversized hoodie. He'd side parted his hair, fixed in place with *my* floral-scented hairspray, something he'd won custody of after our breakup—not that I needed it, preferring wax in my newly-chopped, long pixie-cut.

"I said I'd make the costumes. Not run the whole backstage operation," I said.

"Ava, you co-directed the last show. Someone else should have a turn," Greg said. His tone matched mine, but forced politeness came easily to him. He was smirking beneath the surface of his neutral expression. The president of the theatre society should have been a professional actor; his portrayal of sincerity was second to none.

"I'm not saying I want to direct again. I'm saying that I don't think stage manager would be the best role for me. It's an enormous responsibility and I won't have time to commit to it." I tapped my pen against my notepad in time with my twitching foot, the noise echoing throughout the student union's meeting room.

"Jo did it last time," he said, referring to the vice president who sat next to me and the only member of the committee I could call a friend. "It would be nice for her to do something else. Matt and I are writing and directing, so we can't do it."

"And Chloe?"

"I don't think I'd be a good stage manager," Chloe said, joining the conversation, though her eyes remained fixed on her phone, her acrylic nails tapping against the screen with each swipe left.

How she'd secured a role within the society's committee was beyond me, though I guess it helps when you're the president's housemate.

"You have more experience than me," she said.

"No, I don't. At least, not backstage. I offered to make the costumes as sewing is a hobby and I'd cannibalise the old costumes from last term. I'm trying to reduce my workload, not increase it. My tutors are already riding my arse over late submissions." But Chloe wasn't listening. Now using her phone as a mirror, she dabbed at her false lashes with the tip of her finger, pouted her gloss-coated lips and swept back sleek, highlighted hair.

"Perhaps if you actually turned up to lectures, you might not be behind. All you study is video games. How hard can it be?" Greg asked.

I clenched my jaw as I bit back the snappy retort that I was so desperate to unleash, the squeak of my grinding teeth echoing inside my head.

"Hang on," Jo cut in as she saw I was about to explode. "Greg, I think you'd be a great stage manager."

Greg raised an eyebrow, the compliment catching his attention. Jo always said that flattery got you everywhere. She smiled, dimples forming in the cheeks of her heart-shaped face, wide, brown eyes twinkling with hope. "I didn't think I'd like it either, but it's fun, and you've already shown that you can manage people. And it's something you can put on your C.V."

"I can't direct *and* be stage manager," Greg shook his head, not taking the bait. "As I said, Matt and I are directing this one." He jerked his head towards Matt, who was leaning back in his chair, hands resting behind his light-brown faux hawk, biceps bulging, polo shirt pulled tight across his chest as he nodded along to everything Greg said. Their bromance was a strange one; Matt spending most of his free time in the gym and Greg in the library, but they say opposites attract, and since they'd started writing their script, the two of them were inseparable.

"All those in favour of Ava being stage manager?" Greg raised his own hand, Matt and Chloe following suit. Three to two.

"I guess I don't really have any choice in the matter." I leant back in my seat, arms folded.

"We will try to give you any help you need," Greg said, this time unable to hide his self-satisfied grin, his words an empty promise. Last year I'd been thrilled when Greg had won the presidency, especially as I'd secured my position as secretary for another year. We had amazing plans for my final year at Kinwich University. Unfortunately, it ended up as fun as pushing pins under your fingernails. Funny how much can change in one summer.

I stayed silent for the rest of the meeting, my jaw clenched so tight it ached. The others discussed their plans for this week's so-called rehearsals (not that there was anything to rehearse yet), no longer asking for my input. I wanted to interrupt with remarks about how their drama games were just time-wasting exercises to keep the society members occupied while Greg and Matt wrote their shitty little script. It had already taken them two weeks and was only half done. After all, it was a *student's* production—not the next Phantom of the Opera.

Instead of taking the remaining minutes of the meeting, I started doodling a masterpiece of Greg being stabbed by various bladed objects, everything from a shuriken to a claymore. Petty? Perhaps. Therapeutic? Absolutely.

Just quit, I thought. *That will show them. These idiots don't know what they're doing. Just quit!* But I wouldn't. It was an itch I had to scratch, even if it left me red, raw, and bleeding.

Chloe snapped me out of my trance when she brought up this evening's social event. Organising socials was her one and only responsibility, the role of 'social organiser' having been made solely for her by Greg. I'd never enjoyed the socials, but this one in particular would be torture.

"Club Clique is having a Traffic Light Party tonight and we've already had ten people say they are going. We will probably have more people tag along after tonight's rehearsal."

Well-fucking-done. I don't know what impresses me more: that you organised a social event, or that you can count to ten.

"Are you coming tonight?" Jo asked me.

"Yeah." I fixed Greg with a hard stare. "We agreed to wear amber stickers to keep things civil. Right?"

"Yes," he said. "It's important that all committee members attend the socials to set an example, and this would probably be the best way to prevent any hurt feelings."

"Great. Are we done here? I need a fag." I sprung to my feet, the chair's legs scraping on the floor, making the others wince. "See you outside," I said to Jo as I strode past her towards the door, letting it slam behind me.

When Jo met me in the smoking area for our pre-rehearsal cigarette, she didn't mind listening to me bitch about Greg, even when it continued into the rehearsal itself, and even while we changed into dresses and heels backstage. But she wasn't able to hide her annoyance by the time we were queuing up outside the club.

"Forget about him and enjoy yourself," she said, her breath misting in front of her as her slight frame disappeared into her thick winter coat.

I could barely feel my toes, only just covered in my elegant, yet impractical shoes. The blister on my ankle was begging for a plaster and my thoughts drifted to my Doc Martens lying backstage, waiting for me to pick them up the following morning.

We were near the front of the queue, crammed behind a barrier alongside the club, a shabby-looking building covered with missing person posters—a detail I'd found unnerving in my first year, but had increasingly grown numb to.

"She won't forgive Greg that easily," said Hayley, a student in her second year and one of the few within the society I'd befriended. She linked arms with me and pulled me tightly to her side. Though skinny, she had an iron grip that I couldn't escape. "Typical Scorpio. Too stubborn."

"I prefer the term *determined*, thanks," I said, giving her a playful nudge in the ribs.

"Obsessive."

"I think you mean passionate."

"Rude."

"I'm *not* rude! Just honest. *You're* rude!" We grinned at each other.

I rarely took teasing well, but I didn't mind it coming from Hayley. Though I'd only known her a year, she was more like a sister to me, having bonded over the fact that our biological parents were no longer around, hers having kicked the bucket when she was a baby, and mine preferring the company of their lovers. For my mother that usually meant someone violent, or a drug user. Sometimes she'd outdo herself and find a violent drug user. For my father, that meant cocaine and ketamine. Classy people, my parents.

"If I call you passionate instead, will you get me a drink?" She fluttered her long eyelashes. Not that she needed to; she always looked gorgeous, with full, pink lips, cheek bones a model would envy, and long, golden curls.

"Go on then. First round is on me."

We handed our IDs to the doorman, who waved us through to be greeted by a young man brandishing stickers.

"Hello, ladies," he said. "Tonight's theme is a Traffic Light Party, and so you may choose one of three stickers. Red is a warning to others to keep their hands to themselves. Amber is neutral or playing hard to get." He gave us a cheesy wink. "Green means you are D.T.F or—" He then silently mouthed the words, *'Down to fuck'*. Forming a complete traffic light ourselves, Jo took a red sticker, I took amber, and Hayley took green. "One last thing," he said, "make sure you don't—"

"Walk home alone," we all said in unison, having heard the warning every time we'd visited the club.

"Don't worry, we won't let the goblins and witches get us." I gave Hayley another nudge, who in response rolled her eyes, exasperated that I didn't take her outlandish theories seriously. "Oh, don't get upset, Hay. Come on. Let's get you that drink."

Club Clique was already heaving with people. Unsurprising, as it was the most popular club in Kinwich. The floor was sticky under foot, spilt drinks and bodily fluids. Among the usual stench of stale beer and sweat, the sickeningly sweet smell of mixers and spirits assaulted my nose.

After paying our entry fees and leaving our coats in the cloakroom, we made a beeline for the bar. As promised, I bought the first round, and then hovered near the bar, knowing that round two was soon to follow.

After round three and a strategic trip to the toilet for a swig from Hayley's concealed hip flask, I was ready to face the dance floor. Jo had spotted one of the taller members of the society within the crowd and we made our way over to join him. I kept my eyes peeled for Greg and spotted him dancing with a girl who I recognised from the theatre society, someone I knew was after a lead role. But at least he was wearing an amber sticker. My mind at rest, I sought other society members. The best thing about clubs is that it's impossible to make small talk. But after enough vodka, I was happy to flail in a drunken stupor, screaming above the music, "*I love this song!*"

Hayley was in her element, her tight, green, sequin dress hugging her slender frame, and long hair tossed from side to side as she swayed to the music's hypnotic rhythm.

It was time for shots. Hayley offered to buy this round, but knowing she was strapped for cash, I paid for mine and Jo's, but gave her a suggestive look when I noticed her buy another for some random guy she'd met. I didn't recognise him from our group, but going by his youthful appearance, I figured he was another student. Dressed entirely in bottle-green, he wore a top hat, tail coat, and matching trousers. A total peacock. Whilst I had no objections to guys in fancy suits, wearing one to a club was so pretentious that normally I wouldn't have given him a second look. Tonight, however, thanks to the ungodly amount of alcohol I'd consumed in such a short time, I would have gladly danced the night away with him—or anyone.

He tipped his hat to Hayley as she handed him his shot, and the four of us knocked them back. I turned to leave them to their mating dance and perhaps find a conquest of my own when I spotted Greg grinding up against the backside of the girl I'd seen him with earlier. But now, emblazoned across his chest, was a green sticker. It seemed to illuminate the entire room, penetrating through the crowds and into my eyes. In that moment, there was nothing else. Just the flash of green that consumed me. I stood dumbfounded, mind racing at an impossible speed but my body immobile. Until something inside me snapped. Heat flared through me, my muscles tensing.

You... You promised me...

As though possessed, I marched up to him, ripped the sticker away, scrunched it into a ball, and threw it at his head. When this received nothing but a sneer, I slapped him—hard—across his repugnant face.

"What?" I could just about hear him force a laugh over the pounding bass—or was that my heartbeat hammering in my ears?

Turning on my heel, I stalked off, pushing through the dancers towards the doors labelled '*Smoking*'. Outside, a wall of fumes and icy cold air struck me.

I blinked back tears, fumbling to open my clutch bag before groping inside, the orange glow of the heat lamp insufficient to see. Retrieving my cigarettes, I put one to my trembling lips, but to my dismay could not find a lighter. I'd left it in my coat pocket, sitting useless inside the cloakroom. I wasn't going back in there. Not until I'd calmed down.

I looked around for a familiar face. No one.

Resigning myself to be *that* smoker—the one who had to scrounge off strangers—I plucked up the courage to ask someone for help, when I caught sight of a bottle-green top hat in the doorway.

TWO

My arm glitched out, flapping in the air, trying to catch the attention of Top-Hat-Man. I grimaced as he started laughing, yet his large, friendly eyes shone with warmth.

"There you are!" His voice carried over the chatter. He slid through the sea of smokers, who shuffled out of his way. He appeared to be around my age, early twenties, his goatee still a little fluffy. It was dark-brown, matching the shaggy mop of hair barely concealed beneath his hat. "I was looking for you," he said with a goofy grin. "Is your hand alright?"

I flexed my fingers, palm still tingling. "Yeah, it will live to see another day." I shook my cigarette packet. "You haven't got a lighter, have you? I need something to calm me down."

He plunged his hand into his pocket, withdrawing a clipper. "Only if you got a spare ciggie for me."

He flashed his white teeth. Strange. I'd not met a smoker with teeth that perfect.

"Seems like a fair trade." I flicked the bottom of the box, a cigarette popping out. "Sorry, I didn't catch your name. I'm Ava."

"My name is Austin. And that's quite the first impression you made!"

"Oh, shut up." I smirked, lighting my cigarette and handing his lighter back.

"I'm only teasing." He sparked his cigarette, turning his face away to exhale a large plume of smoke. "So, what was that all about? Your mate—the tall one—is giving that guy hell. He must have done something pretty bad."

I envisioned Hayley on one of her tirades: her blue eyes bulging and nostrils flaring as she spat venom, always going for the jugular.

"To cut a long story short, we used to date, and now we don't. We'd agreed to wear amber stickers tonight, but he changed his sticker to green." I flicked ash from the end of my cigarette, then cringed. "That sounds really childish, doesn't it?"

Austin rubbed the back of his neck, eyes averted. "Maybe... a little?"

I flicked my cigarette again, more forcefully than was necessary, then sighed. "I shouldn't have slapped him. And I know I need to move on. I've heard it enough times." I adopted a shrill voice and plastic smile that was more like a wince. "'*Oh, just let it go! Forget about him.*' But it is easy for them to judge. When they have their heart crushed, they can go crying to Mummy and Daddy—someone who loves them. But when Greg dumped me, I was once again alone. Completely." My eyes burning, I turned from Austin, taking a deep drag from my cigarette. "Sorry, I can overshare after a drink."

"I'm really sorry to hear all that." Austin was looking away from me.

Perhaps he'd noticed the tears welling and was trying to spare me humiliation, or perhaps I was making him feel uncomfortable. I gave myself a little shake and pinched the tears from my eyes as I regained my composure.

"But you know the best revenge is to be happy, right?" he said. "Just imagine his expression when he sees you don't need him anymore. You're feeding his ego when he sees you upset."

I tilted my head, surveying Austin. "What are you suggesting?"

"Well, you could try to part on friendly terms?"

I snorted. This wasn't an option.

"Or you can fight dirty."

I grinned. "Now you are speaking my language."

Austin ripped the amber sticker from my chest, then tore the green sticker camouflaged against his tailcoat and pressed it across the top of my breast, making my skin tingle on contact. "If he can wear green, why can't you?"

My smile widened. "I like the way you think, Austin."

"Come on, let's go back inside. I'll get you another drink, and we'll dance together."

"What about Hayley, my friend? You seemed pretty keen on her?"

This was the only problem when going on the pull with Hayley. I wasn't overweight, but I wouldn't have minded losing the extra cushioning, and I suspected anyone I went home with would be disappointed after I'd removed my makeup.

"Your friend is lovely, but I have seen her dancing with two other guys tonight. She's probably forgotten about me already."

"I doubt it," I said, looking him up and down and giving the arm of his tailcoat a little tug. It was loose on him; he was scrawny as he was tall. "But if you're sure."

"We could even leave at the same time, so it looks like we're going home together, if you know what I mean," he said, wiggling his eyebrows. "After all, it's dangerous to walk home alone."

His gaze flicked to a missing person poster slapped on the wall, and for a moment I thought his playful expression wavered, but when he looked back at me, his cheeky smile was back in place.

"Just *look like* we're going home together?"

"Who knows what will happen?" He winked before stubbing out his cigarette butt on the wall. I mirrored him. "Come on." He held his hand out to me. I took it.

He guided me straight to the bar. I didn't need another drink. My lips were already numb, but throwing caution to the wind, I accepted the shot he handed to me.

"Cheers." Austin tapped his plastic shot glass against mine before necking it and returned to the dance floor. Hayley threw herself around me, giving me a tight squeeze, pinning my arms to my sides.

"Jo has gone home," she shouted in my ear to be heard over the music. "But she tore Greg a new arsehole. I've not seen her that mad before."

"I'd have loved to have seen that!" If sweet, mild-mannered Jo was losing her shit at Greg, then she was absolutely ready to go home. But I wasn't. "Do you mind if I dance with Austin?"

Hayley frowned, but soon realised who I was talking about. "You go for it! I'm trying to get with Matt tonight."

We looked at the treasurer, his arms around the shoulders of his mates, jumping off-beat to the music. His faux hawk was limp, drooping to one side, and he'd spilt a drink down his shirt.

"Whatever floats your boat, Hay!"

She'd told me she fancied him, but I didn't see the appeal myself. Not that I was complaining; if Hayley were to get jealous, that could ruin my plan, but with her blessing I prepared to make that pompous worm, Greg, squirm.

Austin's hand was at my waist, pulling me into his body, facing him. Blood rushed to my cheeks as I put an arm around his neck.

What do I do with my other hand? And what about my legs? Do I move them? Do I sway on the spot? What do I do?!

I licked my numb lips, the rest of my face now equally anesthetised.

Who cares what you do with your arms and legs? No one will remember in the morning. Have fun!

My instincts took control. One hand in the air, I gripped onto Austin with the other, my hips swaying to the rhythm of the beat. Austin's lips were moving, singing along to the lyrics of whatever trashy song was playing. He bobbed from side to side, stiff, like it was his first time dancing. The hand that had been at my waist slipped down to my ass, pulling me closer. One of his legs was now between mine.

Peeking over his shoulder, I looked around for Greg and soon spotted him, flashing him a wicked smirk before turning my attention back to Austin. He pulled me in even closer, so that now I was grinding against his thigh. Heat radiated up my neck, my mouth suddenly too wet.

"Do you feel that?" he said against my ear.

"What do you—oh!" There was a firmness pressing up against me I suspected was not his keys, sending a spasm through my womanhood.

"I like the way you dance."

I wrapped both arms around his neck, our faces only separated by his height, his breath warm against my mouth. His lips were close. So close. Impossibly close...

I closed the space between us, my lips on his. Soft, smooth, delicious, his fuzzy goatee tickling my chin.

"Whoa! Get in there, Ava!" someone said, but they were a million miles away. Unimportant.

Time stood still.

The hand on my ass tightened, sending another shock wave between my legs, flooding my mind with impure thoughts. *What would Austin look like naked and between my thighs?*

Lights went up in a blinding flash. The spell was broken. How long had we been kissing?

A voice rumbled through the speakers, telling everyone to collect their items from the cloakroom, to '*Go home safely*' and '*Be mindful of your neighbours*'. Those who'd survived to closing time were looking around, squinting, just as dazed as I was.

"So, will you let me w-walk you home?" Austin asked.

His voice wavered as he looked at me with raised eyebrows and a hopeful smile. Drunk as I was, I recognised nerves when I saw them.

"I'd like that."

In the harsh, white lights, I saw Austin properly for the first time. His skin was flawless and full lips so inviting, I wondered how I could have ever considered him '*not my type*' earlier in the night.

As we queued to collect my coat from the cloakroom, I spotted Hayley and Matt ahead, hand in hand. She gave me a wave, miming a scream of excitement before leaving with her catch, leaving me with my own.

"So where is it you live?" Austin asked while helping me on with my coat. I linked my arm through his, unsteady on my feet.

"Near the university, Hillwood Road."

"That's ages away. Want to come back to mine? I live near the park. That cuts the journey in half."

"Sure, go on then." My throbbing feet would thank me in the morning.

Kinwich high street was an ankle killer. I almost tripped on a couple of occasions, its uneven, cobbled paths not suited for drunk girls in ridiculous high heels. But each time I wobbled, Austin held me firmly. We followed a narrow, dimly lit path alongside the medieval, timber-framed houses that lined Kinwich's streets. I should have been wary about venturing down a dark, narrow street with a man I'd just met, but disregarded the thought. Austin seemed trustworthy enough. Besides, I could take care of myself if I needed to. The slap I'd given Greg was mere horseplay. I'd earned multiple exclusions from school for getting into fights, something I'd boasted about in my youth, but now made me cringe.

We turned a corner, passing Kinwich Cathedral. There was still evidence of the ancient city wall. Weather worn stones looked out of place against the more modern buildings. One last turn and we found ourselves on a path heading out of the city centre and towards the outskirts. The heavy, black, iron gates at the park's entrance were unlocked. Like the city wall, they'd been left standing for the historical aesthetic.

"It isn't much further," Austin said. "We'll cut through the park."

The park in which I'd spent my summer looked unfamiliar in the darkness. Naked trees lined the path, beckoning me onward with long, gnarled fingers that cast spindly shadows in the glow of the tall, black lamp posts. The smell of rotting leaves in the dirt wafted on the crisp night air, a welcome earthy scent after the stench of garbage and car fumes that choked the city centre. A layer of frost was forming on the patchy grass of the football field, shimmering in the moonlight.

"I didn't realise there were houses on the other side of the park," I said, tottering along the smooth, tarmac path that had been recently re-laid, much to my ankle's relief.

"There aren't. Just the showmen's yard."

"The what?"

"The site where the caravans are parked."

I was familiar with the site he was referring to. A vast, flat, gritted surface surrounded by fencing. Sometimes, when it was deserted, teenagers would break in to ride their bikes—though how they got the bikes over the fences had always baffled me. I never would have known that empty, dead space had once been a fairground site if it wasn't for the black and white photographs of Victorian-style carousels on one of the tourist information plaques that scattered the city. I cast my mind back to last month, when caravans and lorries had parked up inside.

"You're a traveller?" I asked, but my stomach dropped when Austin sucked in air through clenched teeth.

"We are showmen, not travellers," he corrected me. "Did you see any flyers or posters for the Christmas funfair? Or the New Year's funfair?"

"You run a funfair? That must be exciting!" I'd never met anyone who didn't live in a house or flat before, leaving me with hundreds of questions. "Do you live in a caravan?"

"Yeah. Some families live in posh motorhomes, but I have a small caravan with my... uh... my dad. I-I hope you don't mind. He won't be there. We will have it to ourselves."

I gave his arm a reassuring squeeze, his sudden nervousness endearing. "Only if you promise to keep me warm." I poked my tongue out when he looked at me with raised eyebrows.

He laughed through closed lips. "I promise."

THREE

The Showmen's Yard was as I'd remembered it: rows of caravans and motorhomes on the gravelled ground. Beyond them, shrouded in darkness, I recalled lorries, containers, and other large structures covered in tarpaulin. The only source of light was a dying campfire. A couple of figures sat beside it with their backs to us, and from their exaggerated hand gestures, appeared to be in deep conversation.

"Bit early to be having a fireside natter, don't you think?" I asked Austin.

"Showmen work unsociable hours. We're going to have to climb the fence." He tugged on the padlock. "Our leader has the only key. And keep your voice down. I'm not meant to bring girls home."

I clamped my lips together to stifle a giggle. *An adult, and still having to hide girls from your dad? That's kinda cute...*

Once inside, Austin hurried me onward to hide behind the nearest caravan. "We're going to creep behind the campers. Keep low, under the windows."

"Which one is yours?"

"We're on the end. It's hidden behind some of the bigger ones."

After passing the campers, some at least twelve feet tall, my eyes fell upon the smallest and shabbiest of them all.

As though reading my mind, Austin said, "It's nothing much. But it's just me and my dad."

He rubbed the back of his neck, not meeting my eye.

"It's fine," I said with a wave of my hand. "I'm a student, remember? If you have somewhere that doesn't stink of cat piss, you're golden."

Austin kicked off his shoes as soon as he stepped inside and gestured for me to do the same. After putting his top hat away in a cupboard, he slid out of his tailcoat and threw it into a wicker wash basket. He hit a switch on a small lamp, filling the camper with a warm glow. Sofas to my left were upholstered in a carpet-like material, their floral patterns dull and faded. Between them was a small table, its plastic veneer peeling back to reveal the chipboard beneath. Someone had used layers of duct tape to stick blinds down over the windows, reminding me of how Hayley taped newspaper over her bedroom windows to stop the sunlight from getting in when she was hungover. *Yikes! Looks like Daddy might have a drinking problem!*

"Can I take your coat?" Austin asked with an outstretched hand, but I pulled my coat around even tighter.

"It's bloody freezing in here."

"Don't worry, it will soon warm up." Austin took a step towards me. The caravan was so narrow, I couldn't move. He took another step, his body now mere millimetres from mine, my breasts pressed to his chest with each breath. I focused on his wide eyes, as green as his waistcoat. Then his lips, that twitched into a smile. I swallowed. He seized my hips, and before I could lean in to kiss him, he dropped to his knees. Tracing his hands over my ass and down the back of my legs, he kept his eyes locked on mine. My breath caught... until he reached out to flick a switch on a small heater on the floor. It buzzed into life, filling the caravan with the smell of burning dust.

"There we go." Austin fluttered his eyelashes with mock innocence before releasing his grip on my leg and standing upright. "What did you think I meant? Get your mind out of the gutter, Ava."

I let out a strangled laugh, catching my breath.

"Can I get you a drink?"

"Sure, what have you got?"

I grabbed the handle to a tiny fridge beneath the kitchen working top, but before I could look inside, Austin's hand clenched around mine and slammed the door shut.

"It's... uh... broken." His grip tightened, almost painfully. "I need to get it fixed." A flush of red crept up his neck as his eyes darted to one side. "Will tea or coffee be alright?"

"Tea is fine, but you'll need to free my hand first."

The red flush that had climbed up his neck now flooded his face as he released me. "Sorry, I don't know what's come over me."

He couldn't bring himself to meet my eye as he filled a kettle with water and fumbled with his clipper lighter as he tried to ignite the stove. I flexed my fingers, working the feeling back into them.

"Forget about it. Need any help?" I opened another cupboard looking for mugs, only to find it filled with brightly coloured bottles of different shapes and sizes. "What are these?"

"Would you stop poking around?"

He slammed the cupboard door shut, almost catching my hand as I whipped it back. I narrowed my eyes at him, pursing my lips into an expression I hoped he'd recognise as his first warning.

"Look... I'm... I'm sorry." He turned his face to the floor. "I'm not very good with women, and I'm kinda regretting not taking you back to your house instead of here. It's embarrassing."

His eyes darted to a wall clock. "But if you're really that curious"—he opened the cupboard door and withdraw a tiny, blue bottle with a red gem set in the lid—"you could try this one. Dad collects weird and rare beverages. This one is pretty good and I'm sure he won't notice if a drop or two is gone?"

I looked from the bottle, to Austin, and then back again, wrinkling my nose. Without a label, I couldn't know its percentage, its age, or even its flavour.

"I'll pass. Just tea, thanks."

I made myself as comfortable as the rock-solid sofas would allow. The scent of gas wafted as Austin successfully lit the stove. He made our tea, shoulders raised, tense, hands shaking as he filled a couple of mugs with tea bags and sugar. He looked over one shoulder at me and I averted my gaze, not wanting him to feel like I was judging him, and so instead took in the rest of my surroundings. On a shelf were black and white photographs, yellowed with age. One of a couple at their wedding, and another of men in old-fashioned, army uniforms. They sat beside pieces of bric-à-brac, and an old shoe box lined with dust. The opposite end of the caravan had another sofa, a curtain rail encircling it.

"Is that where you sleep?" I asked.

"Yeah." Austin took the whistling kettle off the stove and poured the boiling water into the mugs. "But as my dad is out, I thought we'd sleep up this end. It unfolds into a double bed."

"Sounds cosy."

After adding a splash of UHT milk, he set both mugs on the table and sat across from me, his knee sliding between mine, sending a shiver through my body. I clasped my hands around the mug, warming my numb fingers, and enjoyed the sensation of the hot steam rising to caress my cheeks.

"Enough about me," Austin said. "What about you? What do you study at Uni?"

"Games Art and Design. I wanted to be a concept artist. But this year I haven't been doing so well. My art is great, if I say so myself, but I've been half-arsing the written work, and skipping lectures. It will be miraculous if I scrape a third at this rate."

"Why is that? Your course sounds really interesting."

"It is. But I'm no academic." I tapped my fingernails against the side of my mug as I contemplated just how much to divulge. I'd already overshared with Austin once before and he'd taken it pretty well. "So, after my mum kicked me out when I was twelve, my grandma took me in. But she died just over a year ago. I was hoping to find a sense of belonging at Uni. Is that sad?"

Austin shook his head, his expression serious as he reached across the table to give my hand a squeeze. "Not at all."

I tested the temperature of my tea. Still too hot. I got up, setting it aside on the kitchen worktop. "That's enough deep, emotional stuff. That's not why I'm here. Is it?" I shrugged off my coat, the heater having done its job. "It is definitely a lot warmer in here now."

"Are you comfortable sitting here?" Austin asked, eyes flicking to the wall clock once more. "We could unfold the bed?"

I grinned. "I like that idea." Together, we converted the table and sofas into the double bed, pulling the sheets tight, and arranging the pillows and duvet.

We stood at the end of the bed. My heart thumped so loud I was sure Austin might hear it.

"We don't have to do anything you don't want to," he said.

"I want to."

I slipped a finger down the front of his waistcoat, tugging him towards me. He didn't resist, his body pressing into mine. My mouth filled with moisture. Turning my face up to his, I planted a soft kiss on his lips. And then another, more vigorously than the first, wrapping my arms around his neck and pressing my chest to his. Our lips were now locked in a furious battle for dominance. He took hold of my ass, pulling my hips into his, grinding up against me. In a frenzy, I nipped at the soft flesh of his lower lip and he pulled back, gasping. For an instant, he stared at me, eyes wide, panting. Then a smirk spread across his face. I attacked again.

With fumbling fingers, I unbuttoned his waistcoat, and yanked it off him, barely registering the ripping noise as I did so. I put my hands to his chest to find yet more buttons on his shirt, while in one swift movement, Austin unzipped the back of my dress, which fell to the floor in a heap at my feet, leaving me in just my bra and panties.

My fingers refused to cooperate while I fiddled with each button of his shirt, climbing my way down. All the while, I felt his eyes upon my body... and then his hands. My skin, now sensitive, prickled as his fingertips brushed over my hips, stroked up over my stomach, cupped my breasts, and then squeezed. His hot, wet mouth was at my neck...

I unfastened the last button of his shirt and pulled it away. His body was slender, almost hairless, soft beneath my fingertips.

A hand unhooked my bra. I shrugged off the straps and let it fall. The cold air hit me, my nipples stiffening. His widening eyes raked my upper body, fixed on my breasts, wetting his lips, the corners of his mouth twitching hungrily as he watched them rise and fall with each panting breath. A pulse shot through my womanhood. Aching. Wet.

He unbuckled his belt, pushed his trousers down, never taking his eyes off me. Now just in his boxers, he guided me back onto the bed, climbing on top of me, his erection nudging my clit as he did so, teasing what was to follow.

He trailed kisses from my neck, down to my breasts, taking a nipple between his lips, grazing it with his teeth, flicking it with his tongue. A gasp escaped my lips as an electric spasm shot through me. His tongue flicked once more, extracting a soft moan I couldn't suppress.

He put a hand to my mouth, hushing me. "I don't want everyone to hear."

I had forgotten that there were others living close by. *Very* close by, only a few flimsy, paper-thin walls separating us. I nodded, pressing my lips together.

He slid my panties away. A finger slipped against my clit, already slick.

"All ready for me, I see," he teased.

I flushed. "Do you have a condom?"

He nodded, smirking.

"Then please, just fuck me." Before he could stop me, I pushed down his pants, his cock springing out of confinement.

I pretended not to watch as he applied the condom, but I couldn't tear my eyes off it...

I lay back, one hand on his arse, and guided him inside, pressing my hips upward, taking him inch by inch.

"Not too hard. But deep," I instructed. "I want to feel *all* of you."

He thrust his hips, sliding in and out, the wet slap of his skin on mine. And again. And again. And again...

He grunted, his body becoming rigid, his cock buried deep inside me.

Oh dear... Game Over...

I was half-asleep. Wrapped up in soft bedcovers, the only defence against the cold. Unable to move. Alcohol still coursed through my veins, leaving me in a dull stupor. I was vaguely aware of a pulling on my arm, but still caught up in a post coital slumber.

I kept my eyes closed, hoping I might drift back into a deep sleep, teetering on the edge of a dream, the smell of sex amongst the bedding.

Another tug on my arm. Harder than the first.

I didn't want to care. The warmth of the bed inviting me deeper into unconsciousness.

A sharp pain pulled me out of my torpidity. A piercing, stabbing into the flesh of my inner elbow.

"What the—" I sat up, the world spinning sickeningly.

Austin, now dressed, sat beside me. His mouth hung open, eyes bulging, unblinking, fixed on my face. He gripped my arm in one hand, a bloody needle in the other.

Am I... dreaming?

I blinked. Once. Twice. Austin was babbling, but I couldn't understand the words. I stared at the needle, then my arm, which I now noticed was wrapped in a tourniquet. Dazed, I yanked my arm free from Austin, my skin slipping against his sweaty palm. Blood was flowing freely from the scratch as I unhooked the tourniquet.

"And that's why I need your blood," Austin said. I could finally understand him, though his voice still shook. His hair was up on end from where he must have been driving his fingers through it. "Please, stay calm."

Reality slapped me.

"What the fuck are you doing?!" A tingling sensation shot through my limbs. With all my might, I kicked him in the chest, knocking him backward off the bed. I checked my arm. The blood was still oozing from the scratch, staining the bedding.

I wriggled free. Whipped my head around, searching for my clothes. But Austin had risen to his feet and shoved me back onto the bed, climbing on top, pinning me beneath his weight.

"You need to be quiet!" He clamped his hand over my mouth.

I writhed beneath him, arms and legs thrashing, tossing my head from side to side. I discovered an opening and snapped my jaws down on his fingers. He yelped and yanked his hand back.

"Fire!" I screamed as loudly as my throat would allow. "Fire!"

Austin shook his head as all the colour drained from his face. Taking advantage of his state of shock, I wrestled him off me and barged past, grabbing my coat as I darted for the door.

"Ava, wait!"

But my hand was outstretched to grab the handle—when it was opened from the outside.

A tall figure stood in the doorway, blocking my exit. His haunting appearance—hollow cheeks, deep-set eyes beneath a prominent brow drawn together into a scowl—set the hairs on my neck on end. Instinctively, I brought my coat up to cover myself before a wave of adrenaline took control. I *had* to escape.

I darted forward, ready to bulldoze past, but he grasped my shoulder with one hand, and with all the effort of someone flicking down a row of dominoes, he sent me hurtling back into the caravan, crashing into a cupboard door, and landing in a heap at his feet.

What the fuck?! How did he... He barely moved...

"Austin," the man said. "Would you care to explain yourself?" He spoke softly, but it felt as though he had shouted, his deep, refined voice full of authority.

I looked back at Austin, a bead of sweat running down his pale face.

"Mr Madigan," he spluttered, his voice getting caught in his throat, "I am so sorry, it's not what it looks like!"

The man called Madigan now fixed his gaze upon me with a stern, stony look that sent a chill down my spine. I pulled my coat around me, desperate to find my clothes, but dared not look away from either of my captors.

Madigan sighed, pinching the bridge of his thin nose. "It doesn't take a genius to understand what happened here."

Withdrawing a key from his pocket, he locked the door behind him.

FOUR

I sat on the edge of the sofa, shaking so violently I was sure my bones were vibrating. I'd pulled on my coat. Though suited to protecting me from the winter's cold, it was useless as a shield against my assailants. My eyes darted between Austin, who sat on the edge of the bed, and Madigan leaning in the doorway, long legs crossed and arms folded, surveying me with cold, grey eyes. Only an inch taller than Austin, he filled his suit far better than Austin had. In fact, it was only now that I noticed his tailcoat was identical in style—thin tails, pointed lapels—but was jet-black, and looked tailored to fit him perfectly.

"Mr Madigan, I was desperate—" Austin said, but Madigan raised a white-gloved hand, silencing him.

"You're a bloody fool, Austin."

Madigan ran his long fingers through slick, dark hair, exhaling through flared nostrils. What was he thinking about? What to do with me? Or Austin?

"I'm so sorry." Austin's voice shook, mirroring his trembling hands. "This was my last chance. I heard Ivan talking about how he'd kill me if I failed harvesting."

"He will kill you anyway if he finds out about this." Madigan ran his fingers through his hair a second time, yet spoke with an eloquent, measured tone. With an accent like his, he could be mistaken for royalty.

My mind raced with questions. Who was Ivan? What did they mean by harvesting?

My stomach dropped.

I darted forward to the fridge and tugged the door open. My knees weakened at the sight of vials containing a deep-red liquid.

Blood...

A hand seized me by the scruff of my coat, wrenching me back, and sent me hurtling to the sofa. The way Madigan could throw me about like a doll left me nauseated.

"Who the hell are you wack jobs?" I said in a strangled gasp, but was gagged beneath a glare so frosty my skin prickled with goosebumps.

"It seems we have two choices," Madigan said, turning his attention back to Austin. "Either you flee, now. Or..." he paused, glancing at me with a grim expression. "We take some by force. I am loath to do it, but under the current circumstances—"

"Can't I have some of yours?" Austin nodded towards the fridge.

"My supply is days old." Madigan shook his head, running a gloved hand over his chin. "Ivan would know it's not freshly harvested."

Austin turned his clammy face to mine, looking at me like a starving dog eyeing fresh meat.

"I will scream," I said, adrenaline pumping through my veins. "If you think I'm going to let you take my blood without a fight, you're dead wrong. What sort of sick fetish is this, anyway? Vampirism or something?"

"I'm just a familiar," Austin said, but that just spawned more questions.

"What the fuck does that mean?" I asked, but before he could elaborate, Madigan was addressing him again.

"What do you want to do, Austin? The decision must be yours. And make it quick. Dawn will soon be upon us, and I cannot help once the sun rises."

I looked at Austin through pleading eyes, praying he would make the right choice. He pursed his lips together, but this didn't stop the lower one from trembling.

"I will leave." His voice was hoarse, like he was trying to suppress tears. "I'm not forcing anyone to do anything."

"Fine. We had better hurry. Get a bag packed. Essentials only. You must travel a great distance to stand a fighting chance. Understand?" Madigan now turned his attention to me. "You, girl. Get yourself dressed." His flinty eyes scanned over me, wrinkling his nose, as though looking at something miniscule and disgusting, like a maggot. I didn't need telling twice—I had to escape these sickos.

It was a squeeze manoeuvring in the cramped space. Austin grabbed various things and shoved them into a bag, while I searched for the clothes I'd abandoned and tried to dress without exposing myself. Fortunately, neither of them seemed the slightest bit interested.

I was pulling on my shoes when a noise made all three of us freeze. Austin looked paler than ever, Madigan's scowl intensifying.

A knock on the door.

Madigan growled in the back of his throat, retrieving the key from his pocket to unlock the door. It swung open. I stood on tiptoes, peering over Madigan's shoulder and into the face of the unhealthiest-looking man I'd ever seen.

He was my height, looked to be in his thirties and dressed in raggedy, old-fashioned clothes. He was bald, and as pale as death. Beneath the shadows of his narrow eyes, his cheekbones stuck out like a pair of blades above the sunken flesh of his cheeks. He looked like a corpse.

"Len," the dead-looking man addressed Madigan. "There's been talk of a disturbance. I didn't realise you were involved." His voice was higher than I had been expecting. His thin lips split into a smile that held no warmth.

"There is no disturbance here, Dominic," Madigan said bluntly, but the newcomer had already spotted me, and his smirk widened into a malicious grin.

"I doubt that." The man named Dominic didn't seem to blink much, and that evil smile suggested he knew *exactly* what had transpired. "You've gained a new friend. I'm guessing this is who Austin tried to harvest from?"

"I don't know what you're talking about," Madigan snapped, closing the door, but Dominic yanked it open again.

"It's *sweet* that you're trying to cover for him," he said, his tone dripping with heavy sarcasm. "I'll remember to tell our master of your loyalty to the boy. I'm sure he'd be touched to hear you've befriended his familiar. But rules are rules, and Austin has broken them."

"I'm begging you," Austin's small voice chimed in. "Just one more night."

"I am sorry"—though he didn't sound sorry in the slightest—"but Master Ivan returns tonight, and he made his wishes to me quite clear. He would return to find you had completed your task, or he would return to your execution. And unlike you, I keep my word to our master."

He clicked his fingers and two figures that had been hiding in the shadows appeared at his side. One was short, had a mass of wild hair, and dressed in a black, leather jacket and biker boots. His hands were in his pockets, emphasising his hunched, rounded shoulders. The other, by contrast, wore a blazer over a turtleneck, his hair so tidy it appeared he'd just visited a barber. Head held high, he wore a bored, lazy expression, looking away as though the unfolding events were beneath him.

"Now then," Dominic said, spreading his arms to gesture to his new companions, "are you going to let us do our job? Or will I have to report you to Master Ivan, too?"

Madigan didn't move, clenching and unclenching his fists, his knuckles cracking. But with a growl, he stepped aside, allowing the two henchmen inside. The small caravan quaked as they wrestled Austin to the floor, knocking me back onto the sofa in the commotion. I wanted to call out, to tell these thugs to leave him alone, but my voice had disappeared, lost deep in my throat.

"Let me go!" Austin screamed, squirming in their grip, limbs thrashing. The mugs we'd set aside crashed to the floor, splattering cold, half-drunk tea over the worn carpet. With ease, they pulled Austin to his feet and hauled him outside. I swayed, putting my hands to my face, then through my hair, nervous energy pouring out of me. All the while, Madigan kept his eyes fixed on Dominic, shoulders tense, rising and falling with each breath. Neither of them moved or said a single word until Austin's screams finally faded as they dragged him away.

"What are your plans for the witness?" Dominic's ravenous, black eyes widened as they fixed themselves on me.

Blood drained from my face, leaving me light headed.

"We'll dispose of her, too," Dominic said. "Unless you want to take her for yourself?"

My heart stopped.

"What do you mean?" I asked, my voice almost inaudible, as though a hand was constricting my airway. Neither of them acknowledged my question.

"Perhaps Master Ivan would like a replacement?" Madigan asked.

"I doubt it. Not after Austin's ineptitude, and I don't need *another* familiar. Neither do Jacob or Sebastian." He jerked his head in the direction his henchman had dragged Austin. "We each have one. You're the only one who doesn't. Can I assume from your refusal to take one in recent years that she's of no interest to you?"

Madigan looked over his shoulder, his attention now on me, one of his eyes twitching. I blinked at him, unsure how I wanted him to respond, yet I knew my fate rested with him.

Sighing, the tight muscles in his face relaxed before turning back to Dominic.

"It will be up to her. In any case, it would need Master Ivan's approval before we accept her into the coven. Allow me to discuss it with her and you'll have your answer by sundown."

"I want an answer now."

"You will have your answer by sundown," Madigan repeated through a clenched jaw. Both men stared each other down, waiting for the other to give an inch.

"Fine." Dominic's twisted smile was now replaced with a glower.

"Excellent. Now, if you will excuse us, we have much to discuss. You should return to your camper. It's getting light." Before Dominic could argue further, Madigan slammed the door shut.

An oppressive silence filled the caravan as Madigan pinched the bridge of his nose, shut his eyes, and let out a long breath. Rather than acknowledge me, he looked at the double bed, the duvet still crumpled and covered with blood. *My* blood.

"Stupid boy..." he said under his breath and pulled the bedding away. I felt as though I was imposing myself upon a private moment.

"Excuse me," I said. "What is going on?"

He didn't reply immediately, but continued to remove the bedding. "It's quite simple really," he said once he'd stripped the bed bare. "You will become my familiar, or you will die."

My mouth went dry. "And what exactly does that entail?"

But Madigan was now preoccupied with the green suit crumpled in the wicker basket. A guttural sound emanated from his throat as his long fingers traced over the rip on the waistcoat.

"I said, what does that en—"

"Does it matter? What part of *'you will die'* is difficult to understand?" He sniffed the tailcoat. "Ugh... tobacco..." He whipped his head around to look at me, "Did *you* wear this? You smell just as bad. You'd better quit that filthy habit."

"Dying is the only bit I understood," I said, ignoring his jibe. "Had it not occurred to you that perhaps that would be my choice if the alternative means serving you?"

The words bubbled out of me before I could stop them. As intimidating as Madigan was, his rudeness was getting under my skin.

Madigan stopped what he was doing and fixed me with a long, hard stare, eyes narrowing, before answering, "A vampire's familiar is like a servant. You are correct: your job would be to serve me. Usually, familiars collect blood on their master's behalf and if they cannot do so, they will offer their own."

"Do you really expect me to believe that you are a vampire?" I said witheringly. "Go on then, show us your fangs."

In a movement too fast for my eyes to follow, Madigan crossed the caravan and was now towering above me, my cheeks in an unyielding grip of his white-gloved hand. I grabbed his wrist, trying to pull his hand away, but it would have been easier to uproot a tree. My stomach flipped, a wave of panic rippling through my body.

He put his face close to mine and hissed, "I think you have been watching too many films, ignorant girl." The grip on my cheeks intensified.

"Ok... I believe you!" I could barely spit the words out.

Madigan looked into my face, a sceptical eyebrow arched.

"You're a vampire, I believe you!" I said again.

Madigan's nose wrinkled and lips pursed together before releasing me. I rubbed my cheeks, already aching from the pinch of his fingers.

My heart felt lodged in my throat, pounding, yet suffocating.

Vampires... Real vampires... Could it be true? Dominic could certainly pass for one. A flashback of his twisted grin made me shudder.

"We drink little," Madigan said as though the confrontation had not happened. "A mouthful or two per night is sufficient. Obviously, a familiar would feel weak if fed from regularly, which is why they'll harvest from other humans. Most importantly, it must be done without getting caught. We never, *ever*, bring humans back to our home. That's just one mistake Austin made tonight."

"And making a mistake is a death sentence?"

"In Austin's case, yes. It depends on a few things. One of which is your master. Austin was the familiar of Ivan. Our coven's leader. He doesn't forgive mistakes easily."

"What is a coven?"

"Look," Madigan said, pulling fresh bedding from a cupboard, "you will have many questions. Some will take time to answer. Time I am not willing to grant right now. The sun is rising and I need my rest. You know enough to make your choice, so I suggest you think on it, get some rest, and give me your answer when I wake." He threw the dirty bedding in my direction. "You can sleep up that end. That sofa can be fashioned into a single bed and there's a curtain for privacy. Do not disturb me before nightfall."

"What makes you think I'll stick around that long?"

"You really *do* have a death wish, don't you? If you think escaping Dominic will be that easy, go ahead. Run. See what happens." He seized the curtain up at his end and was about to pull it around his bed, when he said, "I forgot to ask, what is your name?"

"Ava Monroe."

"Miss Monroe," he acknowledged with a slight bow of the head, "My name is Leonard Madigan."

And with that, he drew the curtain, ending our conversation and leaving me with a harrowing decision.

FIVE

My phone was dead. Typical. If I didn't act fast, I would meet the same fate. Mind made up, I planned my escape.

I sat on the edge of the sofa, fidgeting. My stomach twisted itself into knots as I checked the vintage wall clock every few minutes, expecting hours to have flown by. Though eager to leave, it seemed sensible to wait until the sun had risen. I was being held captive by a *vampire,* after all. Also, I needed to be certain that Madigan was asleep before I made my move.

It wasn't until 8 a.m. that I dared to inspect him, a niggling headache forming in my temples, testing my patience. Perfect time for a hangover—not. Madigan was silent behind his curtain, the lack of snoring disconcerting. My hand shook as I reached out to pull the curtain back. I gripped the thin material, knuckles white, heart pounding. I exhaled slowly before poking my head around the curtain to view my captor.

Madigan was sprawled across the double bed, long limbs reaching every corner. His chest was slowly rising and falling with each breath, eyes closed.

Perfect.

I crept to my section of the caravan, drew my curtain closed, and turned my attention to the window. The tape that fixed the blinds down was brittle, the glue having degraded. It was easy to pull away.

I took my time, keeping the ripping sound low. With bated breath, I pulled up the blind, letting a stream of sunlight pour inside. I considered opening the curtains and watch the vampire burst into flames. That's how it worked in movies.

'I think you have been watching too many films, ignorant girl.' That's what he said the last time I'd made assumptions about vampires...

I couldn't guarantee that sunlight would kill him. What if it just pissed him off? Then I'd be at the mercy of a furious vampire who had already shown his superior speed and strength. This idea discarded, I returned to my original plan. I unlatched the window with a click, pushing the plastic pane open far wider than I'd thought possible. Without a neighbour on the end of the row, I could escape unnoticed. With a grin, I draped one leg over the window ledge, then the other, and let myself fall. A squeal caught in my throat as something seized the back of my coat, nearly choking me as the zipper dug into my neck. I glanced up, expecting the enraged face of Madigan to be glowering back, but sighed in relief, realising my hood had caught on the latch.

After untangling myself, I snuck from one camper to the next, towards the gates and freedom, careful to keep low to avoid detection. Most campers had their curtains pulled, but I wasn't taking any chances. A few times I heard voices from inside and froze in my tracks, straining my ears, gauging how close they were. After creeping with the speed of a sloth, I reached the end of the row of campers.

The gates were in sight. I looked back one last time. There was no one around. It was now or never.

I removed my heels, clutching them in one hand, my bag in the other. One last breath, bouncing on the balls of my feet, gravel scratching beneath them.

Go for it... Now!

I sprinted to the gate. Icy wind whipped through my hair, lashing against my face. Gravel shredded my feet. I ignored the sting, focusing on putting one foot ahead of the other. I tossed my bag and shoes over the gate. Clambered over myself. Darted across the road. Into the park.

I kept running. No one else was around. The frosty morning air burned my lungs. I dashed to the closest familiar spot—a hedgerow I'd nicknamed the '*Stoner Bush*'. I crashed through the branches and dark-green leaves until I reached the centre of the hedgerow, ducking down.

My heart was in my throat. The taste of metal in my mouth. Blood rang in my ears. I filled my lungs, gasping for breath. Beads of sweat trickled through my hair and down my neck.

I peered through the waxy-textured leaves, searching for pursuers. No one. Could it be possible that I'd escaped unnoticed? I couldn't believe that a meeting place for potheads was my sanctuary.

Occasionally checking that the coast remained clear, I caught my breath. My lungs were raw and a stitch in my side ached. Panting, I fidgeted with a fallen leaf among the damp earth, discarded fag butts, joint ends, and broken lighters. Before long, its almond aroma was on my fingers and I'd trapped dirt beneath my nails.

You need to keep moving...

After crawling out from my hiding spot, I resumed my liberation. I kept up a brisk pace, still carrying my shoes in case I needed to break into a run. Constantly checking over my shoulder. Only now did I encounter other people. Mostly joggers and dog walkers. Some wrinkled their noses or rolled their eyes upon seeing me. To them, I appeared to be doing the walk of shame. A group of teenagers gathered in the bandstand called out, jeering. Once, this might have bothered me, but now I didn't give a shit. I had only one thing in mind: make it to the nearest safe place. My house was a thirty-minute walk, but there was someone who lived a mere five minutes away. Greg.

I arrived at his house, my finger hovering over the doorbell. I bit my lip.

What if he's angry about that slap...

Screwing up my eyes, I jabbed the doorbell... and waited. I shifted my weight from side to side, looking back, half-expecting to see Madigan in hot pursuit of me. I rang the doorbell again.

This time, I heard footsteps and the muffled sound of voices. The door opened. Greg stood in the doorway, hair unkempt, yawning. His familiar face, after the nightmare I'd experienced, was like a fresh, spring breeze, and all the dramas we'd been through fell away, unimportant. Irrelevant. Forgotten.

"Ava? What are you doing?" he asked, rubbing one eye. He was wearing grey jogging bottoms and a simple, white t-shirt. "No offence, but you look rough as heck."

I wiped my filthy hands on my coat to little effect, covered from head to toe in dirt and scratches from my dive into the hedge.

"Can I come in? I've had one hell of a night."

He frowned, concerned, but not about my welfare. More like, concerned when someone reads a news report that a serial killer has escaped the local prison. He didn't step aside to let me in. "Tell me what happened," he said, folding his arms.

"I'm in trouble with the guy I met last night. He turned out to be a creeper. I escaped, but he could be following me. Can I stay here, just for a couple of hours? I'll clean myself up and be on my way. I promise."

He didn't answer, but glanced over his shoulder into his living room, then back to me.

"Please?" I asked again.

"You're bleeding." He gestured to my feet. I looked down at the bloody marks I'd left on his porch.

"I cut my feet trying to get away."

Greg tilted his head to one side, thinking. "I have someone over at the moment. They'll freak out seeing you in this state. You can't just turn up to my house like this. It's not fair. Especially after slapping me last night."

"Look, I'm sorry, okay?" I drove my fingers through my hair as my chest grew tight. "But I'm in *danger*, Greg. You must understand, I'm desperate." It was impossible to keep my voice from shaking.

He rubbed his chin, then bit the nail of his thumb, his expression softening into a look of sympathy, one I recognised from when we'd been dating, back when he'd been kind. He opened his mouth to speak again, but someone interrupted him.

"Tell her to go home!" said a female voice from his living room. Greg straightened himself and folded his arms.

"I think you might still be drunk, Ava."

"No, Greg, please!"

"Go home and get some rest. I will see you on Monday." And without a moment's hesitation, he shut the door. I stared at the closed door in disbelief.

How could he do that to me? The tightness in my chest now spread through my body, muscles tensing down to my fingers that curled into fists as the red mist descended.

"Arsehole!" I kicked the door, leaving a bloody mark as a searing pain shot through my foot.

Well, that was dumb...

I sighed, the bubbling anger dissipating, leaving a heavy feeling in the pit of my stomach. I'd been sure that despite our history, Greg would have helped me in my time of need. What a fool.

I looked around. Still no sign of Madigan. Resigning myself to finishing my journey home, I put my shoes on, but thanks to my bleeding soles, my feet slid around painfully inside. After removing them again, I continued the trek as I'd started—barefoot.

By the time I reached my front door, my feet felt as though they were on fire, blazing pain radiating up to my ankles. I unlocked the front door, and avoiding the scratchy doormat, stepped onto the cool, ceramic floor tiles, treading carefully as not to slip. It was bliss after walking on tarmac. On autopilot, I headed straight into the kitchen. There was no one there to greet me except a stack of dirty dishes beside a pool of stagnant water in the limescale-encrusted sink. Keys still in hand, I unlocked the backdoor and stepped out into the garden.

I sat myself on the flimsy, wooden stool we kept outside and lit a cigarette, inhaling, holding it in my lungs before breathing out the smoke.

It was peaceful outside, the only sound was the twitter of a robin sat on the garden fence. Everything seemed so familiar. So normal, that last night's shit show could have passed for a nightmare. My temples throbbed, as the hangover I'd ignored during my escape now flared into life once again.

As I brought my cigarette to my lips, the scratch inside my elbow from Austin's harvesting attempt twinged. An enormous bruise had formed, and in the centre a tiny, red pinprick.

I swallowed, my lower lip quivering.

Keep it together... Keep it together... No crying allowed...

I shook myself, taking another puff, refusing to let the weight of what I'd been through drag me down. The sun inched across the sky as I smoked one cigarette after another, extinguishing each with a hiss as I pressed them into the water-filled ashtray. I swirled the end of my last cigarette in the brown water, the stink of stale tobacco fresh in my nostrils. I got up to head inside. Perhaps Charlie, my housemate, was home and would let me scrounge another fag off of him.

I tiptoed upstairs to prevent the fluff from the thin, fraying, red and gold carpet getting into the cuts on my feet, each step creaking beneath my weight as the floorboards bowed. I knocked on Charlie's bedroom door, but no luck. He was probably in lectures, like I ought to be. But that wasn't happening. Not today. Today was about recovery.

After necking some painkillers and forcing down a bowl of cereal, I used the communal bathroom to clean myself up. I brushed my teeth, ridding myself of the sour flavour in my mouth and furry texture on my tongue. I'd made jokes about how you needed a tetanus jab before using the dilapidated shower, but it was worth it when the hot, steamy water ran down my body, brown and red streams swirling down the drain.

Once out and dry, I inspected the cuts on my feet. From the way they stung, I imagined deep lacerations, but they weren't as bad as I'd pictured, more akin to a child's scraped knees, though they still seared as I applied antiseptic cream and plasters.

Desperate to lay my aching body down, I made for my bedroom. I lit a stick of incense—a gift from Hayley—to cover the musty scent of the mould growing in one of the water-stained corners, then switched on my Xbox, and crawled into bed, my mattress sagging beneath me, bed springs digging into my back. I scrolled through the menu screen, replaying the horrors inside my head, on repeat.

Controller abandoned on my side table, I laid back and closed my eyes, my headache still lingering beneath my temples, untouched by the paracetamol, and slipped into unconsciousness. But even sleep didn't free me from my torment.

In my dream, a man in a top hat tied me down, strapping up my arm and sharpening an axe, tapping the blade with the whetstone with a *tink tink*.

I woke with a start in a cold, clammy sweat, my short hair sticking to the back of my neck. Night had fallen. My room was in darkness. The only light was a harsh glare from the TV screen. I heard a strange tapping noise, a low *tink tink,* like metal on glass.

Good. Sounds like Charlie is home.

I wriggled out of bed to answer the knock at my door. Only to find an empty hallway. I closed the door.

Damn it, Ava, you're losing the plot...

I shook myself, shrugging off the dream that still haunted me. And turned... to find the source of the noise staring at me.

A deathly pale face at the window. The vampire who'd caught Austin. *Dominic.* His wicked, little eyes alight with excitement, and thin mouth split into a smile that stretched across his face, ear to ear.

My blood turned to ice as he surveyed me with the expression of a cat watching a bird in a cage.

SIX

My scream caught in my throat, barely escaping my gaping mouth as a strangled squeak. Dominic's smile widened, muffled laughter penetrating through the closed window.

SMASH!

With a single strike, he punched through the double glazing like it was a canvas. Glass rained over me, scratching my arms as I protected my face. With sweaty palms, I fumbled with the door handle, my fingers tangling themselves together. There was shattering of more glass as my stalker clambered through my bedroom window, and laughter as I struggled with the doorknob, slippery in my hand.

The knob twisted. I yanked the door open and slammed it behind me. I darted to the stairs, lost my footing, and slid down on my backside. One step after another. I landed in a heap at the bottom, scrambling to my feet, a twinge in my lower back. Dashing through the kitchen, agony shooting through my feet and up my ankles with each step. But I kept going. Into the garden. I half-sprinted, half-hobbled, biting back pain, ready to make the jump over the fence.

Something crashed into my back, driving me down onto the ground. The taste of earth and blood in my mouth. My attacker was on top of me. I was pinned. I scraped at the ground, trying to crawl free, but only pulled up fistfuls of grass. My fingernails bent back as I clawed at the dirt.

"HELP!"

A hand clamped over my mouth.

I don't want to die!

I screamed into his palm, but was almost completely muzzled into silence, before a second hand seized me by my hair. *He is going to break my neck!*

The face of my grandma flooded my mind. *I'm not ready! Please no!* I exhaled what I thought would be my final breath.

"Dominic," said a voice above me. "Would you mind removing yourself from my familiar?"

I tried to jerk my head upward, but was restrained so tightly my efforts proved futile.

"She made her choice," my assailant said with a sharp tug at my hair. "She was mine the moment she ran away."

"I instructed her to come home and collect a few of her belongings," the voice said slowly, as though explaining something simple to a child. A pair of polished, black Chelsea boots appeared in my line of vision. A moment's silence. The grip on my head slackened, and I looked upward to identify my rescuer.

Madigan.

His arms were folded, head tilted, a look of exasperation on his face that matched his drawling tone. "Isn't that right?" He directed the question at me.

I nodded as much as Dominic would allow, and with a grunt, he released me, getting to his feet and dusting himself down. I gasped, my lungs drinking in air, almost choking on it until my head swam. Madigan offered me his hand, which I accepted, getting up off the ground and leaning on him, my knees threatening to give way. A sharp pain at the base of my spine flared into life—the consequence of my tumble down the stairs.

Madigan turned his focus back to Dominic. "I would appreciate it if you didn't get involved with my familiar again. I know familiars rarely last a month, but it would be nice if *this one* could survive a single night."

Dominic squared up to Madigan, craning his neck upward to maintain eye contact. "We both know you're chatting shit, Len. You won't be able to cover for her again, and the next time she tries to escape"—he ran his tongue over his upper lip—"I will drain her of every drop of blood she has."

"Understood," Madigan dismissed with a casual wave of his hand.

With a scowl so venomous it could shame a sulky teenager, Dominic departed, looking back only once, glaring at me through dark, narrow eyes.

"Are you hurt?" Madigan asked.

I nodded. With each passing second, the pain in my back and feet burned brighter. Lips pursed, I suppressed the urge to vomit as the sour taste of acid burnt my tongue.

Madigan shifted his weight from one foot to the other as his eyes scanned me up and down, sharply inhaling through his nose. "I ought to leave you with your injuries. Then perhaps next time you'll think twice before doing something stupid."

Though desperate to snap back, I dared not open my mouth in case my stomach's contents reappeared.

"I will speak plainly," he continued. "I didn't expect you to run. The risk of death suffices to persuade most people to stay. But I was wrong, and I won't make that error again." He bent down, his face inches from mine, studying me with his cold, grey eyes. "Now, either come with me, become my familiar and join our coven, or I will leave and you can do as you please. By all means, run. Hide. Do what you think is necessary. But Dominic *will* find you, and I won't save you a second time. Do you understand?"

I nodded.

Madigan drew himself up to his usual height. "So, what will it be?"

I faced the house I'd called home for the last two and a half years, the light from my TV streaming from my broken bedroom window, then back to Madigan, his brows drawn into the frown that I might spend the rest of my life viewing. I'd spent so much time and money getting myself here, and for what? An ex-boyfriend that didn't care if I lived or died, a university course I was failing, and a shabby, unsafe house with extortionate rent. Perhaps it was the adrenaline clouding my judgement, but after my near-death experience, my decision appeared to be made for me. I swallowed, bowing my head.

"I don't want Dominic to kill me, so I will go with you. I'll be your familiar. But as soon as a moment arises when I can make my escape, I'm taking it. I'll always look for a way out. *Always*."

Madigan snorted, unimpressed. "Very well. Whatever you need to tell yourself to get through the night. Now, collect some belongings you wish to bring with you."

As I began my walk back to the house, I drew a sharp intake of breath as the pain in my back twinged.

Madigan huffed, and without meeting my eye said, "And I suppose, as you're in my care, I can have your injuries seen to when we get back."

The showmen's yard looked different now. The campfire roared with life, and no less than six people sat around it, their shadows stretching across the ground in the orange glow. Laughter carried on the bitter wind as Madigan assisted me over the gates.

"Are these damn things ever unlocked?" I asked through clenched teeth as he caught me, pain shooting up my spine.

"Master Ivan has the only key," he said, echoing what Austin had told me.

I clutched a bag containing my only possessions in the world: mostly clothes, but also a photograph of my grandma, some makeup, and my sketchbook. I'd grabbed my watch after Madigan had made sure I'd left my phone.

"I don't want anyone to track your location. It could cause trouble for us, and where there is trouble, death will surely follow," he'd said ominously without further explanation. Although, he *had* made me send a message to Charlie to explain my absence.

'Hey man,' it read. *'House was broken into. Doesn't feel safe and I need some time to recover. I'm going to stay with my parents for a bit.'*

I'd hoped that he might realise something was wrong by telling him I was staying with my parents, but Charlie wasn't the most observant person in the world and usually forgot that I didn't have such a happy home life. Perhaps my lecturers might question my disappearance. But then again, I was *always* absent, and all that resulted in was passive aggressive emails in my inbox. *Damn...*

I'd tried to persuade Madigan I needed my tablet and computer, on which I had spent most of my inheritance, but he'd met my request with a flat refusal. He did, however, allow me to bring an old handheld video game console when I'd shown him it didn't connect to the internet.

We walked together to the campfire, and Madigan told me to take a seat. I perched on a stump, flinching as I lowered myself down. Beside me was a dark-skinned woman who I guessed to be in her mid-twenties. When she regarded me with one brow arched in curiosity, my mouth fell open. She was *stunning*. Afro hair worn in springy coils. Huge, dark eyes framed by the longest, curliest eyelashes I had ever seen. Her full lips were a deep, ruby-red that curled into a friendly smile, forming dimples in her plump, rosy cheeks.

"Who's this?" she asked.

"Miss Ava Monroe," Madigan said. "My familiar."

"*You* have taken a familiar? What happened to, '*I have no need of a servant, I can do it myself*', Len?" she asked, mocking his eloquent tone.

"Hilarious," Madigan said, rolling his eyes. "I haven't presented her to Ivan yet. Do you know if he's returned?"

"Yeah, he's in his camper with Dominic, who, by the way, looked as miserable as sin. But once he heard Ivan was back, he perked up. He's probably got his nose buried up Ivan's arse as we speak."

The others around the campfire sniggered at this comment. Even Madigan struggled to hide his amusement, the corners of his mouth twitching.

"Then I'd better interrupt them. Can I leave Miss Monroe with you for the time being? It would be helpful if you showed her around and went over the coven's rules before Ivan meets her. Oh, and she has acquired some injuries. We would appreciate any help you might offer."

"Sure, I can do your job for you." The young woman winked at him. "But I warn you, I might steal her for myself."

Madigan didn't rise to the young woman's teasing, but merely rolled his eyes again and headed toward the campers.

"I'm sorry you're stuck with Mr Misery-Guts. My name is Latisha, and it is a pleasure to meet you, Ava. Now, tell me, where are you hurt?"

"Here." I leant forward, touching the base of my spine. "I fell down some stairs. And my feet are all cut up."

"No problem," Latisha said, and turned to the woman sitting beside her. "Hetti, would you fetch what's needed?"

"What would you like?" Hetti asked.

Latisha tutted. "You *know* what's needed. Come on now. No need to get flustered in front of the newbie."

Hetti twisted her fingers in her lap, nodded, then hurried toward the first camper of the row, furthest from Madigan's.

Latisha turned back to me, smiling her warm, friendly smile. "Now then. Introductions. This is Luna and Aurora." She gestured to a set of twins, the only noticeable difference being Luna wore her blonde hair in ringlets, while Aurora's was straight. Everything else, their large, green eyes, flawless, ivory skin, and their pink, rosebud lips, was identical. "Their parents were hippies," she added with a wink.

"Hi Ava." Luna wiggled manicured nails at me in greetings, and Aurora copied. They, like Latisha, were breathtakingly beautiful, a shimmering aura surrounding them, as though they were the ones casting light instead of the campfire.

"And these two," Latisha said, pointing toward the two remaining ladies who had almost gone unnoticed sitting beside the twins, "are Cassandra and Alex."

"They're our familiars," Aurora said.

"And finally," Latisha said, nodding towards the campers, "the woman I sent to get your treatments is Hetti. She's my familiar. Though I'm not opposed to taking a second if Len becomes too insufferable." Latisha winked again.

The bundle of nerves that had been building in the pit of my stomach eased slightly. "Are you all vampires, too?" I asked.

"No," said Latisha. "No one here is a vampire. Myself, Luna, and Aurora are all witches, and I am the witch's representative within the coven."

Witches... Bloody hell... When I thought of witches, these were not the women I pictured. Latisha, Luna, and Aurora were so dazzling I felt unrefined by comparison, like when approaching the popular kids in school. I plucked at my t-shirt that now felt hot and restrictive, and became hyperaware of the dirt that caked my hands and face from my scuffle with Dominic.

"What do you mean, you're the witches' representative?" I asked.

"Each kind of supernatural—witches, shifters, vampires, and werewolves—has a representative within a coven. Witches' familiars are *technically* shifters, but while in the service of a witch they're part of the witches' faction. Shifters who are *not* in service to a witch have their own faction and representative. I'll introduce you to them and the werewolves later if you like?"

"Sure, I guess... but what are shifters?"

"It's short for shapeshifter." Latisha held out a hand to receive something from Hetti. "Let's see what you've picked out."

Hetti handed her a squat, little jar, a cup, and plastic bottle containing a colourless liquid.

"Good choices," she said as she looked them over, before handing me the jar. Inside was a pink, viscous paste with a strong, chemical fragrance. "That's for your feet. Rub it on the cuts and they will heal up within seconds."

I pulled off my trainers and socks and gingerly applied the paste that left a burning sensation in its wake, followed by an itching as the cuts appeared to knit themselves closed. I strained my eyes, sure it had to be an illusion. But as she'd promised, the skin was smooth and whole again. "Holy shit..." I muttered, tracing my fingertips over the place the deepest scrape had been.

"Here." Latisha held out the cup and plastic bottle. The cup contained four pills, two white and two pink.

"What are these?"

"Paracetamol and ibuprofen."

"What?!"

"A painkiller and anti-inflammatory."

Laughter bubbled out of me. "I know what they are! It's just not what I'd expected from witches."

Latisha shrugged. "Some human medicine is just as effective as my own. Slower perhaps—"

"Hey, I'm not complaining. I'll still take it." I knocked back the pills in one go, flushing them down with water from the bottle. "So, witches make things like this?" I returned the jar of paste to Latisha.

"Yeah. We specialise in potions and remedies that can heal, enhance natural abilities, help you sleep, and so on. We can perform a ritual or two. And we can use a glamour." She struck a pose, fluttering her eyelashes, and in that instant, her beauty became so radiant that for a second, my mouth grew wet as I zoned in on her pouting lips. "A witch has these basic skills, but extremely powerful witches have extra abilities... for a price."

"And how powerful are you?" I asked, able to pry my sights from her mouth as her glamour abated.

Latisha inhaled through gritted teeth, looked towards her companions, and then back to me. "No one here has any extra abilities."

Something was going unsaid, but I decided not to press the issue.

"What was Madigan talking about when he asked you to explain the coven's rules?" I asked instead, changing the subject.

"The coven has rules that we all must follow. The first and most important rule is we must all obey our coven leader, Ivan. We remain within the coven until our—or Ivan's—death. If he dies, the coven is disbanded and we go our own separate ways. Or we can elect a new leader and reform the coven."

Death of the leader disbands the coven... That's good to know... "Got it. Is there anything else?"

"Don't bring anyone back to the coven's location. And do not feed or harvest from someone you know personally. This protects us from being identified for what we truly are."

I thought of Austin, wondering what terrible fate had befallen him, and considered asking Latisha if she knew, but decided against it. Ignorance, as they say, is bliss.

"Another rule applicable to you is that vampires that become rabid are executed."

"What do you mean by rabid?" I asked.

Latisha cocked her head to one side in thought. "I believe it has something to do with their... feeding habits. You should ask Len. He knows more than I do. Witches and shifters are more my expertise."

I nodded, making a mental note to follow her advice. "What kind of supernatural is Ivan?"

"He's a vampire."

"Which is why he uses the vampires to be his mini-Gestapo," Hetti muttered under her breath.

Latisha whipped her head around to look at her familiar. "Do *not* get caught saying that," she said, her tone reminding me of an old headteacher I was often in trouble with. "Come on, Ava." She jerked her head toward the campers, smile back in place. "Let's introduce you to the others before the prophet of doom gets back." She got to her feet and headed towards the campers, looking back to check if I was following. "It will be alright. I know it's all a bit of a freak show right now, but you'll get used to it."

She held out a hand, and after taking a steeling breath, I seized it.

SEVEN

Latisha linked her arm through mine, pulling me into her side in a manner that reminded me of Hayley. "That's my camper," she said, pointing out the motorhome from which Hetti had retrieved the remedies for my feet and back pain. "The next two are Luna's and Aurora's. Supernaturals share a home with their familiar and neighbour with their own kind. Beside us, are the shifters."

As if on cue, a door flew open and two men stepped out, voices raised in a heated conversation.

"Why did you come in here?" the older man snapped in a scouse accent. He was slight of build with a worn, lined face. His thinning, brown hair was sticking up on end, like he'd been tugging at it.

"I wanted to see Cuddles," the younger grumbled. Though tall and well-built, with a broad chest and thick biceps, he cowered beneath the glare of the older man. He, too, had an accent—Scottish this time—and wild, bright-orange hair.

"Ask next time, but for now, clean up your mess." The Scouser thrust a torch into the Scotsman's hands. "You'd better find it before it finds you."

Latisha stepped forward. "Hello boys! I'd like to introduce you to someone."

Both men eyed the witch, then me, frowning.

"Y'alright," the Scouser said, looking as though he was about to retreat into his camper, but Latisha seized him by the upper arm and dragged him towards me.

"This is Trevor," she said. "He is a shifter and their representative. Trevor, this is Ava."

"Nice to meet you," I said, shaking his rough, calloused hand. "Um... so who is my representative?"

"Dominic is rep for the vampires," Latisha said.

Trevor made a noise in the back of his throat. "Ugh, do not talk about that little gobshite around me. Don't mean to be rude, Tish, but me and Billy have shit we gotta do."

"We've got an escaped scorpion." Billy waggled the torch. "Pretty venomous one too—"

"The *most* venomous! And soft lad here, let it escape."

"I didn't!" Billy's voice rose a few octaves in indignation. "You're just looking for someone to pin the blame on!"

"Is Cuddles the name of the scorpion?" I asked, suppressing a laugh.

"Naw," said Billy, grinning. "Cuddles is my spider. I can show you if you like?"

"Uhhh..." My mouth went dry. Spiders had too many legs for my liking, but I wanted to make a good impression. "Go on then."

"Wait!" Trevor shouted, "Don't open the—" But it was too late. No sooner had Billy turned the handle, the door to the camper burst open, and a huge, black mass came bounding out, racing towards me. Before I could gasp, its paws were on my chest, leaning on me with such a weight I almost fell over.

"Look at you!" I said as a long, wet tongue lapped at my face. "You daft dog!" I rubbed the sides of the dog's head, who panted at me, tongue now lolling out the side of its mouth. I noted its black and copper fur. "A rottweiler?"

"Yeah," Trevor said, his once haughty expression relaxing as his eyes shone with warmth. "This is Layla." He whistled, and Layla dropped, lolloping towards him, jumping with excitement. "She's my bonded animal."

"Your what?"

"My bonded animal," he repeated, glancing at Latisha. "You've not told her about bonding, Tish?"

Latisha raised a shoulder. "I thought she should see it first-hand."

"Fine, but I'm not doing a full transformation. Not in this cold weather. Are you ready, Ava?"

Trevor's eyes widened into large, black orbs, identical to Layla's. Then his nose and mouth elongated into her muzzle, the same long, pink tongue drooping out the side of his mouth as black and copper fur sprouted over his face. It was one of the most bizarre things I'd ever seen: Layla's head perched upon Trevor's body, all the while the real Layla stood at his side, occasionally nudging him with her wet, black nose. Trevor shook himself, and before I could blink, his tired face was looking back at me.

"That's bloody amazing..." I said in awe, though it didn't do what I'd witnessed any justice.

Trevor stroked Layla's head, puffing out his chest.

"So, shifters become the animal they've bonded with? Is that it?" I asked.

"Exactly. Beginners can only take the full form of their animal," Trevor explained. "With time, they learn to shift into a hybrid. Part animal, part human, like I did just now."

"Or, like this!" Billy grinned as his eyes split into eight black, beady spheres. His mouth became something else entirely, snapping fang-tipped jaws oozing a clear goo.

"That's disgusting! Change back!"

Billy tilted his head back, roaring with laughter as his usual features reappeared. Even Trevor hid a dry, wheezing chuckle behind his hand.

"That's *not* the introduction to Cuddles I had in mind," I said, pouting with mock annoyance, though couldn't keep up the act. Billy's smile was too infectious. "How do you bond with an animal? Can I do it? I'd *love* to shapeshift. Maybe a bird, so I could fly."

I could just picture myself soaring through Kinwich like an angel. *Total freedom...*

Latisha scrunched the hair at the back of her head, thinking. "I wouldn't advise it. It involves a ritual, performed by a witch—"

"Or warlock," Trevor added.

"Or warlock—a male witch," Latisha said. "But that's why some shifters become witches' familiars. They stay with the witch, learn their craft, and become a witch themselves one day. Or they go it alone. Perhaps find a shifter master to serve while they develop their powers, like Billy did. Though you have a familiar of your own now, don't you, Billy?"

"Aye." Billy put his hands on his hips, thrusting his muscular chest out, head held high.

"And yet," Trevor said, "you're still making amateur mistakes like letting the creatures out."

"I didn't!"

"Excuse me," I interrupted, "but why would you remain a shifter when you could become a powerful witch? No offence, guys."

"None taken," Trevor said with a shrug. "Couple of reasons. One is that a shifter's bonded animal lives as long as they do. But becoming a witch or warlock severs the bond with the animal." His hand drifted to Layla's ears, stroking one between his thumb and index finger. "The animal dies. And another thing: becoming a witch or warlock comes at a heavy price. But I'll let Tish explain that one."

"Cheers," Latisha said in a dry voice. "Becoming a witch is..." She tilted her head upward, the stars reflecting in her huge, dark eyes, as she inhaled through gritted teeth, perhaps wondering just how much detail she wanted to divulge. "Well, it requires a contract with a demon. And they pop up regularly and demand more payment to renew it."

"A demon? Like, from Hell?" I'd never have believed Hell existed a few days ago, but then again, I wouldn't have believed vampires and witches were real either.

"Some sort of Hell-like dimension, at least. It comprises nine layers and is a place of eternal torment."

"Nine layers, huh? Dante got that right, then."

"Oh, do you know Dante?"

I blinked at her. "No, not personally. Do *you* know Dante?"

She shrugged. "How well can you really *know* someone? Especially after only a couple of meetings."

My mouth fell open. "Latisha, how old exactly *are* you?"

"I'm not entirely sure. Perhaps over nine hundred? I don't think I've reached a thousand yet. Anyway," she said, ignoring my dumbstruck expression as I gaped at her, "as for payment, it depends on which demon the contract is with. They each have their own preferred methods. The demon I have a contract with is Lascivious."

"Yeah, I bet he is," I said with a snigger. Demons were bound to be sexual.

"Lascivious is his *name*." Latisha folded her arms. "Though it does suit him."

"And if you don't renew the contract?"

"You lose your abilities."

"Is that all?"

"Technically, yes. But bear in mind that a witch's abilities keep them youthful. Without those abilities..." She shuddered. "I've only seen it happen once. A member of our coven didn't pay. She morphed into a... I'm not sure what it was. A decaying creature, not quite animal, certainly not human. I'm still haunted by the sound of her bones cracking into unnatural shapes, blood and entrails pouring out of her. Withering away. Decomposing, but remaining conscious. Had she been able to form words, she'd have begged for death. I put her out of her misery myself."

I was lost for words. *And I thought my student loan contract was brutal...*

"Demons still hound me for a contract," Billy said with a grimace. "The more sinister demons leave me alone now—thank God—but Mischievous and Avaricious still try their luck. Perhaps in a century or two they'll leave me in peace."

Though I hated to admit it, Latisha was right. I shouldn't get involved in this. "Ok, I get the picture. I won't become a shifter. I draw the line at being stalked by demons."

"Good choice," Latisha said. "And just a reminder, Ava, it's not the *type* of supernatural that makes you powerful, but the individual themselves. Shifters have achieved equality in the last hundred years and have got their own factions within covens, but some are still prejudiced, thinking them the weakest among us."

"Like Ivan..." Billy said, so quietly that his lips barely moved.

"Alright, alright," Trevor snapped. "Enough of the history lesson. Listen Tish, we really gotta find this scorpion. Come back later and I'll introduce the newbie to the other shifters."

"Good luck finding it, Billy," I said, giving him a playful nudge.

"Don't worry, I will." Billy clicked the button on the torch on and off a couple of times, bathing his features in a purple hue. "Luckily, they glow in UV light, so it shouldn't take long. But if you get a wee sting in the night"—he pinched my arm—"you'll know I was unsuccessful."

He grinned a wide, cheeky smile.

As I walked with Latisha to the next set of caravans, I heard Billy and Trevor resume their argument over which of them had lost the scorpion.

"Poor Billy," Latisha said, smirking. "But he should have known better than to go snooping in Trevor's camper. Then again, it's Trevor who insists on keeping the bonded animals in there."

"You mean he *sleeps* in there with scorpions and stuff?"

"Weird, right?" Latisha laughed. "I'd be alright with Layla, and the birds are pretty, but the creepie crawlies are gross. And the *snake.*" She shuddered. "I wouldn't get a wink of sleep if it were me."

She stopped at the door of another motorhome and knocked.

A man with a thick, black beard answered the door, his glossy hair tied in a ponytail.

"Yes?" he asked in a deep, gruff voice, slotting his hands into the front pocket of his hoodie.

"Hi, Alfred. Are you busy?"

"Afraid so. I've got the pack with me. We're having a meeting about our plans for our attractions. They need a lick of paint and a few upgrades, if you ask me."

Standing on tiptoes, I peered over Alfred's shoulder and into the camper. A group of men and women sat around a table. Though a couple looked in my direction, most were caught up in their discussion, jabbing their fingers at pieces of paper that littered the table.

Their voices were raised in unmistakable enthusiasm rather than conflict; the opposite of meetings I'd grown accustom to.

"All work and no play, Alfred?"

"*Someone* has to. I spoke to Ivan about having a relaunch and getting some new machines in, but he doesn't give a toss anymore. What's the point in posing as showmen if he won't run the funfair properly? I mean..." Alfred lowered his voice, leaning close to Latisha, so that I could barely make out what he was saying. "We have *got* to keep up the appearance. Ivan doesn't believe the rumours of the Hallows return. But perhaps he's forgotten that *some of us* are hiding from our own kind, as well as humans. Appearance is everything." Alfred narrowed his eyes at me, only now realising I was there. "Who's this?"

"This is Ava. Len's new familiar. Ava, this is Alfred, the werewolf rep."

Alfred winced. "Is she actually Len's? Or has Ivan palmed her off, like he did Austin? Sorry, Ava, if I do not get too attached. Humans don't survive very long here. Good luck though."

"Gee, thanks," I said. "Very reassuring."

He shrugged. "I say it as it is. Look out, Tish. You got company." He pointed behind us.

Turning, we saw another figure approaching and this time I recognised them; it was the tangle-haired, leather-clad vampire that had assisted in Austin's abduction.

"Jacob," Latisha said through a clenched jaw, forcing a tight smile. Before I could say goodbye to Alfred, he'd closed the door to his camper.

"Latisha!" called Jacob. "Bring the girl to the campfire. Master Ivan wants to see her." My stomach twisted as I watched him head into the grandest of all the motorhomes.

"Come on." Latisha took my hand and gave it a squeeze. "Time to meet our master."

We headed back to the campfire where the witches were still sitting. As soon as we arrived, they rose to their feet, looking beyond us. Following their gaze, I saw Jacob exit the motorhome, accompanied by the other henchman who'd captured Austin, still dressed like he'd walked out of a photo-shoot. Next was Dominic, and my insides seemed to melt away as I caught his smirking expression. And finally, Madigan, along with a behemoth of a man towering above him and about twice his width.

"That's Ivan," Latisha said in a hushed voice as they approached, her lips barely moving. "Always address him as Master, or Master Ivan. Do not answer back. Be respectful. You don't want to make him angry."

My heart was hammering against my ribcage. Unsure what to do with my hands, I crossed my arms, but thinking that might give a poor impression, settled with holding them behind my back.

Ivan stepped into the glow of the campfire, his broad facial features illuminated for the first time. He had icy-blue eyes behind a pair of small, square-shaped spectacles. He dressed in a beige, striped suit, the buttons on his waistcoat straining to accommodate his immense frame. His thick lips split into a smile that did not reach his eyes as he flicked open a zippo lighter and began puffing on a fat cigar that was dwarfed by his sausage-like fingers.

"You must be Ava Monroe." His voice was a deep rumble. "I've heard interesting things about you."

EIGHT

Ivan leant down close, his face mere inches from mine. The heat from the end of his cigar burnt my cheek, but I stood my ground, clenching my fists, refusing to let the sharp, blistering pain defeat me. His exhalation smelt oddly metallic, mixed with the usual scent of smoker's breath. I locked my eyes onto his, unblinking, until they watered.

"I hope Dominic Chase is mistaken. He thinks you ran away from the coven after being offered a position with us?" Ivan removed his spectacles, cleaned them with a cloth from his breast pocket, and replaced them on his nose before scrutinising me.

I hated lying, but what choice did I have?

"He was definitely mistaken." I threw Dominic a filthy look. "Madigan told me to collect some belongings, but Dominic interrupted me. He damn well nearly broke my neck. I mean no disrespect, Master Ivan, but I think that dog needs a leash."

Ivan's eyes widened and nostrils flared. For a horrible moment, I thought I'd overstepped the mark, but he let out a short laugh, turning his head towards Dominic.

"Ha! She doesn't like you."

"Like I give a shit what she thinks," Dominic said, just audible over the crackling fire, but Ivan ignored him.

"I'm surprised Leonard Madigan allows you to call him by his last name only, and not Master Leonard or *Mister* Madigan. It's highly unusual, and the sort of disrespect I enjoy stamping out of my familiars."

Someone who refers to people by their full names probably shouldn't lecture about what's unusual... I clenched my jaw until my teeth ached, scared my thoughts might come tumbling out.

Ivan glared at Madigan over his shoulder, before returning his gaze to me, looking up and down, head tilted to one side. "He's always been too affectionate, but perhaps that's why he has chosen a *girl* as his familiar, if you know what I mean."

Madigan shifted his weight from one foot to the other, tugging at the cuffs of his tailcoat, shooting me a warning glance not to rise to the taunt.

"Still," Ivan said, "I'm glad he has broken his self-imposed isolation. Perhaps you might survive long enough to be converted. I hope you won't cling to your mortality for long. I like familiars to undertake their trial and join the ranks of the supernaturals swiftly. We should wash away the stench of humanity, do you concur?"

"Absolutely!" Though unsure of what he was talking about, I figured it would be smart to agree with him.

His smile widened, revealing yellowing, tombstone-shaped teeth biting down on his cigar. It was anything but reassuring. A bead of cold sweat ran down the back of my neck and trickled down my spine, sending a shudder up my back that I tried to conceal.

"We usually give vampire familiars a month to complete their trial. Only then are they officially recruited into the coven. But given your eagerness, I think a fortnight should suffice."

"Master Ivan." Madigan stepped forward. "I must protest. We give new recruits a month so that they have adequate time to prepare. A fortnight isn't long enough for Miss Monroe to receive the proper training."

"Ha! I disagree," Ivan said with a mocking laugh. "She has two weeks. One week to train. One week to complete the task. If she's as keen as you say, two weeks is perfectly sufficient. Perhaps this time, you will fulfil your duty properly and we won't need to execute this one! I was foolish to have left my familiar in your care."

Madigan stepped back. Although only illuminated by the campfire, I could see that his already pale face was whiter than usual. It was disconcerting to see the calm and collected Madigan rattled. I tried to swallow, but found my mouth had become dry, in contrast to my body that was now slick with sweat, causing my t-shirt to stick to my back.

Ivan paused, exhaled smoke from his cigar through his nostrils, and slowly cracked his thick neck to one side. He turned back to me, his insincere smile in place. "Speaking of which, I think you should witness what happens to recruits that fail their trial within the allotted time. I assume you know what your task will be?"

"I have to harvest blood from a human?" I guessed, recalling the conversation between Madigan and Austin.

"Correct. There are rules to be followed, but I'm certain that won't be trouble for you. It would be a pity if you broke them."

Ivan turned to Dominic and nodded. Dominic must have understood what this gesture meant. He walked away, taking Jacob with him, presumably to carry out the silent order. Within a few minutes, their orders became apparent as high-pitched screams of terror reached us before they came back into view. They returned, dragging Austin between them, who was digging the heels of his feet into the ground in a vain attempt to pull himself from their grip.

He looked dreadful; his hair was limp and scraggly, soaked with sweat, eyes puffy and bloodshot, one encircled with a large, purple bruise, and his lower lip split. When he screamed, I noticed gaps of missing teeth. The noises issuing from Austin churned my stomach, similar to the sounds of a tortured animal. I'd never heard such fear. They brought him before Ivan and threw him to the ground.

"Master Ivan." Austin's voice was high, strangled by terror. "Please have mercy on me."

Ivan knelt down to his level and pinched his cheeks in one hand, puffing smoke into the boy's bloodied face, the false smile teetering on the edge of a wild, sadistic grin.

"Shush now." Ivan's voice remained calm, but the pleasant facade that he had reserved for me had disappeared, the monster within rearing its head. "As poor a mentor as Leonard Madigan was, accept that your fate is your own responsibility."

"No, please! You're right—he was a terrible mentor. I am *your* familiar. I want to be trained by *you*."

"You do not deserve my tutelage. Perhaps if you had simply failed to harvest in time, I would show you the mercy of a quick, clean death. But you broke our rules—a betrayal—and for that, you need a sufficient punishment."

They looked into each other's faces. Austin's was filthy, streaked with tears and sweat, whereas Ivan's was verging on gleeful.

"I think death by *pressing* would be suitable."

"NO!" Austin screeched and tried to get to his feet, but Dominic and Jacob immediately seized him. "I'm sorry! I'm sorry! Please, not that!"

Ivan simply waved a hand. "Take him away and prepare him for his execution. Leonard Madigan, Sebastian Lawrence."

Madigan and the smartly-dressed vampire stood to attention.

"Summon together all the vampire familiars and get the execution site ready. You know what's required." They nodded, but Madigan kept his head bowed, unable to meet my eye.

"Latisha Abara." Ivan turned to the witches around the campfire. "Gather everyone else—the werewolves, shifters, and their familiars—to witness the execution. This coven is getting lax, and I think I need to send a message."

"Yes, Master Ivan." Latisha nodded. She, too, seemed to avoid eye contact with me. "Witches, we have our orders."

All the women gave a small bow to Latisha and then Ivan before dispersing, leaving me alone with the giant.

"Have you heard of pressing?" he asked. "It's an ancient method of execution with a fascinating history."

I shook my head, not sure I *wanted* to know. The firelight danced in his eyes as his excitement bubbled beneath the surface of his otherwise relaxed expression.

"Don't worry. This isn't something you'll forget. It's exactly what I want you to think about next time you have any ideas of running away."

"But I didn't—"

"Do you take me for a fool?" His smile vanished, fixing me with a look that made my bladder feel weak. "I *know* you tried to run. I feel it in my blood. Let's get one thing clear, Ava Monroe. There is only one way out of this coven, and it is a slow, painful exit. I've been ruling over this coven for decades. The coven of Kinwich. One of the most significant cities for supernatural beings in the human world, with a long, bloody history. And if you think I'm going to let you—an infinitesimal pustule upon the Earth—mess that up by exposing our existence to the humans, you're *dead* wrong. And perhaps, this little demonstration will be a reminder of that next time you get itchy feet."

I was alone with Ivan beside the campfire for over an hour, obsessively checking my watch only to discover a few minutes had passed. On the couple of occasions I tried to speak, Ivan raised a dinner plate sized hand as I drew breath, shooting me a dark look that plainly said, '*Do not speak*'. He returned his gaze to the fire, the blaze reflected in the lenses of his spectacles.

Without warning, his head snapped upward, and he looked behind him. Following his gaze, at first, all I saw was darkness, but soon identified the dim outline of Madigan's unmistakable coattails.

"Everything is prepared, Master Ivan," Madigan said when he reached us, his eyebrows knitted together in a grim expression. "Everyone has assembled and we await your presence."

"Very good." Ivan stood, drawing himself up to his impressive height. "Let's not keep them waiting. Keep your familiar close." His lips twisted into a sickening grin. "Newcomers usually faint when witnessing their first execution."

Ivan shoved past Madigan, who nearly lost his balance.

"Are you ready?" he asked, rubbing his shoulder where the giant had knocked into him.

I opened my mouth to answer, but my voice had disappeared. I wanted to tell him the truth, that I *wasn't* ready, but I was still wearing the mask of someone braver than myself. Perhaps it was a trick of the light, but Madigan's expression appeared to soften, lips parted as though he wished to offer words of comfort but didn't know how.

"Come on," he said after a pause. "Stay close."

I accompanied him to a part of the yard I'd not yet been, beyond the campers, lorries, and containers. Once past them, we came upon another locked gate and climbed over it to find woodland. I almost tripped as I navigated a narrow, muddy path in the darkness. Vampires, and perhaps all supernatural beings, must have better eyesight than humans. I shadowed Madigan, stepping where he stepped. It wasn't long before mud and dead leaves caked my trainers and my mind drifted back to my Doc Martens sitting in the cupboard backstage, and the old life I'd abandoned—for now, at least. But I couldn't dwell on it for long, concentrating as I manoeuvred over rotten, fallen trees, the damp moss slimy beneath my hands, adding to the grime that already coated them. Among the musty smell of earth and decaying wood, there was a smoky scent on the wind that grew stronger the further we walked. Soon enough, I made out an orange glow ahead—a fire that lit a small clearing within the woods.

The scene that lay before me stopped me in my tracks. Wooden boards upon the ground. A gathering of people stood in a circle around them. The shadows cast by the dancing flames warped their faces into demonic grimaces. Jacob and Sebastian held Austin, who was shirtless, kneeling in the mud. His head was bent downward so I couldn't see his face, but from the way his body shook, I knew he must be sobbing.

I've walked into Hell...

Madigan noticed I'd frozen and took me by the elbow, leading me towards the crowd. I recognised the witches and their familiars, as well as Trevor, Billy, and Alfred among them. Latisha spotted us and left her group.

Putting an arm around my shoulder, she whispered, "I'll stay with you until this is over."

Ivan stood upon the wooden boards and placed something small in the centre before advancing on Austin. Straining my eyes, I realised it was a small rock, perhaps the size of a clenched fist.

"It's time," Ivan said, and his minions pulled Austin to his feet. Weak as he was from his struggles with the vampires, Austin continued to writhe in their grip, grunting with the effort of trying to free himself.

"Looks like you will have to force him into position." Ivan couldn't keep the amusement from his voice.

The vampires wrestled with Austin, forcing him to lie with his spine pressed against the rock, before Ivan seized another wooden board and lay it on top of the terrified boy, so that only his head and feet were now visible. I squinted, mind racing. Yes, it appeared uncomfortable. But fatal? I didn't understand.

"Keep him in place," Ivan said as Austin thrashed beneath the board. Jacob and Sebastian kept him pinned while Ivan turned his back to retrieve something nearby, obscured by onlookers. When he returned, my stomach twisted, vomit pushing up my throat, but I forced it back down. In one hand he held a metal, trapezium-shaped weight with a ring handle—the kind you usually saw in cartoons.

"No! Please don't do it!" Austin's face was glistening in the firelight with sweat, tears, and mucus streaming from his nose.

His cries turned into ear-splitting screams as Ivan lowered the weight onto the board with a heavy THUNK. The weight expelled the air from Austin's lungs and escaped his mouth in a choking gasp. Screaming between shallow wheezes, he fought for breath.

I clamped my hands around my mouth, stifling a cry as the realisation of what I was witnessing hit me. Ivan looked from Austin, to me, grinning, a wicked glint in his eye, before retrieving another weight. I couldn't stop the shakes that vibrated through my entire body. Every instinct told me to run, but the grip of fear paralysed me to the spot, my legs unresponsive, heavy as the weights Ivan was lifting. Latisha's grip around my shoulder tightened.

Jacob and Sebastian stepped away; Austin had no chance of escaping now.

THUNK. Ivan added another weight. Austin's screams turned into shrieks that could have shattered glass.

THUNK.

Ivan let out a bark of laughter. "Ha! This one is a fighter! Don't give up now, Austin Blane. We have a long way to go!"

"I c-can't watch." My body was shaking so violently that my teeth chattered. Even my bones were quivering. My stomach felt like it was trying to force itself up into my throat. I looked away, instead watching the coven. Most had their sights set on the grotesque spectacle before them with unwavering determination. Billy had a white-knuckled grip on a curly-haired youth's shoulder, who, like me, was trembling, his eyes wide and face pale.

"I'll tell you when it's over," Latisha said in a hushed voice, "but look up when I tell you. Ivan will be watching."

I lowered my head and screwed my eyes tight shut, but there was nothing I could do about the sounds that assaulted my ears.

THUNK.

The shrieks that continued to issue from Austin penetrated my soul.

Make it stop... Please make it stop!

THUNK

Ivan's mirthful voice was just audible over Austin's bloodcurdling howls. "What's wrong? Didn't think you were the type to *crack* under pressure?"

THUNK—SNAP!

"Look up!" Latisha hissed in my ear.

I jolted my head upward, just as terrified of being caught out by Ivan as I was the scene before me that burned into my retinas.

The board had lowered considerably, and there was something dark oozing from beneath it. Austin's mouth opened and closed as he gasped, his screams growing quieter, but the wet gurgles in his throat went on, and on... and on...

He'd turned his head to the side, his wide, haunting eyes pinned on *me*. The dark liquid was now bubbling in his throat, trickling out of the corner of his mouth.

Please, just die. This has gone on too long. Please, Austin, just die...

My ribcage felt too tight. I clutched at my chest, gasping for breath, my head swimming. I felt another hand—Madigan's—seize my arm and steady me.

"Hang in there," he said. "It should be over soon."

But it wasn't soon enough. It was a long wait—perhaps fifteen minutes—until Austin went quiet and still. The only remaining sounds were the crackling fire and my pounding heart. Austin's un-focused, glassy eyes were still fixed on me, his slack mouth open from his last silent scream.

Ivan snapped his fingers and immediately Jacob and Sebastian began removing the weights, and finally the wooden board. I retched. Austin's torso was a bloody mess, broken ribs bursting from his sides, his flesh ripped and pulpy.

"So then, Ava Monroe," Ivan said at last, stretching, his shoulders clicking. Now it wasn't just Austin, but the entire coven with their eyes on me. "I think you'd better get training. You wouldn't want to end up like this"—he nudged Austin's head with his foot, a sickening smirk on his thick lips—"would you?"

NINE

We walked in silence, but Austin's screams still echoed in my brain. The image of his broken body flashed before my eyes, making my stomach writhe, an acidic taste at the back of my throat. I quickened my pace, almost stumbling in the dark, desperate to return to the caravan. I broke into a half-jog when the campers came into view, the pressure in my stomach almost at its peak.

"Good luck, Ava Monroe." Ivan's cruel voice stopped me as I grabbed the door handle. "I look forward to officially accepting you into the coven. And remember, break the rules, and I will break *you*."

I nodded in response, the sour taste in my mouth intensifying.

Unable to hold it back, I crossed the threshold, went straight to the sink, knowing what was about to happen. My stomach crunched, and a spasm ran through my body as I erupted, vomit splattering into the washing-up bowl.

I opened my mouth to apologise to Madigan, but before I could spit the words out, my insides contracted, and I had to release into the sink again. My hair was slick to my forehead, soaked in a cold sweat. I spat, head bent down, afraid to emerge too early.

"Oh, dear," Latisha's voice said from the doorway. "I thought she looked peaky. Don't just stand there, Len. Help her out!"

Someone was rummaging in one of the kitchen cupboards beside me, but before I could pay them any mind, a third wave of retching interrupted me. My stomach crunched, but I was running on empty and had only a burning, yellow liquid left to give. I raised my head, dripping with sweat, a stream of mucus running down my upper lip.

A pale, long-fingered hand appeared in my line of vision, holding a square of kitchen towel. I took it and wiped my face before turning to my companions, clinging to what remained of my dignity.

"Where is it?" Latisha said from inside the cupboard, pulling out a purple, glass bottle. "This is your potion stash, isn't it? Where is the Mollifier?"

She pulled out more bottles. One I'd seen before—the small, blue bottle with a red gem set in the lid—the one Austin had suggested I take. The next, a darker shade of blue, patterned with silver moons and stars.

"I... uh..." Madigan's white cheeks flushed red. "I've run out."

"I topped you up this month! What have you done with it all?"

"I had a tough week..."

"It isn't for recreational use." Latisha gave him a small backhanded slap on the arm.

Madigan's nostrils flared, the redness in his cheeks deepening. "It wasn't recreational," he said through clenched teeth, lowering his voice. "Those accursed humans were celebrating with *fireworks*. Night after night. It's sufferable when they're set off at midnight, but New Year has become a week-long celebration for those cretins."

"Ahhh, yes." Latisha gave an understanding nod, smiling weakly. "Well, be careful. Overdosing can have strange side effects." She turned her attention back to me. "Ava, I'm going to get something from my camper. I'll be back in five."

She left, and I was alone with the vampire.

"Latisha will be back soon," he said, drumming his fingers on the kitchen counter while I cleaned the sink. Each time I looked at him, he turned his head, avoiding eye contact. It felt like a long five minutes, but as promised, Latisha returned with a vial containing a sunny-yellow liquid.

"Drink it all," she said as she handed it to me. I gave her a dubious look. "Go on. It will help."

I knocked the liquid back. It had a pleasant flavour, almost floral, leaving a warm sensation in my chest like doing a shot of vodka. Almost immediately, a wave of calm washed over me. The tension in my shoulders eased as my muscles relaxed and the warmth in my chest spread through my body. I let out a long breath as the tightness in my chest dissipated. Even my squirming stomach unwound from the knot it had tied itself up into.

"Sit down," Latisha said, gesturing behind me.

I obeyed, leaning into the sofa that felt squashier than I remembered. Latisha handed Madigan a larger bottle with a cork stopper containing the same yellow liquid.

"Make this last until November, and I'll replenish it for Bonfire Night."

Madigan inhaled so that his nostrils pinched and gave her a curt nod. "I appreciate it."

"Ava." Latisha's huge, brown eyes were on me again, and I smiled at her, fighting back a strange urge to laugh, feeling dopier by the second. "I want you to rest up. If you can't sleep, use this." She shook the small, blue bottle with the red gem lid. "A couple of drops will make you drowsy. The whole lot will knock you out. You can start your training with Len tomorrow night. Do you understand?"

"Uh huh..." I said, and dribbled down my front. I tried to wipe the drool from my chin, but my hands wouldn't do what I wanted, like trying to play a game with the controls reversed. "Woah, this stuff is crazy..." My voice sounded slower and deeper than usual.

"Len, take care of her. You know how easily influenced people are after a shot of Mollifier."

Latisha left, but before she could close the door, Madigan addressed her, again keeping his voice low. Despite his efforts, I could still hear them.

"Thank you for your help, but I'd be grateful if you wouldn't undermine me in front of my familiar. She's unruly enough as it is."

"I'll stop undermining you if you stop trying to be a big, bad, *scary* vampire. You know you're not like the others, Len. Stop pretending to be."

She closed the door, once again leaving me alone with Madigan. I averted my gaze, pretending I'd not been listening.

Madigan pinched the bridge of his nose with eyes closed, before surveying me with an expression someone might give a troublesome puppy. "I'm going to"—he whirled about, like he was searching for something—"tidy up."

There was nothing to tidy; Madigan was obviously one of those types that cleaned as he went. Nevertheless, he reorganised a few things in the illusion of busying himself. I felt useless sitting there watching him, but the Mollifier was still coursing through me, making the world seem hazy. After a few minutes of arranging some tatty, faded books on a shelf he removed his tailcoat, tutting as he examined flecks of dirt and blood visible against the black fabric.

"Why do you wear that?" I asked. My lips were numb, but I was relieved that I'd spoken without dribbling this time.

"It's what I like to wear," he said with a shrug, now leaning back against the kitchen counter, arms folded. "Though modernised, it reminds me of the fashion I wore as a young man. Black is my preferred colour. But I have others. Red, blue, green..." His voice trailed off. I knew why. He must have thought of Austin. "Those are for special occasions."

"And the top hats? I've not seen you wearing them. What are they for?"

"I have those for when I'm working. I run the funfair's haunted house attraction, and it goes well with the general ambiance."

Of course he runs the haunted house. As if he wasn't weird enough already.

"Speaking of my clothes, the laundry will be one of your responsibilities. Mine, and everyone else's. But take extra care with mine; they're tailor made, and expensive."

"No problem," I said, plastering on a confident smile, though a fluttering in my stomach suggested that the Mollifier was already wearing off. "What else will I have to do?"

"The other familiars have their own jobs, but should they become incapacitated, we will ask you to cover their work, too. As for your role within the funfair, I imagine you will be just litter picking and drawing in crowds like..."

Like Austin used to...

"Like others have done before you. Do you have any useful skills?"

"Well, I can sew, so laundry duty is perfect for me," I said, giving him an over-the-top thumbs up. "But besides that, I studied art for video games at Uni, which I doubt is a transferrable skill."

Litter picking didn't sound like it would be much fun, but a lot of students did menial jobs after graduation, so in that sense, my situation wasn't dissimilar.

Madigan's mouth twitched as if trying to suppress a rare smile. "You studied video games at university?" I noted a hint of amusement in his voice. The cheeky bastard was judging me!

"Concept art *for* video games," I said slowly, as though speaking to someone stupid. "It's ok if you don't understand. How *old* exactly are you?"

His eyes widened, either impressed or shocked by my gumption. "I am one hundred and thirty-something. Or is it forty-something?" He rubbed his chin. "I think it's thirty. Most of our kind lose track of their age during our second century. And yourself?"

"Twenty-two. So, a bit of an age gap, huh? Shame. It will never work between us."

Madigan ran his hand over his mouth and I was certain that, once again, he was trying to hide a smile.

"Is it weird looking younger than you really are?" I asked.

"Age is relative. Compared to other vampires, I am considered young. When I became a vampire, the man who sired me was around eight hundred."

"Damn…" I rubbed the back of my neck, frowning as I tried to imagine what the world was like eight hundred years ago. "That *is* old."

"Yes, he was. But looked to be in his forties—the age he became a vampire. Our kind does not age while we feed regularly, but should we stop feeding, our bodies age rapidly. The older we are, the faster the ageing process, and even vampires cannot live in a body that ages beyond function. So, as you can see, it is important we feed. Which is why we recruit familiars to assist us in obtaining the blood we need, whether harvested from another human, or themselves."

"Damn…" I said again, lost for words. I'd figured vampire lore I'd picked up from books and movies couldn't be entirely accurate, but it was strange to talk about it in such a matter-of-fact way. "Why did you join the coven? No offence, but I don't think it was the best decision you've ever made. Ivan is a bit of a tyrant, isn't he?"

Madigan grimaced. "Speak quietly if you're going to say such things." He slid down into the seat opposite me, leaning on his elbows as he leant in close. "I was in a dark place when I joined. My former master was murdered by a group that called themselves the Hallows—an organisation that kill supernaturals—and it was not a swift death. Ivan and his coven assisted me in taking out the Hallows responsible and wiped out their infestation within Kinwich. The price for their help was my membership. Since I required help locating the culprits, it seemed like a good idea... at the time."

"And not anymore?"

He fixed me with a hard stare, possibly thinking of how he should respond, weighing up if he trusted me enough to be completely honest. "There have been rumours of the Hallows recent return that Ivan has dismissed. Those of us acquainted with the Hallows are somewhat... frustrated. But it doesn't matter. We can't leave, and Ivan remains in charge unless someone challenges him to a fight to the death for leadership."

"I can't see that happening," I said with a snort of sarcastic laughter. "He's built like a brick shit house."

"And he has Dominic guarding him."

"Dominic doesn't look fit to guard anybody. He looks like he might keel over at any moment."

"Don't let his appearance fool you. Even I'd be no match for him," Madigan said with a scowl.

"But you're bigger than him. You're taller, more muscular."

"He looks the way he does because he drinks a lot more blood than I do." Madigan wrinkled his nose with the same look of disgust he'd given me during our first meeting. "I limit myself to a mouthful each night. If a vampire drinks too much, they become a monster. We call it *'going rabid'*. Human blood is highly addictive and if we indulge in our addictions"—he inhaled through his teeth as he searched for the right words—"we lose the humanity we have left. We lose our self-control, our self-awareness. You might say we lose our soul and become nothing but a mindless beast. Those monstrous, fanged depictions of vampires you've seen in films were inspired by rabid vampires. We call them Brain Eaters, as they're no longer content with merely drinking blood, but eat the brain, too."

"That's bloody disgusting!"

"Yes, it is rather distasteful."

"So, how is Dominic able to control himself?"

"He is teetering on the edge of going rabid. If he keeps drinking as he does, it won't be much longer. Ivan views him as a wild dog, and when Dominic takes it too far, Ivan will just stick a leash on him. He kept a Brain Eater called Beckett for *years* like that, until... the accident..."

I didn't know how to respond. This was information overload. I thought vampires were straightforward: they drank blood, didn't age, had enhanced speed and strength and couldn't walk in daylight. The End. But they were more complex than that. I felt sick again. The Mollifier must have worn off.

"I think I might be out of my depth here," I said with an unconvincing laugh. "There is so much to remember. Vampires with and without fangs. Shifters who serve witches and shifters that don't." I rubbed my temples. "How am I meant to process this?"

"You'll be fine. After all, you attended university. You must have *something* between your ears."

"Well then, I really *am* screwed. Did I mention I was failing? I thought university would be good for me, but I was wrong. I wanted to be part of a community, and student life sounded like fun. So much freedom, y'know? After Grandma died, all I wanted was to belong somewhere."

"I am sorry for your loss. I assume you have no other family?"

I looked into his eyes, biting my lower lip. This wasn't territory I usually walked with strangers. Was he genuinely interested? Or was he probing to find out if he needed to explain my disappearance to them? Or worse—finding out if there was anyone he needed to dispose of? It didn't matter either way.

"My mother, but I haven't seen her since I was twelve, after she got herself a new boyfriend."

I played with my fingers as I thought about her. Madigan would have difficulty finding her, and even if he did, I didn't care what happened to her, or *Darren*. I shuddered at the mere thought of his name.

"And I've had no contact with my father. They deemed him an '*unfit parent*'." I sketched quotation marks with my fingers. "That's all, really. I don't know if I have family on my father's side, and my mother was an only child. Grandma was all I had." I shrugged, feigning nonchalance, but I had already shared more than I usually would.

"I'm... I'm sorry to hear that. I've lost loved ones, too." Madigan turned his face away, looking at the old, black and white photographs framed on a shelf. Only upon closer inspection did I realise Madigan was the groom in the wedding photo, as well as one of the soldiers in the other. "My wife. Our child. My dearest friend..." He swallowed, but his stony expression remained fixed.

"I'm sorry. That must have been shit."

"Yes. That's one way to describe it." Madigan didn't take his eyes from the photos.

If a friend had dropped this bombshell, I might have known how to comfort them, but Madigan was still a mystery to me. An uncomfortable silence followed as I wracked my brain to change the subject.

"Latisha said I should rest."

"You know where your bed is." Madigan nodded towards the other end of the caravan. "It's as you left it."

I hauled myself to my feet, my legs sluggish.

"I'm going out," Madigan said, mirroring me, standing. "Is it safe to assume you will still be here upon my return?"

"Don't worry," I said, getting ready to draw the curtain around my bed, "I'm not going anywhere."

"Miss Monroe." Madigan's eyes shifted to one side as he tugged on his shirt cuff. "I want you to enjoy your time here as best you can. Is sewing a hobby of yours?"

I nodded.

"Could you repair this?" He pulled the bottle-green waistcoat that Austin had borrowed from a cupboard. "It has a rip at the shoulder. Normally I'd be furious at the person who'd damaged it but, on this occasion..." His voice trailed away.

"No problem," I said, sparing him the need to finish his sentence. He didn't need to know that *I'd* been the one to damage it.

"The sleeping draught is there if you need it." He pointed to the small, blue bottle still set on the kitchen counter. "Make sure you get some sleep. We'll begin your training tomorrow."

"Thanks, Madigan. I appreciate it."

He coughed into a clenched fist, the palest of red tinges appearing on his cheeks. "It would probably be best if you addressed me as Master Len, or Mr Madigan."

"Alright, *Madigan*, I will keep that in mind." I winked at him before drawing the curtain, ending our conversation. I listened to him rummaging as he readied himself to leave, muttering under his breath, and though I couldn't make out exactly what he was saying, I was sure one of the words was '*petulant*'.

Now finally alone—or as alone as one can be in a small caravan—I closed my eyes, and exhaled slowly. Austin's remains flashed before my mind's eye and I flinched. *I've only one option,* I reasoned with myself. *Keep your head down, follow orders, play Ivan's game, and then*—my stomach gave a sickening lurch as I contemplated the consequences of failure—*when the time is right, get the hell out of Dodge.*

TEN

T raining with Madigan was crap. He'd been surprisingly patient while showing me how to draw blood, but when he'd offered his arms for me to practise on, my attempts had been unsuccessful, either unable to draw blood at all, or bruising him so badly that if I'd harvested for real, I could expect a fight with my victim, as I'd done with Austin.

"I think that's enough practise for now," he said, pressing down on his inner elbow as blood leaked from the scratch, none of which had reached the vial I'd failed to attach. "Besides, you have another duty to attend to." He picked up his laundry basket and dumped it into my arms. "I'm going out to harvest. If you have time to take a break, I'd advise you to practise on others, should they allow it."

That evening I learnt a valuable lesson: laundry duty was shit. Some of the fancier motorhomes had washers and dryers which I took advantage of. Jacob and Sebastian were among those who *didn't* let me use theirs, preferring to leave their baskets outside and letting me struggle. I didn't even bother asking to use Ivan's. Besides, his suits, like Madigan's, needed to be hand washed.

It wasn't long before my elbows ached from the constant scrubbing, and my back muscles seized up from being hunched over the wash bucket while sat on a stool. My fingertips wrinkled from how long I'd submerged them in the water, but I didn't rush, working meticulously as I washed out the stubborn reddish-brown stains from Ivan's jacket.

"You not finished yet, hen?" Billy's jovial voice called. My neck clicked as I looked up from the wash bucket to see him heading my way.

I shook my head in indignation. "I'd like to see you do it faster."

"Easy." A pair of arms burst from Billy's sides.

"Show off. Don't you have lunch to prepare? I'll be disappointed if it's as bland as breakfast."

He and his familiar were tasked with the coven's catering.

"Ouch! Bit harsh," he said with a laugh as he sat himself on the step up to Madigan's caravan. "Growing extra limbs certainly helps get the job done faster. That, and having a familiar. W-why are you staring at me like that?"

"If you can grow extra limbs, could you let me practise drawing blood from them?"

Billy winced. "I hate needles."

I looked at him pleadingly.

"Oh, go on then. As it's for a good cause. You can practise on these after lunch." He flexed the muscles of his extra arms, then pouted his lips, blowing me a kiss.

I spluttered with laughter. "Never mind your muscles. I bet having extra *hands* makes you popular with the ladies." I wiggled my eyebrows, smirking.

"Anna's never complained."

"Oooh, who's *Anna*?" I asked, intrigued. But rather than his usual cheeky smile, Billy's expression dropped. "What's wrong?"

"I shouldn't have mentioned her." Billy retracted his extra arms and adjusted his shirt as he looked about, as though concerned someone was eavesdropping. He fixed me with a serious expression. "Please don't tell anyone."

"Of course, but why?"

Billy swallowed, his eyes flicking from side to side as he focused on each of mine, running a hand over his mouth before the words tumbled out. "Alright, fine. Anna is my girlfriend, but she's human. Ivan doesn't know about her. If he found out—"

"Say no more." I raised a hand. "I understand."

"Cheers, Ava. Only Trevor and Tish know about her. It just sort of slipped out."

"It slipped out? I bet you say that to all the girls." I winked, and Billy's sombre expression cracked into his usual grin.

Before he could retort, the sound of a door slamming interrupted him. I sprung to my feet. I'd not realised how on edge I was, but already adrenaline was coursing through me, ready to face whatever horrors would present themselves. But it was Latisha that had emerged from Ivan's camper, now storming away from us, towards her motorhome.

"Uh oh, what's happened now?" Billy muttered under his breath, before calling out, "Here, Tish!"

Latisha turned around to face us, her scowl softening. She paused, weighing up whether to continue on her path, or to double back. With a sigh, her shoulders relaxed and she trudged towards us.

"Hey guys," she said in a heavy voice.

"What's going down in crazy town, Tish?" Billy asked.

Latisha made a guttural noise in her throat, shaking her head. "U gh... just had a meeting with our *master*." She folded her arms, leaning against Madigan's caravan, scraping the toe of her shoe against the gravelled ground as she spoke, focusing on it, rather than us.

"Lucky you," said Billy. "Looks like it went well."

Latisha shot him a warning glance, not in the mood for his jokes. "It was regarding the rumours of the Hallows return. I was trying to convince him to investigate. I even volunteered to do it myself. And do you know what he said? He asked if I was going senile or wanted to relive the glory days. Sick bastard..." Latisha clamped a hand to her mouth, looking behind her, as though expecting Ivan to be standing there. She turned back to us and continued in a whisper, "I tolerated his cruelty when I thought he would protect us from external threats. But now... I don't know... Makes me wonder what's the point of being in a coven. But I suppose such speculation is pointless."

Madigan's words from the previous night echoed in my mind. *'Those of us acquainted with the Hallows are somewhat... frustrated'.*

Before I could question Latisha further, Ivan's camper door swung open again. This time, it was Dominic and his familiar, a scrawny human around my own age, named Randall. As soon as they were outside, they talked together in lowered voices, looking directly at *me*. I whipped my head around, wondering if there was something behind me. But there was nothing. Dominic remained where he was, but Randall strutted towards us, twitching with nervous energy. His lips twisted to the side in a pouting smirk as he swept back his short, sandy-brown hair. He passed Latisha, who eyed him suspiciously, but Billy got to his feet, squaring up to him, blocking his path.

"Can I help, pal?" Billy asked, folding his arms and thrusting out his chest like a bouncer who'd been handed a phoney ID.

The tension that had built up inside me relaxed slightly, my heart swelling with gratitude.

Randall craned his neck to look up at Billy, who stood at least a head taller. "I need to speak to Ava. Master Ivan's orders," Randall said in a nasally, shrill voice that suited his rat-like appearance perfectly.

"Did he specify you needed to speak with her *now*?" Billy clicked his neck.

Randall glared at him, baring his oversized front teeth, before saying, "No, but—"

"Well then, jog on. She's got work to do."

"Master Ivan said—"

"Look whose clothes she's washing. You think Master Ivan will be happy if you interrupt her and he has to walk about naked for the next week?"

Randall's long, pointed nose wrinkled as he sneered, "That's *her* problem."

"You want to take that risk?"

There was a moment's silence while they stared each other down, but Randall conceded.

He stood on tiptoes to peer at me over Billy's shoulder. "I'll see you later, washerwoman," he said before slinking back to his master and the two of them headed into Dominic's camper.

"Slimy git," Billy said with a growl. "Be wary of him, Ava. He's definitely up to something."

"Probably part of his initiation," Latisha said darkly. "He's passed his harvesting trial, so Ivan's probably testing him before making him a vampire."

"And that test involves me somehow?" I asked. "What is Ivan's problem with me?"

"It's not personal," Latisha said with a shrug. "He just hates humans."

"I *am* human. That makes it personal." I drew Ivan's enormous suit jacket from the bucket and twisted, squeezing the water from it like I was wringing someone's neck.

"Don't do that!" Latisha snatched the jacket, water splashing everywhere. Billy cried out as it doused his jeans, but Latisha ignored him. "You'll ruin it, wringing it out like that. Here, do it like this." Latisha rolled the jacket in a towel before unrolling it and adding it to the washing line I'd set up. "Let's not give Ivan another excuse to torment you further."

"Come on," said Billy, retrieving the last items from Ivan's basket, handing one to Latisha. "Let's get this done. You can take a break with us."

After a quick lunch of soup that tasted like hot water, I sat with the shifters and, as promised, Billy let me practise drawing blood from each of his arms, until he'd finally had enough.

"Sorry, Ava. Shifting this much is exhausting."

"What about this one?" I poked his normal right arm.

"I need this one in good working condition. It gets lonely around here and I need to *take care of myself*," he said, smirking.

I spluttered with laughter.

"It would be funny if he was joking," said Marcus, Billy's freckled, curly-haired familiar, as he threw another log onto the fire, sending a cloud of glowing embers into the air. I raised my eyebrows at Billy, who shrugged unapologetically, his mischievous smile fixed in place.

"Very well. Any other volunteers?" I looked at everyone sitting around the campfire individually, but no one would meet my eye. When Marcus noticed me watching him with an expectant expression, he hurried away to the campers.

"Seriously?" I called after him. "You aren't afraid of spiders, but you're afraid of a little needle? Pussy!" I turned to his master. "No offence, Billy."

"So rude," he said, grinning.

"You can practise on me," said Latisha, rolling up her sleeve.

I bowed my head in appreciation as she took her seat by the fire and I gathered up my equipment. I was running low on needles. Madigan had given me some of his supplies to practise with, but he and the other vampires needed them for themselves, and stealing from local hospitals and doctor's surgeries wasn't easy.

Last attempt for tonight... You can do this, just take your time and remember what Madigan showed you.

Latisha offered her arm, and I placed the tourniquet above her elbow. My insides squirmed as a large, juicy vein bulged outwards. I readied the needle as Madigan had showed me while running my thumb over Latisha's vein, feeling for the best place to insert.

Madigan's words echoed in my head. *'Insert at a 20-to-40-degree angle. Pull the skin taught before your insert.'* I pierced the skin and felt some give. My heart jolted. Could this be it? My first successful draw? I attached a vial to the barrel of the needle, waiting for blood to flow.

Nothing.

"Fuck!" I grit my teeth. My skin prickled and my clothes felt restrictive as my armpits and the back of my neck became wet. *Don't get flustered... Don't get flustered... Perhaps the angle was wrong?*

I tried to adjust it, but Latisha flinched, gasping. Still nothing. I sighed, pulling the needle out, not wanting to hurt her further. Another failure.

"It's alright." Latisha gripped onto my shoulder and squeezed. "No one gets it right away. You just need more practise."

"Hopefully not *too much* more practise," I said, stretching as I got to my feet, tugging at my t-shirt that was now sticking to my body, the chilly night air cooling me off.

"I'll second that!" said Billy, ducking out of reach before I could swat him.

"Leave it for tonight," Latisha said. "You won't get it while frustrated."

She was right, of course. After finishing the last of my laundry duties, I returned to Madigan's camper and sketched costume designs, attempting to clear my mind. Apart from a gothic tailcoat design I could picture a long-limbed vampire wearing, most of the designs were lousy. I couldn't block out the thoughts that I should be practising. *I can always try again tomorrow.*

Except, I didn't. The following night, Madigan had other plans.

"The ability to draw blood is vital, but without someone to draw from, your skills are useless," he said.

That night we left the showmen's yard and headed into Kinwich City centre. It was bizarre being back, watching people go about their normal lives. It was a Saturday night, and Kinwich was buzzing with students falling in and out of clubs and bars. Madigan attracted a few puzzled looks from people as they eyed his strange clothes, but he was completely oblivious or chose not to acknowledge them.

"Students can be a suitable target, as you discovered first-hand," he said.

"Yeah, thanks for the reminder."

"Getting into pubs with your supplies isn't difficult, but don't be tempted to do what your predecessor did, and leave your supplies at home to get into a club. Always take them with you."

"Got it. Austin screwed up. I'd worked that out for myself, actually."

"Of course, picking the target isn't the difficult bit. The target does a good enough job of picking themselves. Again, as you did, by getting drunk and going home with a total stranger."

"Okay, I'm feeling attacked now."

"The tricky bit is getting them to a location from where you can draw from them undisturbed. If you're taken to their house and can be certain no one will interrupt, great. But if not, you may have to resort to some underhanded tactics."

Madigan unzipped the bag that he'd brought with him. Inside, I saw more needles and vials, but he rummaged deeper and withdrew a bottle I recognised from his stores—the blue bottle decorated with moons and stars.

"So, what's that then? Chloroform?" I asked with a laugh.

"Yes," he replied, and now I spotted a white rag inside the bag, too.

"You have got to be shitting me."

"Well, it's not *really* chloroform. It's a potion that goes by the name of Slumber Smoke. But it functions in the same way. Not to be used regularly, you understand. But in a desperate situation, it's better to use it than come back empty-handed. And remember, should you get caught while drawing blood, it's this"—he shook the bottle—"or you'll have to kill them. You can't let them leave and go blabbing to the police, or their families, or anyone. Better they wake up with a pounding head, wondering if it was a hallucination."

I didn't like what I was hearing, but I knew he was right.

"The best targets," he said, "are lone, homeless people, especially if they are drunk or high on other substances."

"That's offensive. Not all homeless—"

"Spare me the political correctness lecture. It's my job to tell you the facts and keep you alive. An inebriated individual is an easier target than someone who is sober. Someone difficult to trace is a preferable target over someone who lives in a house, pays bills, has a job and a family. Understand?"

"Yes..."

"Good. Then let's find our target. In the meantime, make yourself useful." He thrust the bag into my arms. It wasn't heavy, but after walking around the city for a few hours, the strap cut into my shoulder and I started to fidget with it. Madigan's grey eyes narrowed as he watched me hoist it from one shoulder to the other, but didn't offer to take it back.

Whenever he saw a potential target, he would point them out with a few comments.

"You see those two over there? One of them looks ready to pass out. You could wait around to see if they go their separate ways. You see the old man on the bench? The presence of his sleeping bag suggests he's homeless, but appears sober. You could return later to see if that remains the case."

And on it went until the early hours of the morning, until my feet throbbed and I carried the bag in my arms instead of over my shoulders. Madigan sauntered up and down the cobbled paths and alleyways, whilst I jogged a few steps to catch up when flagging behind. I was going to ask if we could return to the showmen's yard, when I noticed a girl in a glittery dress laying on the stone steps leading up to Kinwich Cathedral.

"I think we have acquired our target." Madigan nodded in her direction.

"You can walk on church grounds?" I asked.

"Yes. Why wouldn't I?"

I shrugged. "I just thought perhaps vampires wouldn't be able to."

Madigan raised an eyebrow. "Vampires aren't inherently evil, you know. Demons on the other hand... But I digress. Come on."

We approached the girl with caution.

"Hello?" I kept my voice low, stroking her hair to see if she would stir. Nothing. If it wasn't for her breathing, I could have mistaken her for dead. Madigan hauled her up over his shoulder with ease, taking her to the churchyard around the back where we would be less likely to be seen. He drew blood from her quickly, his long-fingered hands almost a blur with the speed at which he prepared his needle and vial. My mouth fell open, half in awe, half in despair. How the hell was I going to master this?

Before we left, Madigan rummaged around in the bag again, taking out a thin blanket and draping it over her shivering body.

"What?" he asked when he saw me looking at him, mouth still agape.

"I just… didn't expect you to be so caring."

Madigan's eyebrows drew together. "I suppose I should take that as a compliment."

On the Sunday night, I practised drawing blood from members of the coven again. Billy and Latisha were the first to offer their arms to me. Madigan watched on, and would occasionally stop me from what I was doing to give some advice, but despite this, all attempts were unsuccessful.

"I just don't understand why I can't do it!" I said as Alfred, the last of my test subjects, returned to his motorhome, rubbing his sore arm, leaving me alone with Billy, Latisha, and Madigan by the campfire. "I've seen it done so many times now, and Madigan has gone over it again and again with me. What more can I do?"

"Have you asked the other familiars and vampires for help?" Latisha suggested.

"I think Dominic or Ivan have told them not to help me."

I found it ironic that I was a vampire's familiar, and yet the other vampires wanted nothing to do with me, whereas the witches, shifters, and werewolves were perfectly friendly, and often helpful.

"It was probably Dominic," Billy said, wrinkling his nose. "Excuse my French, but that guy is a slimy cunt."

Latisha and I sniggered, and even Madigan looked like he might smile, but Latisha's laughter died when both she and Madigan suddenly sat upright, tense.

"Ivan is coming," Madigan said, a slight tremor in his voice.

Within a few seconds, I heard the footsteps of the giant approaching. Billy got up to leave.

"Sit," Ivan's voice barked. Billy slowly sat down, eyes wide and unblinking, fixed on his master. Ivan reached us, and from my seated position, he appeared even taller. Dominic followed behind, along with the other vampires and their familiars. Ivan smiled a wide grin that did not reach his cold eyes as he lit his cigar, puffing foul-smelling smoke into the air.

"Ava Monroe." The friendly way he spoke my name made my skin tingle. "It is good to see you practising. You're almost halfway through your first week. How are you getting on?"

"Training hard," I said in a small voice. It wasn't a lie, but the leer on Ivan's face stated plainly he knew what was going unsaid.

"Ha! Excellent." He sat beside Madigan, gesturing for his minions to do the same. "Perhaps you would like to show me the results?"

I looked at Madigan, whose stony expression had not changed, but gave a small nod.

"Ok," I agreed. "Do I have any volunteers?" Before a single person could respond, Ivan raised his hand.

"I do," he said, the smirk on his face never faltering.

"No problem." I tried to sound confident, but my treacherous voice broke.

Ignoring this minor loss of composure, I collected up my equipment. I didn't need to kneel in front of him as I had done the others. He was so large I could do it standing. I rolled up his shirtsleeve and applied the tourniquet, pulling it hard to wrap around his huge, beefy arm, praying he wouldn't notice my shaking hands.

A vein bulged straight away, fat and purple. Step-by-step, I readied the needle, then the vial, and prepared to puncture his skin. *He is the same as everyone else. This is no one special. No one important.*

With a deep breath, I inserted the needle.

At first, nothing happened. I could feel the weight of everyone watching with baited breaths. *Stay calm... You can do this...*

I adjusted the needle slightly. A red line—blood—appeared at the base of the barrel where I would attach the vial. My heart skipped a beat. I was in.

I swallowed and exhaled slowly, my chest having become tight. With my free hand, I grabbed the vial and attached it to the barrel. The smallest trickle of blood flowed into the vial—and then stopped. I tried adjusting it again, but I knew... it was game over.

"Amazing," Ivan said, blowing cigar smoke into my face while his minions snickered. "I am truly blown away."

"I was just nervous." My face flushed as my eyes stung with humiliation, causing Dominic to laugh harder still.

"That is understandable." Ivan rolled down his sleeve, his tone casual, like we were discussing the weather. "May I suggest you get a better grip on your nerves? It would be *crushing* to lose you."

I nodded, but this wasn't enough for him.

"The words you are looking for are, *'Yes, Master Ivan'*. Say it."

"Yes, Master Ivan."

"Very good. At least get *that* right next time."

He got up and started towards his motorhome, pausing only to lean into Madigan's ear and say, "Teach that girl some respect, unless you want *me* to teach her."

Ivan's minions followed him, Dominic bringing up the rear, turning back to flash one last wicked smile before scurrying after his master.

I felt the eyes of my companions on me, Madigan's in particular boring into my soul. The trembling I'd been suppressing had taken hold, my body shook violently as my stomach performed somersaults.

"I have to piss," I managed to spit out, before turning on my heel and walking away, face burning.

ELEVEN

Latisha spun on the spot, the light skirt of her dress fluttering around her. I'd figured that once it whipped up to reveal her bare arse she'd stop—but she didn't. My eyes snapped upward as I forced them to focus on her beaming face as my mouth became wet and heartbeat quickened. Perhaps it was the glow of fairy lights and the exotic, perfumed scent of burning incense, but there was an aura around her that engulfed me, making me hunger... for her. I lowered my sights and bit my lip, smirking.

"You stop your perving!" She came to a standstill, laughing, as blood rushed to my face.

"Sorry!"

Latisha laughed harder, pulling up the skirt and flashing me her lady bits. "Go on! Get a good look!"

"Damn hussy. Want me to make you some matching undies to go with your dress?" My cheeks still burned, but I gave her a sheepish smile. "Don't you get cold?"

"Evidently, I do." She thrust out her chest, her nipples visible beneath the thin fabric.

"Stop it!" I bunched up a scrap of cloth and threw it at her. "How am I meant to concentrate when you're flirting with me?"

"Concentrate on what? You have finished the dress."

I snorted, shaking my head. "Bloody tease."

"Sorry Ava, it's just my witch's glamour. It has an alluring effect on people."

"It's not always this strong," I mumbled, looking away as I rubbed the back of my neck.

"I can control it to an extent, but it's always stronger when I *feel* beautiful." She twirled once more. "Thanks for the dress. It's gorgeous."

My embarrassment died as I basked in the warmth of her compliment.

"We were lucky to find that sewing machine in the storage container, weren't we?" she said.

"Yes, lucky..." Was it luck? This Singer sewing machine was the same model as mine, sitting unused in my student housing, gathering dust. We'd also found an older model, one I would have been less adept at using, along with rolls of fabric, and a case containing scissors, tape measures, seam rippers, and everything else a seamstress might need.

Why does the coven have an expensive sewing machine without a seamstress to use it? Before I could ponder who the mystery seamstress might be, Latisha dumped another roll of fabric onto the table.

"You must make more for me. I like this cloth, and you could use these, too." She gestured to the various brightly coloured throws that decorated her camper.

I'd fallen in love with her home the moment I'd stepped inside, greeted by the soft tinkle of a wind chime as I'd opened the door. It reminded me of a crystal shop I'd visited with Hayley. At the far end was a bookcase, packed full of thick books, some with gemstones set into the spines. I'd scanned the titles, but they were written in untranslatable symbols. The deep reds and purples of the upholstery and squashy cushions looked so inviting that I didn't want to leave.

"Len will be pleased. He spends a small fortune on his suits. You should make him one." She nodded toward the bottle-green waistcoat folded on the table, the ripped shoulder repaired. I didn't want to confess that I'd never made a suit from scratch and was more complicated than the simple pattern I'd memorised for her dress.

Latisha opened a cupboard, admiring herself in the full-length mirror that hung on the door. "I'll wear this in summer. Ivan likes us to dress up when running the attractions. He would approve of this."

"How do you work during the summer?" I asked. The question had been playing on my mind. "I mean, you can't walk around in the day, can you?"

"Witches can. Nocturnal shifters can, too, they just prefer not to. It's the vampires that burn, but even they can cope with a lotion I make. It acts as a powerful sunblock."

I spluttered with laughter at the mental image of Madigan applying suntan lotion, dressed in sunglasses, shorts and a garish Hawaiian shirt. "So why don't they use it all the time?"

"All witch's remedies have side effects if used long-term. Speaking of which, I don't suppose you've noticed if Len's been using any more of the Mollifier I gave him?"

In all honesty, it wasn't something I'd paid attention to, and my chest tightened at the thought that perhaps I should have. "Not that I'm aware of."

"Good. I know he's been struggling. But that stuff can have the opposite effect if abused, and I don't want him putting you in danger."

My stomach lurched as I recalled our first encounter and the ease with which he'd thrown me across his caravan. At least *Darren* had mortal strength when he'd drunk too much. I shuddered, pushing aside the memories of mother's boyfriend. I had to change the subject.

"Latisha, I was wondering if you would let me practise on you before I go."

"Practise on me?" She looked at me through the mirror's reflection as she tied the discarded scrap of cloth I'd thrown at her around her head like a headband. I tapped the inside of my elbow. She took a steeling breath.

"Take it from someone who knows, you need a break. Yes, practise will help, but pushing yourself too much will only make it worse. You will doubt yourself, and it will only go downhill from there. One night off won't hurt. In fact, it will help."

"Please?" I clapped my hands together in the prayer position. "I can't stop thinking about it. Just one go?"

"No, Ava. If I'm honest, I'm still pretty bruised from last time, so I doubt you'll get any blood from me anyway, and that will dishearten you. Maybe Len will help you later."

She turned to look at me properly, and from her slight frown I knew she was serious.

"I'll have to wait until he gets back." I reclined in my chair, folding my arms. "He's always going out."

"Can you blame him? He doesn't get along with the rest of the vampires and we usually keep to our own. He's always been a loner. But you two get on alright, don't you?"

I shrugged. "He tolerates me, I think."

"Well, that's a start."

We packed away the sewing equipment and stashed it away in a cupboard. After promising to make Latisha another dress and gathering up Madigan's freshly steamed clothes, I headed back to his caravan, expecting it to be empty. My heart leapt when I found he'd returned early, pulling off his tailcoat with a yawn.

"Ah, Miss Monroe," he said, stretching. "I'm running low on jackets. Have you—"

"Here." I gave him his clean clothes. "All hand washed and steamed. And I repaired this." I handed over the waistcoat, holding my breath as I waited for his reaction. He frowned, taking the waistcoat and examining where it had been damaged, poking and pulling with his long fingers before turning his eyes on me.

"This is excellent work. Thank you."

He placed a hand on my forearm. I studied his face, looking for a tell of sarcasm, but it never came. Instead, his usual critical scowl was replaced with a *smile*! Not the lip-twitching, suppressed smile I'd grown used to, but a smile that reached his eyes, lips pulled back so I could see his straight, white teeth, making him look about ten years younger. I couldn't help but grin back at him.

"I didn't know you could do that!" I said with exaggerated surprise.

"Do what?"

"Smile."

Madigan rolled his eyes. "Such impertinence."

"You love it."

He raised an eyebrow, smirk still in place, as though he were fighting with himself to maintain his moody appearance, and failing.

"Well, you're certainly amusing at times. I'll give you that. But enough of this silliness. How is your training progressing?"

My body felt heavy beneath the weight of the albatross around my neck. "I'm trying."

"Yes, you are *very* trying."

My head snapped upward to squint at him. Though his serious expression had returned, he still winked, the corner of his mouth twitching. *Cheeky bastard...*

"Perhaps you will let me practise on you?"

"Well, I suppose after you repaired my waistcoat, I should return the favour," he said.

His hand drifted to the cuff of his shirt, unbuttoning it before pulling the now loose sleeve over his elbow. He took a seat, reclining, and spread his long legs as I knelt between them. Being so close, I noticed he had a sweet sort of scent, like vanilla. My hands trembled as I applied the tourniquet and readied the needle.

"Insert between 20-and-40-degrees. Did you feel it go in?"

Did you feel it go in? I suppressed the urge to make a joke. Perhaps it was from my position between his legs, but heat flooded my cheeks, my heart fluttering. *Concentrate, Ava. Concentrate. This is not the time or place.*

"I think so." The words got caught in my throat.

"Attach the vial," he instructed, and I did as I was bid. Blood streamed into the vial, filling it faster than I had been prepared for.

"Ah! Holy shit! I... I did it!" I blinked, shook my head, then blinked again, expecting the blood to have disappeared, all an illusion. But there it was, flowing into the vial. "What do I do now? Do I take it out?"

"No, take the vial off first."

The small vial I was practising with didn't take long to fill, unlike the larger ones I'd use during a real harvest. I popped it off the barrel and set it aside.

"Now, remove the tourniquet. This can be tricky one-handed, but you must keep hold of that needle. Good. Now, prepare the cotton wool to cover the insertion point, and remove the needle. Remember to press down hard when the needle is out."

I followed his instructions, taking my time, keeping my breathing as steady as possible, almost laughing with relief. I'd done it! I'd successfully drawn blood. So caught up in the moment, I didn't notice that he too was holding down the cotton wool on his arm, his fingers pressed to mine.

"You can release now," he said, amusement in his voice.

I looked into his face. "You're doing it again."

"Doing what?"

"Smiling. Twice in one day must be a record."

He shrugged. "I've had little to celebrate. I knew you'd get it, eventually. Just remain calm, and don't get inside your own head." He examined his arm, and once sure it had stopped bleeding, discarded the cotton wool. "I will retire to my bed now. I have some laundry for you."

"Yay," I said with a sarcastic fist pump. "Can't wait."

I tilted my head as I watched him unbutton his waistcoat and toss it into the basket, on top of his tailcoat. He was wearing braces tonight, something I'd not noticed him do before. I bit my lip. The way he slid his thumbs up the underside up to his shoulders to remove them was mesmerising, but a gasp hitched in my throat as I caught sight of his bare torso as he removed his shirt. Deep, bumpy scars covered the left side, entire chunks of flesh missing.

Madigan caught me staring and frowned.

"Military service. I'd rather not discuss it. Some scars heal better than others, if you understand what I mean." He tapped his temple with a finger.

Now feeling I was intruding on a private moment, I averted my gaze as he continued undressing, my insides squirming with conflicting, confusing emotions.

When he handed me his now full laundry basket, I attempted to maintain eye contact. Although I'd learned his actual age, I was struggling to determine the age that he appeared on the outside. Perhaps in his late twenties or early thirties? Not a single trace of a grey hair.

Nor any creases at his eyes, but there was a sadness behind them that appeared as old as he was.

As much as I tried to focus on his face, I saw from my peripheral vision he was down to his boxer shorts. I swallowed.

"Would you like to go scouting with me again later?" he asked. The question was a cold slap of reality, the brief luxury of playful banter interrupted by the burden of the trial and the consequences of failure.

"Actually, I think I should probably go on my own."

He arched a brow. "Really?"

"I want to see how I fare on my own. I probably won't harvest immediately, but I want to see how I handle it solo. Is that alright?"

"I don't see why not. Usually, I would think it is too early, but given the circumstances, I suppose it would be best to throw you in at the deep end."

"Great!" I said, plastering an enormous smile on my face, but inside my guts were threatening to exit my body.

TWELVE

The wind bit me as the icy rain smashed down. My nose was streaming and cheeks tingled, my thick coat ineffective. I held onto the hood with numb fingers, shivering to my core until my muscles ached. My feet squelched in my sodden trainers as I walked my third lap of the city centre, searching for my target, hoping someone would stand out. A gaggle of girls dressed in cheerleading outfits passed, laughing and chanting, undeterred by the lousy weather.

Some people are too peppy... I wrinkled my nose at their sickly sweet perfume and shrill voices. Those kinds of girls stuck together; shadowing them was a waste of time, despite their inebriation.

After a few more laps, my heart stopped as I spotted my first potential target. A young man, perhaps in his twenties, taking shelter in a shop doorway, his waterproof jacket wrapped around him and a frayed woollen beanie pulled down low. Eager to make my move, I considered the best way to get him out of sight.

Hello, Mr Homeless Guy. How about we go down this dark alleyway together? Perhaps not...

Madigan said to bide my time and watch for patterns in behaviour. Maybe he'd find somewhere secluded to sleep? I'd have to be patient.

I stood in a doorway opposite, checking my watch, pretending I was waiting for someone. I kept up the charade for about thirty minutes, but soon grew twitchy as unwanted thoughts plagued my mind.

How long do I keep this up? Is he looking at me? I'm sure he was... Does he know what I'm doing?

I shook myself and steadied my breathing, regaining composure.

Get a grip. How could he know?

The target got up, grabbed his pack, and walked away. My stomach fluttered as I prepared myself to begin the chase. I waited until he'd disappeared around a corner before pursuing him, but as I followed, I was caught up in a tangle of students pouring out of the nearest pub. I pushed through the crowd, searching for the target... when a familiar face caught my eye.

It was *mine*. Staring at me, smiling, in black and white, across a missing person poster, almost lost among numerous others against the wall.

'MISSING', it read. *'AVA MONROE. Ava, 22, was last seen on Thursday 7ᵗʰ January in Kinwich. She is described as white, approx. 5'6", with white and brown piebald hair. She was last seen wearing a black dress and high heeled shoes.'*

"Oh, you fucking idiots..."

Instinctively, I peeled the poster away from the others. The police had used a photo at least a year old and, indeed, depicted my distinguishing white tuft of hair, the rest a dark-brown. Problem being, my most distinguishing feature was currently bleached.

"Guess I can't count on the fuzz to find me then."

Not that I had much confidence in them anyway.

What to do? Should I replace the poster and hope that *someone* would recognise me? Then again, what would happen if I was? What would the police do? Rock up to the showmen's yard and arrest Ivan? Yeah—right.

I'll ask Madigan what I should do...

I folded the poster—there were bound to be others littered about Kinwich—and abandoning my mission, I thrust my hands into my pockets and marched towards the park to take the usual shortcut, head bowed against the downpour. I assumed the park was empty. The only sounds were the smattering of rain and creaking branches as the bitter winds swept through the trees and hedgerows.

"There she is!"

The shout pierced the quietude like a needle through flesh. I whirled around. A pair of shadowy figures that had been sheltering in the park's bandstand approached. I should have ignored them, but curiosity kept me rooted to the spot. My insides dropped as they passed under a street lamp. Dominic and Randall.

"Can I help?" I asked with forced politeness, though my limbs tingled, readying myself for whatever they had prepared. Dominic stopped beneath the streetlamp, leaning against it as he watched his familiar draw closer to me.

Randall flicked his sandy-brown hair out of his eyes and looked at me with a wrinkled nose, like he could smell something particularly nasty, like sour milk on a hot day.

"I need something from you, Ava. Master's orders. And it looks like you haven't got your eight-legged freak here to protect you this time."

"What do you need? My autograph?"

"I need what all vampires crave. Are you going to give it willingly? Or will I have to fight you?"

I glanced at Dominic. His small, dark eyes creased into a sneer as he watched on. I clenched my fists as adrenaline surged through me. The frustration, anger, and despair that I'd bottled up over the last week overflowed, my face contracting into a grimace, my muscles tensing, blood pounding in my ears.

"I'm afraid you are going to have to fight me," I snarled.

Randall blinked, his facial features twitching, and looked back towards Dominic for a second.

"What's wrong?" I asked. "Need Daddy's permission?"

He returned his gaze to me, flushing. "You're going to regret not cooperating with me when you had the chance." He stepped forward and raised his fists, bouncing from one foot to the other.

Cocky little shit...

I stood on the balls of my feet, tense, ready to pounce as the fight-or-flight response pulsed through me. "Come on then!"

With a roar, he threw the first punch. I ducked, raised my fist and smashed it into his jaw. He staggered, dazed and blinking.

I spread my arms, drunk on adrenaline. "What was that?! You want to go? Let's go!" I went to strike again, but he charged, crashing into me.

We wrestled in the muck for dominance, cold mud slapping into my face, clogging my hair. He was on top of me, blood splattering into my eyes from his gaping mouth. With a primal snarl, I drove my knee between his legs, and he rolled off me with a yelp. I scrambled to my feet, but someone seized me from behind in a tenacious grip that could only belong to Dominic. I thrashed on the spot, feet slipping in the mud.

"Get up, Randall!" Dominic's crisp voice commanded.

Randall groaned, but hauled himself up, hand over his privates, face contorted, oversized front teeth bared, eyes wild. He balled up his fist and thrust it into my stomach. Winded, my knees buckled, and Dominic shoved me down. A boot struck the side of my head. Lights burst before my eyes as my head hit the ground, mud filling my ears and mouth.

A hand pulled at my hair, yanking upward, and hot breath washed over my face.

"Learn your fucking place, you little ratbag." Dominic's high voice pierced through my head before the hand released my hair. My vision blurred; the last thing I saw was Dominic's skull-like features before being swallowed by darkness.

I don't know how long I laid in the dirt, but even as my consciousness returned, I kept my eyes closed as my head pounded. When I prised my eyes open, I found to my relief the blinking lights had gone, but my vision remained blurry. The sun hadn't risen, but the sky had turned from black to dark-blue.

I picked myself up, only now noticing my aching ribs, and the unmistakable bruising inside my elbow from where they must have stolen my blood, the sleeve of my coat ripped open. *Bastards...* I staggered back to the showmen's yard. It was a tough climb over the fence. I reached the top and swung my legs over and braced myself for the drop.

"Fuck me, Ava! You're filthy!" A tall figure stood below. Even through my blurred vision, I could tell from their muscular physique and crop of ginger hair that it was Billy. I hadn't noticed him approach the gates and was now looking up at me. I squinted, making out his face. He was frowning, head tilted to one side.

"Need a hand?" He reached out and assisted me with the climb down. "What happened?"

I shook my head and instantly regretted it as it made the throbbing in my temples flare.

"I don't feel too good," I said through clenched teeth. "Will you take me back to Madigan's?"

"Aye."

He put an arm around me and let me lean on him as he guided me toward Madigan's caravan. En route, we passed the caravans of the other vampires. Jacob and Sebastian were sitting outside Ivan's motorhome.

"Uh oh. Your mates are here." Billy couldn't resist poking fun at me, even in my sorry state.

"They're not my fucking mates."

"What happened, Ava?" Jacob called out to me in his gruff voice. "You're not looking so hot."

Sebastian said nothing, but still smirked at my expense, running a hand over his perfectly styled hair.

Someone pulled back a curtain hanging in the motorhome's window. Ivan leered at me from inside, grinning his wide, toothy smile as he tapped the windowpane, then beckoned me with a thick finger.

"Shit..." I said under my breath.

"Want me to wait for you?" Billy asked.

"Nah, but if you could get Madigan—"

"He is already there." Billy nodded to the motorhome, the door now open. Madigan stood in the doorway, his brows drawn together and his lips a thin line.

"Wish me luck." I took a deep breath and, with all the strength I could muster, walked upright, head held high, into Ivan's home.

The inside was nothing like I had expected. It looked so *normal*. The clean, beige carpets, the maroon, leather sofa, the free-standing lamps. There was even a huge, flat screen TV, but from the layer of dust that had settled, I guessed it was rarely used. I jumped, spotting what I mistook for another figure in the corner, but it was just a sewing mannequin, just as big and broad as Ivan himself.

Dominic and Randall were sitting on the sofa, Dominic leaning back, not looking at me, but picking at the dirt beneath the nails of his spindly fingers. Randall, like me, was caked in mud, clashing against the pristine carpets and furnishings. He pulled his lips back into a snarl, but I just wrinkled my nose in response. Madigan stood beside me and my pounding heart eased slightly.

"Glad to have you join us," Ivan said in his usual, pleasant tone that sent shivers up my spine. He was sitting in an armchair, hands together, fingers interlocked.

"Thanks," I said, then added with a hurry, "Master Ivan."

His lips spread back into a wide grin. "Very good. Now then, to business." Ivan cracked his neck from side to side. "I wanted to clear something up. I've spoken to my subordinates and they informed me that yourself and Randall Johnson got into a minor scuffle. Is that right? Is this your handiwork, right here?" He pointed to Randall's bloody mouth, and then his eye. I'd not realised that in our wrestling match I'd blackened his eye, filling me with a strange satisfaction.

Before I could even open my mouth, Randall cut in.

"You wanted her blood. She wouldn't cooperate, so I took it by force. If she'd not been Leonard's familiar, I'd have killed her for it."

"Fuck off Randall, you little piss mite." The words erupted from my mouth before I could stop them. "You only got the upper hand on me because Dominic got involved. If you want to fight again, let's go!"

Madigan put a calming hand on my shoulder, steadying me, but growled low in his throat.

"You got involved too, did you?" Ivan asked Dominic, an unmistakable danger in his tone. "You failed to mention that."

"That's because it's a load of bollocks." He flicked the dirt he'd been digging from out of his nails. "It's as Randall said. He asked for her blood. She refused. He overpowered her."

Ivan looked at me over the top of his spectacles.

"He's chatting shit," I said. "I was coming back after going scouting and, yes, he asked for my blood. Was I meant to hand it over nicely?

When I refused, he *tried* to overpower me. But Dominic discovered his familiar is a little bitch, so he held me back. Pretty cowardly, if you ask me."

Madigan growled again, this time audible enough for the others to hear.

"Also," I said, "why is Randall allowed to beat people up for their blood, while I have to stealth mission for it?"

"He's passed his harvesting trial already," Dominic said, rising to his feet, but Madigan stepped forward defensively. "All Master Ivan said was Randall needed to acquire your blood. Any means necessary."

"Any means necessary?" I shouted, standing on tiptoes to view him over Madigan's shoulder. "Did that include getting you to fight his battles for him?"

Ivan smirked in amusement as he lit up a cigar, watching our exchange as though it were a comedy performance.

"Ava Monroe," he interrupted, "you were coming back here with something for me, I hope? No? How disappointing." He puffed smoke into the air, eyes turned upward in thought. "Well, with his word against yours, I suppose we can't learn the truth. Dominic Chase, you've been campaigning for Randall Johnson to make a full conversion to a vampire. He's been harvesting for a couple of weeks and has the bloodlust required; he's one of the most promising recruits we've had. But losing to a girl?" He snorted with laughter, flicking ash from his cigar into an ashtray. "That's pathetic."

"Master Ivan—"

"Silence!" He raised a hand, then withdrew a vial of blood from his breast pocket. "That said, he completed the task I assigned him." He tilted the vial, the blood—*my* blood—sliding from one end to the other. "And I'm a man of my word." He stood, still examining the vial before saying to me, "You don't mind if I hang onto this, do you?" It was a rhetorical question.

In three strides, he crossed his motorhome to the kitchen, opening the fridge. My mouth fell open as I caught a glimpse inside. Like Madigan's, it contained vials of blood. Unlike Madigan's, it was packed full, and set inside the door were large bottles filled to the brim with dark liquid, each with a label. The closest was labelled '*Leonard*'. After writing my name on the vial in permanent marker and slotting it alongside the others, Ivan retrieved a bottle from the door.

"Here we are. '*Dominic Chase*'," Ivan said, reading the label. He thrust it into Randall's hands. "Drink."

"A-all of it?" he asked, unable to hide the tremor in his voice.

Ivan's usual sickening smile broadened, his wicked eyes lighting up. "All of it. It's only a litre. What's the problem?"

Randall opened the top, looking inside at the red-black substance, before turning his gaze to Dominic, then to Ivan.

"Do I need to fetch a funnel?" Ivan asked, squinting at him through his spectacles.

"No," Randall said, bringing the bottle to his lips, and began drinking, screwing his eyes shut, gulping down the liquid as fast as he could. He gagged a couple of times, tears seeping between his eyelids, but kept going.

I put a hand to my mouth, dry heaving. Thankfully, Ivan was too preoccupied watching Randall struggling to drain the litre of blood to notice my loss of composure.

Randall gasped for air, wiping blood from his chin and set the now empty bottle on the kitchen counter. His whole body shuddered as he collapsed to his knees, holding his stomach, groaning.

"I don't feel so good."

"Good. That means it's working," Ivan said.

Randall's body spasmed again, and he fell into the foetal position, his groans growing louder.

"That's going to keep him busy for a while." Ivan stepped over Randall's writhing body and returned to his maroon, leather armchair. "And as for you, Ava Monroe. Come here. Give me your hand."

He reached out towards me. Swallowing, I mirrored him. In a movement too fast for my eyes to follow, he snatched my hand, almost crushing it in his fist as he yanked me towards him so that we were face to face. I resisted the urge to wince at the smell of his sour breath.

"I am impressed. It's good to see you won't be bullied into submission. A very promising quality. I might not disregard you just yet."

"Thank you, Master Ivan," I said, voice raised to be heard over Randall's ever-increasing wails.

"But"—his cold eyes flashed—"I am growing tired of your rudeness." With a sharp tug, he ripped away what remained of my tattered coat sleeve. "This is a reminder that you are *mine*, and will show our brethren the respect they deserve."

He brought down the tip of his cigar and pressed it deep into the flesh of my arm. I shrieked, as the smell of burning flesh filled my nostrils, white-hot pain radiating through my arm. I tried to tug my hand out of his, but his grip compressed even more so. Only when the cigar was extinguished did he remove it, leaving behind a red and black circular burn. He allowed me to pull my arm back, cradling it, my mouth open in horror, my body vibrating in shock.

"Will that be all, Master Ivan?" Madigan asked, his tone measured yet urgent.

"Get out," Ivan said, waving his hand like he was swatting a fly. "And don't you dare put any potions or healing balms on that burn, Ava Monroe, or the next cigar I extinguish will be in your eyes!"

Madigan grabbed my shoulder and steered me towards the door. I clutched my shaking arm to my chest, covering my burn from the elements with my hand.

Dominic spouted insults as we left, but I barely heard them over the noises issuing from Randall, now less of a groan and more of a scream, still thrashing on the floor of Ivan's kitchen.

As soon as we were inside Madigan's camper, he made me take a seat.

"Let me have a look." He held out his hand, but I kept my arm to my chest, not even wanting to look at it myself. "I need to bandage it."

"Ivan said not to—"

"He said not to put any healing balms on it. He said nothing about bandaging it."

I licked my lips in hesitation, then extended my arm. In the centre of my forearm was a huge, red crater, about the size of a ten pence coin, peppered with black residue and covered in a shrivelled, dead flap of skin that dipped inward.

Madigan inhaled through his teeth. "This will blister soon, and you can expect a nasty scar, I'm afraid. But we'll keep it clean and covered and it should heal up just fine." He cleaned the ash residue away before applying a gauze and bandage. "Perhaps wear long sleeves for the foreseeable future." He tightened the bandage, making sure it was secure, then held my hand in his. His touch was warm, and skin rough. "Would you like to tell me everything that happened in the park?"

As I went into detail of my fight, his eyes became hard and flinty.

"Bastards... Perhaps I might pay Dominic a visit later and—"

"No." I put my free hand on his. "I don't want you getting into trouble, too. I just want to get on with completing my trial."

For a couple of seconds, we looked at each other and I noted once again his soft, vanilla scent that caused a warmth to spread through my chest. He flushed, suddenly releasing his hold on my hand.

"Besides your confrontation with Randall, how did your scouting go?"

"Not great," I said, before remembering the reason I'd returned early. "I found this." I retrieved the poster from my pocket and handed it to him.

Madigan unfolded the piece of paper, his eyebrows rising slightly as he ran his eyes over it, the corner of his mouth curling slightly. "Is this you?" he asked, referring to the picture.

I nodded. "I didn't know what to do. What if the police come looking for me?"

Madigan didn't respond right away—he was looking at my picture again, the curl of his mouth threatening to become a full-blown smile—but when he realised I was awaiting an answer, he said, "I understand you'd like to be rescued. However, I'd advise against attracting police attention. It wouldn't be the first time they have come here, and Ivan *always* gets his own way. Perhaps you should adopt a disguise while harvesting. And remove any more posters you find." He folded up the poster and handed it back to me. "Let us not provoke Ivan's wrath further."

"I'll second that," I said, putting a hand to my bandage. "Did Ivan torment you when you first joined?"

"Not exactly. I was already a vampire when I joined. All I needed to do was provide a blood sample, albeit... unwillingly. I'm sure you noticed Ivan's supply is plentiful."

"Plentiful is putting it lightly," I said, my stomach lurching as I recalled the bottles of blood. "Why does he have so much?"

"The larger quantities are for transforming humans into vampires, as you saw for yourself. But the smaller samples—such as the one Ivan requested Randall obtain from you—are for tracking. Using it, he'd have Dominic detect where you've been, much like how a dog can follow a scent. Vampires—and Dominic in particular—have a powerful sense of smell. That's how we traced you back to your home; you left a trail."

I licked my lower lip, thinking. "He uses blood for tracking us down," I said, more to myself than Madigan, processing the information. "He uses the *blood* for tracking us..." My pulse quickened, my muscles tensed, and I looked Madigan dead in the eyes before saying with a trembling voice, "So, you're telling me, that all this time, I could have fucked off and he wouldn't have found me?!"

Madigan's eyes widened, blood draining from his already pale face. "Dominic and I found you without—"

"You found me because I left a trail, yes?"

"Well... yes, but—"

"And you didn't feel it necessary to tell me this until now? *After* he's taken my blood?!" My body quivered with a rage that longed to burst free. I rose to my feet, unsure of what I was going to do, but I had to do *something*. My fists clenched. Unclenched. I wanted to pace, but the space was too tight. Just enough room for me and the man before me. My *captor*. "You... you..."

I lost control, and without thinking, I raised my palm and swung it, aiming for his face.

The next thing I knew, Madigan was standing over me, my wrist in his hand, glowering, eyes darker than I'd ever seen them. Though my anger still burned, a cold pulse of panic rippled through me, along with another feeling that I couldn't quite identify—suddenly reminded how much taller and stronger he was. And he was close. *Very* close. I caught the waft of vanilla again.

"Don't. Do. That." He spoke calmly, but his tone was low, firm, *dangerous*. I yanked my hand, but his grip was too tight.

"So help me, if you come between me and my freedom again, I'll... I'll..."

"I'm sure you'll give me a jolly good slap. Yes, yes." He released my wrist, rolling his eyes. "Look, I didn't realise that he'd not yet acquired your blood. I haven't taken a familiar in well over a decade and if truth be told, I forgot, alright? I'm sorry."

I massaged the feeling back into my wrist, not looking at him, ignoring his apology.

He let out a deep sigh. "Look, I have... I might have a solution."

I snorted a sardonic laugh. "I'm sure."

"I'm uneasy about discussing it here, where we may be overheard, and sunrise is almost upon us. But, if you're willing, tomorrow night I'll take you somewhere private, and offer a suggestion that might benefit both of us. Is that agreeable?"

I gave him a sideways glance. I wanted to tell him where he could shove his suggestion. But, I couldn't deny he'd piqued my curiosity, and if it really could help me get out of here...

"Fine."

THIRTEEN

"As far as I am aware, no one else comes here," Madigan said as he led me deeper into the wood. It was unpleasant passing through Austin's execution site, but as we drew farther away, it was like leaving the rest of the world behind. "This woodland is only accessible through the showmen's yard, and the coven avoids it... for obvious reasons."

I clasped his hand, near blind in the darkness, but Madigan could either see perfectly, or had memorised the route, sliding through the trees with ease. His hand was warmer than I'd been expecting, his palm rough and grip strong.

"This is it." He guided me through the final rows of trees, greeted by the sparkling moonlight reflecting off the surface of a nearby lake. "Sit here. I'll get some firewood."

He indicated to a fallen tree beside the remains of a firepit before heading into the darkness of the woodland.

I seated myself, examining the deep ridges of the tree bark between my fingers before slotting my hands into the front pocket of my hoodie, my breath misting in front of me, as though the absence of Madigan had left me frozen. I shivered.

"Cold?" Madigan asked, returning with his arms full of logs and branches.

"Yeah. Thanks to the combined efforts of Randall and Ivan, I no longer have a coat."

"Here." Madigan removed his tailcoat and draped it around my shoulders, still containing his warmth and scent.

"Thanks," I said shortly—I wanted him to know I was still annoyed with him, but his gentlemanly behaviour was making it difficult.

I looked around. Empty acorn husks littered the floor, among the distinctly shaped oak leaves. In the distance, I heard an owl hooting and the trickle of the stream feeding the glimmering body of water. I understood why Madigan had kept such a tranquil spot a secret. Even vampires needed sanctuary from their day-to-day (or night-to-night) troubles. His hands were a blur as he rubbed two sticks together, and soon had a small, crackling fire danced in the pit.

As he worked, I couldn't help but admire him from behind. Each time he leant forward, his waistcoat rode up, teasing his braces beneath. My lips twisted into a devilish smirk, wondering if this made me a pervert. He stood up and stretched. His legs appeared disproportionally long, or perhaps it was just the way he shifted his weight from one to the other, never standing squarely on both. I scanned up his legs to his backside. *He has a gorgeous ass! Shame it's always covered by his coattails...*

The memory of him taking his shirt off plagued my mind. I'd been so shocked by the scars that covered his side that I'd almost forgotten the modest, yet toned muscles down his chest, leading to a tuft of dark hair beneath his belly button...

"Are you alright, Miss Monroe?" he asked as he took a seat beside me, snapping me out of my thoughts. He was looking at me with an almost *knowing* expression, eyebrow raised, lips twitching.

Can vampires read minds? God, that would be embarrassing. I'm not sure what's come over me... Loneliness, I suppose...

"Yes, thank you," I answered, perhaps a little too quickly. "This place is stunning. Thank you for bringing me here."

"It's nothing much. But it's mine."

"How often do you come here?"

"Perhaps twice a week, just for a few hours." He tugged on the cuff of his shirt sleeve. "Though perhaps more often recently. Sometimes I just need to escape the tension of the coven."

"I don't blame you." I shuddered, not from the cold, but from the memories forever burned into my mind, created by Ivan. "Though a few hours aren't long enough, if you ask me. I'd prefer an eternity."

"Which is why we're here: to discuss a proposition that I don't want overheard." He turned to face me, tugging on his cuff once more and let out a deep, steadying breath. "You are not the only one who wishes to escape the coven. I, too, wish to leave, and have concluded that there are two ways in which we might succeed. The first, is to obtain our blood samples from Ivan. This would mean breaking into his motorhome and stealing them. Without our samples, finding us would be far more challenging for Dominic. The second way we might escape, would be to kill Dominic, a method I have tried in the past... and failed."

"You tried to kill Dominic?" I asked, almost disbelieving.

He nodded. "Fortunately, Ivan thought we'd simply got into a fight, and that my beating was punishment enough. But without Dominic and his near-Brain Eater's sense of smell, Ivan would have to rely on Jacob or Sebastian. Yes, Blood Drinkers have powerful olfaction, but we don't fixate on blood like a Brain Eater does. But I digress. The point is, I believe if we can obtain our blood samples from Ivan, we have a greater chance of escape without being caught. But it's not something I can do alone. Until now, I've not had anyone I can trust enough to assist me."

"You trust me?"

"I trust you want to escape as much as I do. And this might be the only way. Can I count on you?"

My pulse raced at his words. "Yes. If you can get me out of here, I'll do anything you ask."

Though he maintained his usual serious demeanour, his eyes sparkled, the fire dancing within them, reflecting his excitement. "Then listen carefully. At the end of the month, there is a full moon. The werewolves will be in lockdown, and the witches within their Sacred Ground to pray to their Moon Goddess. I'll need you to provide a distraction. You'll tell Ivan that the Hallows attacked you, and are plotting to do battle with Ivan's coven. With only the shifters to call upon for help—a faction Ivan has little respect for—he will undoubtedly call upon the vampires to hunt them down, as he has done in the past. During this time, I'll break into his motorhome and steal the samples."

"Won't he ask you to go with the vampires?"

"Not if I make myself scarce, but he may ask you to escort them to the Hallows location. We can decide where we'll stage their hideout at a later date."

"And you're sure you can break into his home?"

"Of course. I've been an accomplished picklock since I was a boy." Madigan toyed with his cuff, and I noted a sense of pride as he spoke. "But Ivan has vampires guard his home, which is why we need to remove them. And without the witches and werewolves to battle the Hallows—"

"He and the vampires will have to do it themselves," I said, finishing his sentence, processing the information.

"There is, however, one complication."

"And what is that?"

"As I said earlier, the full moon isn't until the end of the month. Your deadline to harvest will have come and gone. I need you to complete your trial and keep your head down until then. Can you do it?"

He seized one of my hands in his, warmth seeping from his skin and into mine.

I swallowed. *Could* I do it?

I nodded. "Yes. I can."

His face cracked into a rare smile.

He really is good looking when he smiles... My mind was momentarily invaded by the memory of him undressing again, making my heart thump as warmth flooded my body, but as suddenly as he had taken my hand, he dropped it, looking away, flushed.

"Madigan," I said, my own face burning at the question I was about to ask. "Can you read minds?"

He gave me a sideways glance, a ghost of a smile on his lips. "No, but I can smell moods."

"You can *smell* moods?" I repeated sceptically.

"In a sense. While Brain Eaters focus almost entirely on blood, Blood Drinkers can enjoy a greater variety. Providing I'm close enough, I can tell one person from another from their scent. I can smell when someone is stressed, or sick... or aroused..."

Blood rushed up into my face, burning as I comprehended *how* he'd known I'd been thinking impure thoughts about him. Though difficult to detect in the firelight, I was certain he, too, was blushing. A corner of his mouth twitched. I became hyperaware of the space (or lack of) between us. The heat radiating through me was not from the fire. It was, in fact, emanating from him.

"You're warmer than I thought you'd be." I raised a hand towards his face. "May I?" He blinked rapidly before nodding in response. I brushed my fingers against his hollow cheek. "Is that another vampire thing? You're warm?"

He nodded again.

"Would you... Would you warm me up?"

He flushed, swallowing so hard his Adam's apple quivered. "Alright." He raised an arm and jerked his head, indicating for me to shuffle closer to him.

I closed the gap between us, sliding across the fallen tree to sit beside him. He put his arm around me, his hand on my shoulder, and rubbed it up and down my upper arm. Heat permeated from his body and into mine, melting my innards as though he'd lit a fire inside me.

His hot breath caressed my cheek. Turning towards him, my eyes zoned in on his inviting lips. My stomach squirmed, like something was bubbling violently inside me. I leant in closer and I could have sworn that he mirrored my action so that our lips were mere millimetres apart.

In my head, I leant in and kissed him, massaging his lower lip between mine, and pulled his body against me. I imagined removing his clothes, how it would feel to have his bare skin pressed against my own, how he would feel *inside* me...

"Is that better?" he asked, his voice cracking, pulling me out of my fantasy.

"I'm sorry?"

"Are you warmer now?"

"Yes... Thank you."

"Good." His face was still inches from mine, lips slightly parted. "Then perhaps you will answer a question for me?" His voice was low, almost a whisper.

"Anything."

He examined my face with an intense stare. Was this it? Was he really going to kiss me?

"I've been meaning to ask, how is your arm?"

The fire inside me was brutally extinguished.

"Oh! Yeah..." I pulled up my hoodie sleeve before peeling back the bandage, revealing the oozing mess beneath. "It popped today. So gross."

He examined it, his warm hands brushing my skin tenderly. "Well, it doesn't look infected, which is a blessing."

He smiled again, and a moment passed where we simply stared at each other, until Madigan finally broke eye contact, coughing into his fist.

"We should probably get back and patch you up again," he said.

"Can we come back here again sometime?"

This wasn't the *real* question I was asking, and from his soft expression, I knew Madigan had read the subtext.

"Yes."

He held out a hand to help me to my feet, which I accepted. The fire in my soul blazed once more.

FOURTEEN

When I awoke, the first thing I saw was the disguise I'd prepared after letting Madigan patch me up. Tonight was the night. I could feel it.

The ginger wig beneath my beanie made my scalp itch. As my coat now had a ripped sleeve, I'd borrowed an ugly, brown one that I'd found among the werewolves' piles of old clothes. It smelt like dog. Though accustomed to wearing ripped jeans, these were a size too big, and I had to repeatedly pull them up over my hips. The dirt I'd rubbed on my hands caught under my fingernails. I could have easily passed for homeless person on Kinwich's streets.

I carried sandwiches in a paper bag, my trembling hands numb in the frosty night air. My heart leapt when I espied my target, a huddled figure sat on a bench outside Kinwich train station. A sleeping bag in a roll and a scrappy-looking bag beside them. I stood outside the Lagoon Lounge, a live music venue that attracted artsy clientele, watching the figure, completely invisible among the patrons in their snazzy outfits.

I took a seat beside my target, scrutinising him. He had a thick beard, flecked with grey hairs, and dirt had accumulated in the wrinkles on his face. He didn't acknowledge my presence, keeping his head bowed. This was it. I was going to harvest from him. My heart pounded in time to the dull beat of the bass emanating out of the Lagoon Lounge.

"Would you like one?" I opened the bag of sandwiches, offering him one. He frowned at me, then dropped his eyes down to the sandwiches and swallowed, before returning his gaze to mine.

"Just ham and cheese," I said, "and the bread is a bit stale."

"What's the catch?" he asked. His voice was low and raspy, and I noted that his few remaining teeth were blackened.

I feigned as friendly a smile as I could muster. "No catch. I just want some company. I've not been in my situation for very long. Maybe just over a week, and it gets pretty lonely."

"I know what you mean." His expression softened, and he took a sandwich with a grubby, calloused hand. "It's a tough life, but better than the one I left behind."

"How long have you been on the streets?" I asked, taking out a sandwich myself and taking a bite. My stomach was knotted so tightly I had to focus on chewing, swallowing, and forcing it down.

"Years. When I was younger, I had a few friends I stuck with. But they're gone now."

"Back home? Or did they get council accommodation?"

"Neither."

I withdrew a hipflask from the pocket of my coat. The floral smell of the sunny-yellow liquid tickled my nostrils as I opened the screw top.

"Want some? I'm not sure what it is, but it does the trick, if you know what I mean. Got it off someone I met in the park," I said, as I offered the flask.

"You didn't get it off the guys that hang out in the bandstand, did you?"

My heart skipped a beat. "Friends of yours?"

"Fuck no. I'd keep away from them if I were you."

You don't need to tell me twice...

I pretended to take a swig, only allowing a drop to pass my lips, then offered it to him again. The sweet, sticky substance slid down my throat. I was careful not to have too much; even that small sip was enough to relax my muscles. "Go on," I said, handing it to him. "It's the only thing that helps me sleep."

He took the flask and knocked some of the liquid back before returning it.

"That's nasty." He coughed, wiping his mouth on the back of his sleeve as he dribbled into his beard. "It's like syrup."

"Yeah, but as I said, it does the trick."

I mimed another drink from the flask and continued chatting with him while watching the masses falling in and out of the Lagoon Lounge, occasionally handing him the flask. The more he drank, the more he opened up to me. I even shared some half-truths with him, telling him I had to leave my home when my mother's new boyfriend had got aggressive.

"Mum asked me to come home, but I'd rather be here than living with that wanker. I don't care how sorry he *says* he is."

"People are cunts," the old man slurred. He handed me the now empty flask, not bothering to wipe the spittle from his chin. "You're better off staying away from the whole bloody lot of them."

"I'd drink to that if we had any left," I said, attempting to appear equally inebriated. If I was overacting, he was too spaced out to notice. "I can get more. Want to come with me?"

He cocked his head, his glazed eyes darting from side to side.

"If you want to avoid the group from the park, I can leave you halfway and meet you afterwards? I know the perfect spot where you won't be bothered."

He bit the inside of his cheek in thought, before nodding slowly. "Why the hell not?"

Shakily, he got to his feet, stretched, and picked up his belongings.

I led him toward Kinwich Cathedral, my plan being to get him to the same spot Madigan had harvested from the girl in the glittery dress a few nights back. The walk took a little while; he was dragging his feet and even stumbled a few times. Perhaps a whole flask had been excessive. My pulse was in my throat and my palms were sweaty despite the bitter cold. Every time we had to pause, the knot in my stomach tightened, half hoping that he would collapse in sight of others and I'd have to abandon my plan, but he kept going.

Eventually we reached the cathedral, illuminated by the yellow glow of spotlights, the steeple acting as a beacon. I guided him into the churchyard and into darkness, helping him to sit in the same spot that Glittery-Dress-Girl had been. Although she was gone, the raggedy old blanket remained, shredded and covered in dirt.

"Wait here," I said. "I will be back soon."

"I suppose I could come with you. For protection?" The words hit like a blow to the stomach.

"No, it's just... I don't want you to see what I do to acquire it. The guy I get it off..." I paused for dramatic effect, sighing and shaking my head. "He doesn't accept *money* as payment."

The old guy nodded, settling on the filthy blanket. "I understand."

I wandered into the darkness of the graveyard, following a narrow, stone path leading through the tombstones and towards a mausoleum. Though surrounded by black, iron railings, someone had still broken in and covered it in graffiti. I hid around the back, crouched down low and waited, picking at the freshly mown grass and rolling the blades between my thumb and fingers as I listened out for the sounds of voices or footsteps following behind me, but only picked up the noise of the wind through the branches of a dead tree. My ribs ached as they restrained my thundering heart, and just as I wondered how long I should keep waiting, I heard a distant, snorting noise. Could that be snoring?

I crept back to where I had left him, using the gravestones as cover. As I got closer, his snores grew louder. By the time I reached him, there was no doubt that he was unconscious, head back, mouth open, a trail of saliva running from his lower lip into his wiry beard.

This is it...

I knelt beside him, opened my bag and withdrew my equipment, a single item at a time, and placed each piece down in order of need.

With a deep breath, I tried to roll his sleeve back, but his coat was too thick.

Shit, shit, shit... I took another breath, trying to calm my pounding heart and think clearly.

I slowly unzipped his coat, manipulating his arm until free. He was wearing a thick, woollen jumper, but this time I could roll the sleeve back, exposing the soft flesh of his inner elbow.

Stay calm. You've got this...

I attached the tourniquet. His veins were invisible in the dark, but I ran my thumb up and down his arm, feeling for them. His skin felt strange. Bumpy. Textured like nothing I'd felt before. But I couldn't feel the squishy vein I'd been hoping for.

I had a torch with me. Did I dare use it? He snorted loudly, a raspy, wet noise in the back of his throat. I'd risk it. He seemed pretty intoxicated.

I took my torch from my bag and shone it on his arm. My blood ran cold as it became clear why I couldn't find his vein. Not just his inner elbow, but most of his inside arm was covered in small, circular scars. My eyes and nose tingled with emotions that threatened to overpower me.

I'm so, so sorry...

It felt so wrong to puncture him with another hole. But what choice did I have?

I hope you're not ambidextrous....

After removing the tourniquet, I pulled the sleeve down before removing his other arm from his coat. I froze, pulse raging in my ears as he snorted, only to settle, and I exhaled the breath I'd been holding. As I pulled back the sleeve, I saw more scars, but far fewer this time. This would be my best chance.

I applied the tourniquet and an electric pulse of excitement shot through me as I saw a vein bulge. Making sure I had my vials ready, I inserted the needle, holding the torch between my teeth until my jaw ached. I waited for a red line of blood to appear, prepared to attach the vial.

Nothing.

He snorted again.

I removed the needle a millimetre at a time. I'd started shaking, and my chest felt tight.

Breathe. You can do this. Just calm down. You can try again. There is no one else here. Take your time.

I felt for the vein and inserted the needle.

This time, he coughed, and his eyelids flickered. He sat up, looking at me through bleary eyes.

Shit!

I pulled the needle out, praying he was too delirious to notice, but he was already looking down at his arm, at the tourniquet, and rolled back sleeve.

He gaped at me with the same expression of horror I'd given Austin. "What the fuck are you doing, you little bitch!"

I fumbled in my bag, rooting around for the blue bottle and rag that I'd stupidly forgotten to prepare, but he shoved me backward and kicked the bag out of reach. I fell onto my arse, scrambling back, digging my heels into the dirt and pushing, my hands slipping in the mud.

"It's not what you think!" I said, holding out my hand as though it were a shield, but he was already towering over me.

He seized me by the front of my coat, yanked me to my feet, and smashed a fist into my face. A sickening crunch echoed in my head as the punch knocked loose a tooth from the back of my jaw, and my mouth filled with blood. Sent flying, I crashed onto my back. I rolled onto my front, spitting out the loose molar, before he hauled me back up again.

"Please... stop..."

But he struck again. Once. Twice. And sent me hurtling into a gravestone. Smacking my forehead with a crack. Something warm and wet dripped down my face. Collapsing in the weeds, I crawled as fast as my limbs would allow towards the cathedral. I looked back. He stumbled toward me, the aftereffects of the Mollifier hindering him. I clambered to my feet.

"Get back here, you little cunt!"

My legs had turned to jelly, but I lurched forward, falling upon one of the cathedral's stone walls, propping myself up against it as I hobbled around to the front of the building. I seized one of the cold, metal rings on the double doors and pulled. Locked.

My attacker's face appeared around the corner, teeth bared as he lumbered towards me, grabbing me once again from the front of my coat.

"You're dead, bitch!" he said with a snarl, eyes bulging out of his skull.

"No! Let me go!" I thrashed in his grip. Animal instinct took hold, and I sank my teeth into his hand.

With a yelp, he wrenched back his hand, and seizing the moment, I freed myself from his clasp.

"Just fuck off!" Propelling myself forward, I bulldozed into him, throwing my entire weight behind it. He staggered, taking a step back. Then a second. In what felt like slow motion, he lost his footing at the edge of the stone steps. He tumbled back, falling down one step after another, smashing his head on the corner of one, landing in a crumpled heap at the bottom.

I stood frozen, waiting, watching to see if he would get up again.

He didn't move. A pool of blood seeped from beneath his head.

I cast around, unsure if I wanted to find someone to help, but was completely alone, except for a stone angel whose blank eyes stared at me in judgement.

My body acted on its own as I collected up my belongings from the graveyard and ran.

I found myself in the park, hidden in the Stoner Bush that I had used as shelter when fleeing the showmen's yard, unable to recall how I'd got there. The only thing on my mind was the crunching sound as the old man's head hit the stone step. My stomach writhed, followed by a sour taste in my mouth.

Oh no...

My stomach crunched, and I vomited.

I remained in the Stoner Bush for hours, huddled in a ball, sobbing. It wasn't until the sky had turned from pitch-black to a dark-blue that I found the use of my legs and hauled myself back to the showmen's yard. For a second, I'd considered returning to the cathedral to collect blood from the corpse, but the thought of going back to the scene of the crime made me want to hurl again. Besides, someone might have discovered his body by now.

Madigan had not yet returned from his own night time outing, and I bundled myself into the tiny shower. I washed away the dirt and blood, but not the harrowing thoughts that haunted me. I jumped as I heard the door of the caravan open and close.

"Ava, is that you in there?" Madigan called through the bathroom door.

"Yeah, it's me," I said, clutching my chest in relief to hear his familiar voice. "I'm knackered, so I'm going straight to bed after this, if that's ok."

"Do you need me to bandage you up?"

My heart stopped. "W-what?"

"Your arm. Do you need a new bandage?"

"Oh!" I'd almost chundered again in panic. "No, thanks. I'm going to let it breathe while I sleep."

"Then I shall bid you good night. Or good day, I suppose."

I waited until I'd heard Madigan draw his curtain before emerging from the bathroom, giving him plenty of time to fall asleep; I wasn't ready to relive the experience by retelling it. Gathering up my clothes and the bloodied wig, I tried to conceal them as best I could as I dumped them into the wash basket, for the first time grateful that the laundry was *my* responsibility. I crawled into bed, the cut on my forehead and the hole where my tooth had been only now flaring with pain. My limbs felt heavy and my vision blurred as a wave of nausea washed over me.

It wasn't real... It wasn't real... It wasn't real... I told myself over, and over, until I fell down into a deep darkness.

FIFTEEN

My skull was splitting in two. An intense stabbing as it cracked down the middle and a metal rod plunged in deep over my left eyebrow.

My eyes snapped open and my body jerked upright with a sharp, ripping noise as my face peeled away from the pillow. My head swam and a wave of sickness flooded through me. Dried blood covered the pillow, soaked in sweat and a yellowish, foul-smelling goop. Memories of the previous night rushed back.

Shit... What have I done?

I brushed my hair away from my forehead to discover a clump of it had dried in the open wound. The pain in my head seared and blood flaked away as I tugged my hair free. I gathered up my bedding and dumped it into the wash basket with last night's clothes. Checking Madigan was still asleep, I crept out of my corner of the caravan and into the bathroom.

The face reflected in the mirror wasn't mine. Clammy, deathly pale, with dark shadows beneath sunken eyes. My forehead had disappeared under a reddish-brown carpet of dried blood. I washed my face and bloodied hair in the sink, taking great care to avoid the oozing lesion that was the source of the yellowish goo. I gingerly brushed my teeth, bypassing the crater left by my absent molar, now filled with a large clot. Even after brushing, my mouth felt furry and my throat tender and swollen.

I exited the bathroom, grabbed the wash basket, then snuck out of the caravan. The sun was setting, casting a red glow over the showmen's yard. Billy and Marcus were fooling around, laughing and joking while building the campfire and setting up for breakfast.

I made a beeline to Latisha's camper, slamming my fist on the door.

"Just coming!" Latisha opened the door, dressed in a blue and orange silk dressing gown, yawning as she scratched her head, her spiral curls dishevelled and sticking out at odd angles. She rubbed her eyes, frowning as she examined me. "Ava?" She rubbed her eyes again, her sleepy, bleary-eyed expression replaced with a frown. "I didn't recognise you at first. What the hell happened?"

"Can I speak to you? Alone?" I asked, my voice breaking as I tried to remain composed.

"Of course." She turned her head to address her companion. "Hetti, we need privacy. We can meet at the campfire with Luna and Aurora."

Latisha's familiar didn't argue. I lowered my head as she passed, hiding my face, then stepped into the camper.

The vibrant throws and tapestries blurred into a swirling pool of colour, the fairy lights sparkling like tiny, floating stars. The incense that had once been inviting now made my stomach churn. Latisha told me to take a seat, but I had already plonked myself on one of the squishy sofas, my legs shaking so vigorously I thought they might give way.

"Can you help me with this?" I brushed my hair aside so that she could examine the deep laceration. Latisha's mouth dropped open.

"I can. But It's going to require something rather potent," she said, getting a closer inspection, running her thumb over her lower lip. "It needed stitches, but it's too late now. I can give you an ointment that will kill the infection and accelerate the healing. Should take about an hour, but you'll have a scar, I'm afraid."

"I don't care. Would the ointment heal a tooth socket? What about a headache?"

"Yes, for the socket, not the headache. For that, I have good old paracetamol."

"I'll take anything you have."

First, she brought me the white pills and a glass of water to knock them back, then began pulling oddly shaped bottles out of a cupboard, each containing a different coloured liquid of varying viscosity.

"This is the one," she said, withdrawing a jar of paste that appeared similar to the one she'd given me for my feet on my first night with the coven. The only observable difference was that it was a deep-red instead of pink. She cleaned my forehead with cotton wool and warm water before applying the paste to my forehead, leaving behind a hot, tingling sensation, but almost instantaneously the pain subsided. She let me apply it inside my mouth, its bitter flavour somehow worse than the sour taste that had been gradually building.

"Stay here until the wounds have closed. How the hell did you do it?" Her eyes diverted to the wash basket. I'd arranged the laundry to hide the blood staining, but from this angle she'd see a few tell-tale droplets.

"I..." I couldn't think of a lie, my thoughts consumed by the image of the old man's unmoving body. My lower lip trembled. "I..." The muscles of my face contracted into a grimace.

Keep it together... Keep it together...

"I..."

I couldn't keep it together.

I broke down into hyperventilating sobs, my face instantly soaked in hot, salty tears, snot streaming down my upper lip. Though I wiped it away on the back of my sleeve, it didn't stop the unrelenting flow. I spluttered my story through deep, gasping breaths, my nose now blocked. Latisha listened, eyes growing glassier with each detail.

"Oh Ava…" She took the seat beside me and wrapped her arms around me, pulling me into her body. "It is ok. You're in a safe place now. I got you."

I clung to her. She didn't seem to care about my snotty face as I buried it into her shoulder. She rocked me, saying nothing, her cheek resting against the top of my head. Once I had calmed down enough that my nose had cleared and I could breathe in the sweet fragrance of her perfume, I pulled back and wiped my face.

"I'm sorry, Latisha."

"Don't apologise." She squeezed my hand, nudging the half-drunk glass of water closer towards me. "If it's any consolation, everyone here has a story like this. You're not alone."

"Even you?" I asked, taking a sip of water.

Latisha let out a short, humourless laugh. "Yes, even me. Especially me. I won't bog you down with the details now; it's pretty grim. But I've had to kill or be killed. The cost of becoming a supernatural is high."

Though reassuring to know Latisha and the others had all experienced something similar, I was grateful she'd spared me the gritty details. I stayed with her until the wounds had closed and I was—physically—like my old self again.

"I'd suggest you stay at the showmen's yard tonight," she said, raising a hand as I opened my mouth to protest. "You still have just under a week to complete your first harvest. If you go out again tonight, I guarantee you'll panic and mess it up."

Despite the ticking clock hanging over me, I was glad for the excuse to avoid venturing out again.

"I'll help you with your laundry duties tonight," Latisha said.

"Don't you have your own jobs to do?"

"That's what familiars are for. I might have healed your head wound, but you're likely still in shock. Come on. Let's get set up."

Madigan was gone by the time I got back, and though Latisha assisted me in setting up the wash bucket and washing line outside his camper, she soon left to collect everyone else's clothes and use their facilities. We figured the coven members would have a harder time saying no to her. It was a pity, as I could have used her company.

The old man's face kept invading my mind. His wild, crazed expression as he charged at me. The way his eyes widened for a split second as he lost his footing, and though I never saw his face again after his fall, I imagined a blank, glassy stare, like Austin's.

It could be you next if you fail again… My airway tightened.

I kept working, focusing on scrubbing out the stubborn dirt to prevent flashbacks. When Latisha had finished her half of the laundry and asked if I wanted to join her for a lunch break, I remained where I was. Though the other coven members might offer a welcome distraction, I didn't fancy sticking on a false smile and pretending everything was fine.

I was working on my last garment when the sound of footsteps reached me. I looked up from the wash bucket, my neck clicking as I did so, but instead of Latisha's silhouette to greet me, it was a skinny, male figure. Randall. I groaned inwardly, taking a deep breath and readying myself for the jeers about to be hurled my way.

"Not tonight, Randall," I said.

But the taunts never came. Instead, Randall held his face, covering his eyes, head bend down, like he had a migraine.

"Randall? Are you ok?"

He let out a moan, stumbling slightly, tripping over his own feet before propping himself up with his free hand against the side of Madigan's caravan. His hair was limp and greasy, flopping over his face, which looked even paler than usual, glistening with sweat.

He peered at me through his fingers, and slowly raised his head, as though only now seeing me. He blinked, tilting his head as his eyes widened.

"Randall? What are you—?"

He pounced, almost too fast for me to see, landing on top of me and knocking over the wash bucket. Warm, soapy water sloshed around me, soaking my hair and clothes as he pinned me to the floor, legs on either side of my hips, one hand on my chest.

"Get off me!" The words came out as a choking wheeze, the crushing weight of his hand restricting my breath. I flailed beneath him as a wave of panic rippled through me. I raised my hands to drive him off, one on his face, the other on his chest, but it was like pushing against a brick wall.

He licked his lips as his eyes raked over my upper body before settling on my neck. I knew what he was planning. He opened his mouth and bore down as I raised an arm to protect myself. His teeth clamped on the soft flesh of my forearm. I gritted my teeth, still trying to free myself, ignoring the sharp pain of his bite. But his jaw tightened, his teeth penetrating through my skin, forcing a scream from me as something hot and wet gushed from his mouth. I thrashed harder. His teeth cut deeper.

Something crashed into him, shoving him to the floor beside me. I scrambled away, holding my bleeding arm to my chest until someone seized me from behind, yanking me upward and clasping me to their side. Billy. He wrapped several arms around me, trying to lead me away, but I dug my heels in, whipping my head back, looking for Randall.

Madigan was on top of him, a hand round his throat. He hauled Randall to his feet and slammed him into the side of the caravan. Randall squirmed but was as defenceless in the stronger vampire's grip as I'd been in his.

My scream had drawn a crowd. Coven members shoved past each other to see what had happened. I noted Trevor's grim expression as he put a hand on Marcus's shoulder, whose eyes were wide with fright. Alfred tutted, shaking his head before murmuring to another of the werewolves, who nodded in response, their lips pursed in disapproval. Latisha reached us, trying to get a look at my arm, but I kept it pressed to my chest and looked past her, watching Madigan and Randall.

"What's all the commotion?" drawled a high voice. It was Dominic. He pushed his way to the front of the crowd and surveyed the scene, smiling as though mildly amused. His dark eyes strayed to me, flicking down to my bleeding arm, and his smile widened.

Madigan threw Randall to the ground at Dominic's feet. "I believe *this* belongs to you." Though he maintained his clipped, precise accent, he spoke with a snarl, jaw clenched, eyes wild with fury, the utmost contrast from the irked expression he'd worn while rescuing me from Dominic. "We do not feed from another's familiar within the coven."

"She hasn't passed her first trial yet. She isn't an official member."

"We do not feed from another's familiar! Randall is still *your* responsibility!" Madigan jabbed a finger into Dominic's chest.

Randall was still on the floor at his master's feet, but kept his ravenous eyes locked on me, blood and saliva dripping from his lips. He didn't even flinch when Dominic took hold of him by the scruff of his shirt, like someone takes a dog by the collar.

"He is suffering from blood sickness," Dominic said with a dismissive air. "It will pass once he's finished the transformation."

"I know what blood sickness is, you dolt! It's not an excuse to let your familiar run rampant!"

He snatched Dominic by the front of his shirt and yanked him close so that the pair were face to face, Dominic's turned upward, his smile wider than ever, Madigan's contorted with rage, one of his eyes twitching. "Keep him under control, or so help me, I will—"

"You'll do what?" Dominic swatted Madigan's hand aside, breaking his hold. I'd forgotten Madigan's warning about Dominic's hidden strength. And so, it seemed, had Madigan, who clenched his fists in a manner of someone readying themselves for a fight.

"Len." Latisha's voice barely registered.

"Any harm that befalls Miss Monroe shall also befall you," Madigan said to Dominic through gritted teeth.

"Len!" Latisha shouted, and the two vampires turned their faces to her.

She nodded towards Ivan's motorhome. So caught up by the confrontation, neither of them had noticed Ivan's enormous frame looming in the doorway of his camper, watching the pair of them, lips curled into a smirk just visible beneath a haze of cigar smoke.

"Master Ivan." Madigan stepped forward, uncharacteristically bold. "I must insist Dominic be held accountable for the maiming of my familiar. Randall is his responsibility and, in a fit of blood sickness, has bitten Miss Monroe."

Ivan cocked his head with a smile that could have been mistaken for pleasantness. "Let me see."

I still had my arm in my hand. It was hot to the touch, wet and sticky. I didn't want to let go. Madigan held out a hand towards me, indicating for me to step forward. I looked up at Billy, who released me from his many arms and nodded.

I kept my hand clenched around my arm as I approached Ivan, and reluctantly uncovered my bite, allowing him to view it. A colossal bruise enveloped the side of my forearm, red and swollen, exhibiting a ring of deep-set, bleeding holes.

Ivan raised his eyebrows. "He certainly tried to take a good chunk out of you, didn't he?"

I withdrew my arm, suddenly feeling sick and lightheaded.

Ivan addressed Dominic with the demeanour of a teacher reprimanding their favourite student. "You can't let Randall bite the human familiars. As temping as it may be."

"I'm sorry, Master Ivan." Dominic bowed his head.

"Keep a close eye on him. It won't be much longer until he regains some self-control. Now, be off with you." He then raised his head to address the coven. "All of you. There's nothing to see here anymore."

Some of the coven members immediately set off towards their campers, though a few of them, such as Trevor and Alfred, allowed themselves a critical glance at their leader before dispersing. Randall, who appeared to be oblivious to everything going on around him, still stared at me as Dominic pulled him to his feet, dragging him back to their camper.

Ivan narrowed his eyes. "That includes you two. William McGregor. Latisha Abara."

Billy wrinkled his brow as he gave me a parting glance, then hurried after Trevor and Marcus. Latisha glared at Ivan, and for a second, I thought she was going to disobey, but begrudgingly she, too, withdrew.

"Ava Monroe," Ivan said, "let me see your arm." Once again, I held it out for his inspection, but he laughed. "The other arm." My stomach twisted as I showed him the burn he'd given me. He pursed his lips, nodding. "Oh dear, you are in a sorry state, aren't you? Fortunately, I'll allow you to find a healing remedy for your bite. No sense in allowing someone *else* to mark you."

"Thank you, Master Ivan," I said, and with one last self-satisfied smirk, Ivan disappeared into his camper.

"Miss Monroe." Madigan didn't look at me, but had his head bowed, jaw still clenched. Was he angry with me? "Get yourself inside and lock the door." He pressed a key into my palm. "Answer to no one but me. I will get you a remedy from the witches. Do you understand?"

I nodded and did as I was bid. I sat on my bed, holding my bleeding arm close as it throbbed, yet it wasn't the pain that had me shaking. Madigan soon returned with a jar in his hand, and for the second time that night, the red paste stitched my wounds. We watched as the holes in my arm closed. I expected to cry but didn't. Instead, there was just a hollow feeling inside.

"Something troubles you?" Madigan's voice wrenched me out of my thoughts.

He was still holding my arm in one of his hands, the residue of red paste on one of his fingers.

My chest felt heavy as I braced myself for my confession. "I hate that you've had to rescue me. *Twice*."

Madigan raised his eyebrows, opening his mouth to speak, but I cut him off before he could do so.

"It's not that I'm ungrateful. I'm just used to fighting my own battles."

Madigan considered my words before responding. "I understand. But there is no shame in accepting help when it's needed."

"I don't like needing it."

"Everyone needs it from time to time."

"If you say so."

I sat back, leaning my head against the wall. My eyelids ached, and my rumpled duvet was calling to me.

Madigan squinted at me beneath a furrowed brow. "Forgive me if I seem forward, but you do not resemble yourself today."

"Don't I?"

"Not at all." His frown deepened. "No quips. No arguing back."

"Perhaps I've just learnt my lesson from Ivan," I said, not meeting his eye.

"I doubt that." He placed a hand on mine, the warmth of his touch permeating into my skin somewhat comforting. "I realise that I've not been the most emotionally available, but as your master, I hope you feel you can confide in me."

I paused, scrutinising him for a hint of a lie, but his eyes were earnest. My gaze dropped to his hand on mine.

"I tried harvesting last night and... and..." The words seemed to stick in my throat, but I swallowed, bracing myself. "I killed someone." I couldn't look him in the face, instead speaking to our hands.

His grip tightened as he drew a long breath. "Does anyone else know?"

"I told Latisha."

"Anyone else? Were there any witnesses?"

I shook my head.

"Good." He cleared his throat, perhaps trying to think of some words of comfort. "I... uh... I'm glad you were not hurt."

"I got hurt pretty bad. But Latisha patched me up."

"Why didn't you tell me?"

I forced myself to make eye contact. "I didn't want you to look at me with *that* expression."

"Concern?"

"No. Pity."

Madigan narrowed his eyes, tilting his head. "I admit, I have some sympathy for your situation. But I do not pity *you*. Though we haven't known each other long, I wouldn't have picked you for a familiar if I didn't think you had inner strength. You've shown great resilience in the face of adversity."

I gave him a weak smile. "You think so?"

"I do. You still have time to try again. But you must keep going. If you can pass your trial, we can escape before the month is out. I *know* we can."

"But what if I kill someone else?" My voice almost disappeared as I asked the question more frightening than the vampires.

Madigan sighed, lowering his head, before looking back at me with lips pressed into a wry smile. "Don't hide it from me next time."

SIXTEEN

I awoke Saturday evening, dread looming over me. The squeaking of hinges as Madigan rummaged through his cupboards for his clothes seemed to mock me, as the idea of getting up and dressed just made me want to hide deeper beneath the folds of my bedding. I pulled the covers up over my head, curling into the foetal position.

"Miss Monroe? Are you alright in there?" Madigan said through the curtain.

"I'm fine. I'll get up in a sec," I called back to him.

"I'm going out. Did you wish to accompany me?" He sounded uncertain, like he knew something was wrong.

"No, I'll go on my own. I need to... I need to try..." Spitting out the last words proved impossible.

"I understand. I will see you later. And good luck."

I hid beneath the covers until Madigan had gone, then finally emerged from my cocoon, sitting upright and running my fingers through my dishevelled hair.

I will get out of bed, but I'm not getting dressed, I bargained with myself.

I will get dressed, but I'm not going out...

Following this step-by-step process, I got myself out of the caravan and into town to find my target. I identified a few potentials: a huddled figure sat on a bench; a young woman waiting for a bus; a drunkard

in a kebab shop. But each time I considered approaching them, a jolt
of panic consumed me. My heart raced, vomit rising in my throat and
a cold, clammy sweat soaked through my clothes. I halted, paralysed,
before turning on my heel and hurrying away, putting as much distance between myself and the lost target as possible.

Sunday was no better, and I returned to the showmen's yard at a
snail's pace, empty-handed. Madigan was sitting at the table, playing
solitaire with a battered looking deck of cards. Had he been waiting
up for me?

"How did it go?" he asked, but I didn't respond, instead just kick-
ing off my trainers before drawing the curtain around my bed.

When I woke up on the Monday night, I immediately felt a churn-
ing in my stomach. The deadline was terrifyingly close.

Three nights left...

The temptation to hide beneath the covers was ever enticing, but
I sat up, closed my eyes and focused on breathing, mentally bracing
myself, coming to terms with what needed to be done. Perhaps Austin
had been filled with the same steely determination. Like Austin, I'd
have to break the rules if I was to succeed. Unlike Austin, I wouldn't
get caught.

*Monday night is a theatre society night. I'll go to the social and find
someone to harvest from. And if I fail tonight, I have a second shot on
Wednesday...*

No need to disguise myself, I dressed in my usual clobber, and even
applied some smoky eye makeup before heading to the university. The
session was just ending by the time I arrived.

Everyone was standing in a circle, taking it in turns to perform some
improv, too preoccupied to notice me slink through the double doors
into the hall. That is, until Hayley halted mid-monologue, looked
around dramatically, and spotted me.

"Ava?" Her eyes widened, mouth hanging open.

All heads whipped around. Most expressions mirrored Hayley's.
"Ava!"

Hayley marched towards me, pushing through the circle. I couldn't
tell if she was going to hug me or slap me, but was relieved when she
wrapped her arms around my body, pinning my arms to my side, and
squeezed, enveloping me with the smell of cigarettes. Instead of the
usual cravings it triggered, I was somewhat repulsed. I suppose Ivan's
habit for puffing smoke into my face had *one* benefit.

"Where the fuck have you been?" I couldn't see Hayley's face, but
her voice wavered, like she was holding back tears.

The next thing I knew, I was surrounded by people. Jo. Matt.
Chloe. Even Greg. Everyone seemed happy to see me, even the members
I barely knew.

"I thought you'd been kidnapped. We all did." There was no mistaking the tremor in Hayley's voice now, and her face, buried in my
neck, was wet.

It took everything I had not to cry, too, but I forced a smile. "I'm
sorry I made you worry. I was burgled and it kind of shook me up, so
I stayed with my mum for a bit."

Hayley released me, looking at me through narrowed, slightly reddened eyes. "Really?" Her voice wasn't shaking now. On the contrary,
the single word was firm, forceful, sceptical. But before I could try to
convince her of the lie, Jo cut in.

"We need to tell the police you're alright." She hugged me. Not as
tightly as Hayley, but the embrace was welcome. *Damn, I've missed
these girls...*

"It's alright," I said, thinking fast. "I've been to the station. They
know I'm ok. In fact"—I was suddenly hit with inspiration—"they

said they'd remove the missing posters, but if we see any they've missed, we should take them down, too."

"Really?" Hayley said again, her perfectly threaded eyebrows drawn together.

"Yes, really."

Her lips pressed together into a thin line. She was not buying this at all. I wondered if I should try to signal to her again that something was wrong, like when I'd used the phrase '*staying with my parents*' in my message to Charlie. Then she'd go to the police and...

No. I couldn't drag her into this mess. What if Ivan found out? My guts writhed at the thought of what he'd do to her. Besides, I had faith in Madigan's plan to escape. But first, I needed to harvest from someone. Anyone. Even if it was one of my friends.

"Seriously Hay," I gave her hand a squeeze. "I'll explain everything when it's just the two of us, alright?"

She grazed her lower lip with her teeth, but she finally let out a sigh. "Fine."

"Come on," Greg said, addressing the entire group. "We can reunite during the social. We'll lose our tables if we're late."

While the others disappeared backstage to get changed, Greg pulled me to one side.

"I'm glad you're ok," he said stiffly, not quite meeting my eye. "I thought... perhaps... your disappearance was my fault. I should have let you stay at my place."

"Forget it," I said. "I'm sure you can make it up to me."

And I know the perfect way to do it, too, involving a needle and tourniquet...

"You could pick next week's drama games?"

"Actually, I think I need a break from the society."

"You... you what?" Greg's mouth fell open. "You can't leave! Who'll make the costumes, and run the social media, and send the emails?"

"I'm sure the rest of the committee is more than capable. I'm not really *leaving*. Just taking a break. Until the end of the month. Then we'll be even, alright?"

"I guess," he said with a sigh.

I smiled at him one last time before heading backstage, leaving Greg the last person in the hall. Alone.

"You getting changed?" Hayley asked me, admiring her reflection in a mirror, having already changed into a little, red dress.

"You could say so." I pulled off my trainers, now permanently stained brown, and dumped them into a cupboard before retrieving my beloved Doc Martens. Reunited at last.

We ended up in the Black Dragon; I was oblivious to how Chloe had been bullied into abandoning her beloved Club Clique, but suppressed a giggle imagining the tantrum she'd have had. Instead of the bass that throbbed throughout a nightclub, the riff of a guitar greeted me as we stepped inside. The pub wasn't especially busy. A group of people covered in tattoos and leather took a couple of tables. Another was taken by two couples, the ladies dressed in polka dot dresses, and the gents in tight waistcoats. I pushed an intrusive thought of another waistcoat-clad gentleman aside and distracted myself, admiring the vinyls hung on display against wallpaper decorated with pin-up girls.

The theatre society filled the rest of the pub, taking the remaining tables. I sat beside Jo and across from Hayley, intending to move between tables under the pretence of socialising, but in reality, to gauge who was drunk.

Hayley got out her tarot cards, doing quick readings for anyone who asked. "Come on, Ava. Your turn!"

Desperate for just a few minutes of normality with my friends, I shuffled the deck and returned it. I still had the entire night ahead of me to pick a target.

"This represents the past," she said, drawing the first card and flipping it over. The upside down image of a hooded skeleton on a horse stared at me.

"Death?" I cocked an eyebrow at her. "Gee, great."

Hayley rolled her eyes and continued as if I hadn't spoken. "Death means change. But it's upside down, so you've been resisting change and holding onto the past. Next is the present." She flipped the next card. "The Hermit. This represents soul-searching and self-reflection. And finally"—she flipped the third card—"the future. The three of swords reversed. I'd be concerned if it were upright."

"Why is that?" I looked at the upside down picture; a heart pierced by three swords.

"The three of swords means heartbreak or betrayal. But as it is reversed, it symbolises forgiveness and moving on."

"Well, isn't that convenient." I glanced at Greg's table.

Jo laughed. "Hate to say it, but I told you so!" She nudged me, a cheeky smile on her face.

"Cringe." I wrinkled my nose. "Well, I guess I'd better get started." I picked up my drink, letting another member of the society take my seat for their own tarot reading. "Though I have one question for you, Hay."

She stopped shuffling the deck to look at me.

"How do you know an upside down card is for me, rather than yourself?"

She opened her mouth to answer, then closed it, frowning, as though the answer had abandoned her.

"Ignore me," I said, shrugging. "I'm being facetious."

"No change there," Hayley said smirking, and Jo broke out into giggles.

"Rude!" I said, pretending to be offended, "If you're going to take that tone with me, I'm leaving!"

"Don't be too long," Hayley said, as she resumed shuffling her cards and fixed me with a hard stare. "Jo and I have missed you." She was being serious now.

I blew a kiss, winking, before sliding a chair from another table to join Greg's. I was somewhat disappointed that he was sober. Would it be petty to harvest from him? Probably. But it would have felt just. However, Chloe, still disgruntled about being at the Black Dragon, had been necking shots since her arrival.

"I just can't stand the music," she said, slurring her words. "It's just middle-aged, angry men screaming."

She didn't bother to keep her voice down, even as a fresher was selecting songs on the jukebox. A fat, bearded man at the bar shot her a furious look.

"I know you don't like it, but we have to go to different places to suit everyone's preferences. Otherwise, people will stop coming," Greg said in an irritable voice I'd grown familiar with.

Had *he* overridden her? Impressed as I was that he'd grown a backbone, I kept my expression neutral.

"This place is tragic." Chloe's voice grew louder and higher, her London accent becoming more pronounced. "Everyone here is a fat, old, ugly biker." The bearded guy at the bar drained his pint before cracking his thick, tattooed knuckles. "We should leave soon."

"No! Not until we have had our songs!" the fresher shouted from the jukebox. "We always end up at a club or sports bar. The one time we go somewhere good you want to cut it short!"

"Imma yeet myself outta here if you're staying all night." Chloe shakily got to her feet. "Greg, walk me home."

"Are you serious?" he asked, unable to hide his impatience.

"It's dangerous to walk home alone at night! You want to see me on a missing person poster? No offence, Ava."

I saw my opportunity and snatched it.

"I'll walk you home," I said. "I pass your house on the way back to mine."

Greg looked at me, his eyes wide with surprise. "You wouldn't mind?"

"Not at all."

Chloe eyed me suspiciously.

"We can grab a drink for the walk back," I said, sweetening the deal. "The offie down the road does canned cocktails."

"Thanks Ava," Chloe said. "I am glad *someone* cares about me. Y'know, I've really missed you. Let's get a selfie!"

She raised her phone, and before I could protest, she'd snapped the picture. Even while inebriated, she still looked pretty without a filter. I looked the same in every photo: gormless. My insides felt as though they'd been replaced by eels as I recalled her boasts of several thousand followers on Instagram. But then, the eels were replaced by molten lead. If my harvest attempt went south, like it did at the cathedral, I'd just provided evidence of the last person with her.

Another reason not to fuck it up...

I guided her out of the pub, letting her lean on me as she tottered on her ridiculously high heels. We picked up cocktails from the off licence and strolled back to her house, only stopping to discard the cans once empty.

"So, what happened to you, anyway?" she asked, almost collapsing through the door. "I meant what I said earlier. I really missed you."

"Thanks," I said, my chest tightening.

I'd forgotten Chloe was an affectionate drunk, and for all her flaws, she wasn't as bad as I'd remembered. Compared to the likes of Ivan and his minions, she was positively angelic.

"Come on," I said. "Let's get you into bed." I knew my way around their house from when Greg and I had been dating. I helped remove her shoes and climb the grey, carpeted stairs to her room. Though as drab as the rest of the house, Chloe had brightened her room with pink, flowery furnishings and a Hello Kitty glitter lamp. The only thing she couldn't glam up was the scent of mould that emanated throughout the entire house. I undressed her down to her underwear and tucked her into bed.

"Can I get you anything?" I asked. "Water? A sick bucket?"

"Water, please," she said, wriggling down beneath the covers and closing her eyes. It only took a few minutes to fetch a glass of water, but by the time I'd returned, she was fast asleep, mouth wide open and snoring loudly.

I unzipped my bag...

I poked my head into Madigan's caravan, half-expecting him to be out, but he was sitting with his long legs crossed on the table, reading an old, faded copy of The Hound of the Baskervilles. He peered over the top when he heard the door open.

"Yes?" he asked, his brows furrowed.

"I did it," I said, though the words were barely audible as they got caught in my throat. Saying it out loud made it *real*.

"What?" He closed the book without marking the page and set it down, slowly getting to his feet.

"I did it!" I hadn't put the vial in the bag, but had kept it clutched in my sweaty palm, concealed in the pocket of my hoodie, almost afraid to let it go. As I raised the vial, the dark liquid appeared almost black in the dim light.

"Miss Monroe... I... I'm astounded!" He took the vial, examining it between his long, gloved fingers. "I had tried to encourage you as best as I could—but despite my efforts I—I didn't really think—and only in two weeks..." He was babbling, running his fingers through his dark hair, pacing as much as the cramped space allowed, but then seized my shoulders, grinning broadly in a way I'd not seen before.

"We must show this to Ivan immediately." He pressed the vial into my hand. "I don't know if he's here right now. Wait by the campfire, and I'll see if he's home."

He strode to the caravan door, but then stopped in his tracks, gripping the handle.

"I'm... I'm proud of you, Miss Monroe."

He turned his head to hide his flushed complexion as he left. I realised from my aching cheeks that I, too, was beaming, and only partly due to my success.

I did as instructed and headed to the campfire. The shifters were already there, and soon we were all chattering in excitement, unable to keep my news a secret.

"I didn't think you'd do it." Marcus looked at me with wide, disbelieving eyes.

"You owe me ten quid," Billy said to him with a snigger, hand outstretched.

Marcus rummaged in his pocket for his wallet and begrudgingly handed the cash to his master.

"I am very impressed," Trevor said, nodding, arms folded, smiling pleasantly.

"You owe me *twenty* quid." Billy held out his hand for the money, but Trevor swatted it aside.

"You can fuck off, soft lad."

"You guys were betting on me?" I asked.

"I was betting on you," Billy said. "These two were betting *against* you. Just a reminder of who your real friends are." He threw a strapping arm around my shoulder and squeezed me into the side of his body.

"So, celebration drinks are on you, then?" I nudged him in the ribs.

"Afraid not, Blondie." He lowered his voice to mutter into my ear, "This money is going to a very special, wee lady."

But the banter died as the skeletal form of Dominic hurried towards us, announcing that Ivan was on his way. Sure enough, Ivan's colossal frame soon came into view, followed by Madigan, whose smile had vanished, and the rest of Ivan's minions, except for Randall, who was noticeably absent.

"You have something for me?" Ivan asked.

His expression was hard to read; his lips were tight like he had been sucking on a lemon and eyes narrowed behind his spectacles. I held out the vial to him, which he took from me and examined between his thick fingers. He popped the cap off the vial and tipped a couple of drops onto his tongue and smacked his lips together, like someone tasting wine.

"Well, it is freshly harvested," he said, rubbing his square chin in thought. "It contains so much alcohol, I wonder if you harvested off someone who died from alcohol poisoning."

My stomach dropped. "I thought we could harvest from drunk people!"

"We can," Madigan cut in, his voice steady, but his fists were clenched and eyes cold.

"Yes, you can." Ivan leant down, his face inches from mine, so close that I could smell his sour breath. "But it tastes disgusting. So, tell me, from whom did you harvest this?"

His eyes bored into mine, seeking a giveaway sign of misconduct. I swallowed hard, a trickle of cold sweat running down the nape of my neck. He knew something was wrong. His nostrils flared, reminding me he could smell my stress.

"I didn't catch their name." I forced the words out, my throat suddenly restricting.

"It could be her own blood," Dominic suggested, and Ivan's eyes lit up, his lips curled into a menacing smile.

"That's true. I'll have to test it." He grabbed my arm with one hand and wrenched me upward until my toes barely scraped the floor.

"What are you doing?" I couldn't keep the panic from my voice, and before anyone could answer, he brought a silver blade up to my neck. "Stop!"

I thought he was about to slit my throat, but the blade bit down just above my collarbone. Ivan yanked me up higher, so that I was hanging in the air, my arm feeling like it would pop out of its socket. His hot, wet tongue lapped up the blood now flowing from the cut, making my skin crawl. Again, he smacked his lips, tasting my blood, savouring its flavour.

He dropped me, and I nearly lost my footing. Billy, who was closest, caught me before I could fall. I watched for Ivan's reaction. His eyes narrowed, surveying me, then licked his lips.

"With all due respect, Master Ivan, if she has presented a fresh harvest and it is not her own blood, we have no further reason to suspect her," Madigan said, his hands still balled into fists.

Ivan gave him a hard stare before turning his gaze back to me. He was looking for an explanation for my success. I said a silent prayer that he would believe my harvest had been authentic.

"Dominic," he said, his voice, though calm, was a deep rumble. His right-hand man stood to attention. "If you'd been tailing her, you could have confirmed if this had been a truly successful harvest."

"Master, I... You didn't ask me..."

"I shouldn't have to. You will be punished for this, I assure you." He then turned his attention back to me, leaning in close. "You're safe for now," he murmured so only I would hear. "But when you slip up—and you will—I'll know about it. Until then"—he drew a breath through his teeth, as though pained—"I *officially* welcome you into the coven. I shall speak with your master about your conversion." He turned abruptly and marched toward his camper. "Dominic, with me. Now. We need to talk."

Dominic scrambled after his master, eyes wide with fear. I let out a held breath, clutching at my chest as my heart tried to escape its cage.

SEVENTEEN

Waking the following night, it took a second to recall why there wasn't the usual terror constricting me, but then I grinned, sinking into my bedding as last night's success came rushing back. I considered having a lie in, but changed my mind. Tonight could be an opportunity to socialise without the feeling of impending doom hanging over me.

I drew my curtain, expecting to see Madigan, but he'd already gone, his bed converted into sofas and a table.

Bastard left without saying goodbye! What a cheek!

I showered and dressed, planning to find Latisha or Billy, and exited the caravan to find a group congregated around the campfire.

"There she is! Evening's Greetings, Princess!" Billy's jovial voice carried on the breeze. The rest of the crowd turned their heads in my direction, followed by cheers and greetings, one figure bouncing towards me in her fluttering, brightly-coloured dress. Latisha.

"Ava!" She handed me a glass of red liquid. "Don't panic. It's only wine. Come on, everyone's waiting!" She pulled me by my free hand to the group I identified as the entire coven, except the vampires. "You're an official member of the coven now. We thought we should celebrate!"

"Few vampire familiars make it this far," Alfred said, flicking his long ponytail.

"Ignore the grumpy bawbag." Billy gave Alfred a small punch on the arm. "Though he's not exactly *wrong*."

Alfred glared at Billy, baring his stained teeth and rubbing his arm. "No touching, shifter."

"Boys…" Latisha rolled her eyes. "You can practically smell the testosterone."

I laughed. Dysfunctional as they were, the coven was a family—one that I might have wanted to be part of if it wasn't for Ivan and his cronies. I mingled with the different groups, thanking each of them for coming to my party. Even the antisocial werewolves.

"Any excuse to celebrate," said a female werewolf who, I suspected, was Alfred's mate. "And not attending *another* execution is definitely worth celebrating."

"I'll drink to that," I said, clinking my glass against hers.

She raised an eyebrow at me, her mouth twisting into a disgruntled pout. *Grouchy werewolves…* I left her and the pack to join the friendlier members.

Luna and Aurora huddled together, occasionally glancing at me, like they were up to some mischief and didn't want to get caught, but as I approached, they sprung to their feet, wearing identical grins.

"We've got something for you," Luna said, holding out a small box. I opened it and inside was a yellow gemstone on a dainty, gold chain.

I put a hand to my chest. "I… I don't know what to say! Thank you!" I immediately took it from the box and put it on.

"It's topaz," Aurora said. "The ancient Egyptians believed it contained sunbeams. As vampires can't walk in the sun, we thought you could carry the sun with you instead."

"They're not *real* sunbeams, of course," Luna added. "It's more for sentiment. But it should still benefit you, as a Scorpio's birthstone."

I looked at the twins, mouth agape. *How do they know my star sign? Is all that stuff real?*

But before I could ask, Billy threw an arm around me, saying, "Sorry, Blondie, I haven't got you a present, but I can top up your drink!" He poured more wine into my now empty glass. "You've spent enough time with the hags. Come and hang out with your boys."

"Watch yourself, Spidey, or these hags will pull all eight legs off," Latisha said with a wink.

"You know I meant no offence, my lady," Billy said, adopting a posh voice and doffing an invisible cap, flashing his most charming smile. He steered me toward the shifters. After a few drinks and jokes (most at Marcus' expense), Billy asked, "Where's Len? I get he's a recluse, but you'd think he'd want to celebrate your success with us."

"I don't know," I said. "He was already gone by the time I got up."

"I saw him go into Master Ivan's motorhome at sundown," Marcus said, listening in on our conversation.

"Oh, really?" I drained the last of my wine, setting the glass on one of the stumps that encircled the campfire as I got to my feet.

"I wouldn't interrupt them if I were you," Trevor said, as serious as ever.

"I'm not going to. But I want to hear what they are saying."

The wine was doing the thinking for me. I reached the motorhome but came to an abrupt halt at the sound of Madigan's voice within.

"I will speak to her about it, but I still think it's too early."

"It doesn't matter what you think," Ivan's voice responded. "This is a direct order."

"She's just passed the first trial and you already want her to undergo the transformation? Now?"

My heart stopped.

"Two nights," said Ivan. "That's plenty of time to build up a blood supply for herself."

Two nights?! Two?! But the full moon is a week and half away!

"But... but Master Ivan, I thought perhaps another fortnight would—"

"Your prattle about the Hallows and the alleged threats they pose got me thinking. The faster we can increase our numbers, the better. Though why you are so afraid of them is beyond me. Don't you remember what happened to them last time?"

"I remember." Madigan sounded as though he were speaking through clenched teeth.

"Master Ivan," Dominic's voice joined the conversation. "Shouldn't you test her a second time, as you did Randall?"

"For once, I agree with Dominic," said Madigan. "She's too inexperienced. Another trial will determine if she's ready."

"Don't question my reasoning," said Ivan, and in my mind, I saw his icy glare over his spectacles. "Randall Johnson and Ava Monroe are entirely different and need to be treated accordingly. One was eager to undergo the conversion, and the other, I suspect, isn't. But perhaps she can be persuaded. If not, I'll dispose of her."

There was a moments silence.

"I understand, Master," Madigan said so softly I could barely hear him.

"Good. And don't argue with me again. It would be a shame to eliminate you, too."

"Yes, Master."

"Get out. I've had enough of you for one night. And the rest of you. Except, *you*." I couldn't see who Ivan was gesturing to, but it was probably his henchman, Dominic. "You stay. And your familiar. We have something to discuss."

My heart flared back to life, threatening to leap up my throat as footsteps approached the door. I darted around the motorhome, skulking in the shadows as the door swung open and the vampires exited. Jacob, Sebastian, and their familiars returned to their homes, followed by Madigan, who made for the campfire. I jumped from my hiding spot, running to catch up with him.

"Hey!" I called out before he could reach the party. He turned, a frown on his face that softened as he saw me.

"Miss Monroe! What were you doing back there?"

"I was listening to your delightful meeting." The only thing more sarcastic than my tone was my smile.

"You heard all of that?"

"I heard the end. Ivan wants me to become a vampire in *two* nights."

"Well…" Madigan tilted his head to one side, tugging at his cuff. "To put it bluntly: yes, he does."

"And what of our escape plan?"

"Shush!" He clamped a hand around my mouth and hissed into my ear, "We're outside Ivan's camper you dolt! I agree this needs discussion, but *not* here."

By his grace, I freed myself from his grip. "Then let's go. I need to know what I'm getting myself into."

Madigan nodded. "This time, we are bringing wine."

Like last time, Madigan guided me through the woodland to the lake. After building the fire, he spread a blanket beside it and seated himself, leaning back against the fallen tree, then patted the spot beside him, inviting me to sit. He opened the bottle of wine and took a swig straight from the bottle before passing it to me. It tasted like vinegar, but I still enjoyed the warm sensation in my chest.

"Before we dive into the details of the transformation, I wanted to congratulate you," Madigan said. "It must be a relief to have passed your trial."

I snorted with bitter laughter. "Hardly. Even if we escape this sodding place, if I become a vampire there is no way I can go back to my old life. You have no idea what I'm going through."

"I have *some* idea." He arched an eyebrow at me. "Becoming a vampire wasn't exactly my first choice. But it was that or dying. I chose a life of servitude—until my master released me, that is."

"Your master wasn't like Ivan, then?"

"No." He rubbed the back of his neck, eyes drifting to the fire. "He was a good man. A good mentor. He gave me a lot more time to undergo my training. A *lot* more time."

"Was there the threat of death if you failed?"

"In theory. All vampire masters are supposed to dispose of their familiars if they fail their training, but Master Tobias was... different." His voice trailed off. I didn't need him to tell me how fond he had been of his master; I could tell from the way his voice cracked when he spoke of him. His vulnerability softened my temper.

"We don't have to talk about it if you don't want to," I said, handing him the bottle of wine.

"It's alright," he said, taking a drink. "Master Tobias wasn't traditional. He didn't join a coven, choosing instead to take me and my friend as familiars in exchange for saving our lives." He touched the left side of his torso absentmindedly, but then, realising what he was doing, ran his fingers through his hair. "We travelled, keeping to ourselves. It was a simple life, difficult to adjust to perhaps, but we were free. That is, until he was murdered."

He flicked an acorn husk into the fire, the light dancing in his shiny eyes as he gazed into the flames, hypnotised as he relived his past.

"It's difficult losing someone you care about." I pulled the photograph of my grandma from my hoodie pocket. "I think about my grandma every day... and how disappointed she'd be."

Madigan put his arm around my shoulders, squeezing me into his side. My stomach flipped over.

"I'm sure she would be very proud of you." Handing the half-empty wine bottle to me, Madigan looked at the photograph. "That's your grandma? She looks young enough to be your mother."

"She was only fifty-five when she died. Both she and my mother had kids young."

I looked at the photo, noting her large, brown eyes and unusual hair—dark-brown, with a tuft of white at the front—just like mine when it wasn't coated in bleach. I returned the photo to my pocket before my eyes could start stinging. I took another swig from the bottle, then scooted closer to Madigan, resting my head on his shoulder, warmth seeping from his body and into mine, and for a while we remained silent, watching the fire as we finished the remaining wine and cast the bottle aside.

"So," Madigan said with a sigh, finally breaking the silence, "I suppose we should discuss your conversion."

"Do we *really* have to?"

Ivan was right; I didn't want to become a vampire. It was difficult enough harvesting to pass my trial. To do it regularly filled me with dread. And the sun: I'd miss the sun. I clutched at the necklace the twins had given me. As touching as the sentiment was, the yellow stone wouldn't replace the feeling of the sun soaking through my skin. Or the beauty of golden light shining over the horizon, or the red glow of sunset. I wondered how severe the long-term side effects of Latisha's sunblock lotion were, and if it was worth the risk.

"Look," Madigan twisted to face me, gripping me by the shoulders and stared into my eyes with a look of determination. "As you said yourself, you won't be able to return to your human life, but we *can* still escape the coven. This is just another obstacle to overcome."

I stared back. My temper longed to flare again, but what good would that do? I felt the fight bleed out of me. "Fine. Tell me about the conversion."

"Well, as you know, you'll be required to drink vampire blood."

"A litre? Like Randall had to?"

Madigan nodded, his perpetual frown set in place.

"Will it be your blood?"

He nodded again. "After drinking a vampire's blood, you shall slowly become one of us. It takes about a week for the process to complete."

"A week?! It will take that long?"

"Afraid so. And it's not a pleasant week. Every cell in your body will ache as your DNA is rewritten. You'll have moments of boundless energy, only to crash minutes later. And possibly the toughest thing is the craving for blood. Anyone's. Human. Vampire. Animal. It's not unusual for those undergoing the conversion to drink their own in desperation."

Without thinking, I put a hand to my arm, covering the spot Randall had bitten me. "Blood sickness," I said, recalling the term Dominic and Madigan had used.

"Correct. But I'll take care of you. Rest assured of that." He looked at me, half-smiling, and my insides melted. "And not just during your conversion, either. After the transformation, you'll battle your addictions to human blood. It's during this time that most vampires become Brain Eaters."

I shuddered as I recalled Madigan's explanation of the vampires that became so addicted to human blood they became monsters.

"That's why most of our kind travel to the Vampires' Nest for their conversion," Madigan continued. "It's a sacred place for our people and it's easier to undergo the conversion with the support and knowledge of different types of vampires. Unfortunately, Ivan doesn't allow such things."

"What do you mean by different *types* of vampires?"

Madigan scratched his chin, cocking his head to the side, considering the best explanation for me. "Well, I've told you of the Brain Eaters."

"Yes, I remember. Big yikes."

"*Yikes*, indeed," Madigan chuckled. I'd never heard him laugh before, the sound of which gave me butterflies, eager to make him laugh again. "There are Blood Drinkers, such as myself. And finally, there are Soul Suckers. They are the most powerful of our kind. They have an arsenal of abilities, such as glamour, wallcrawling, as well as ungodly speed and strength that make the rest of us seem feeble by comparison. But it comes at a price." He fixed me with an intense stare. "To become a Soul Sucker, a Blood Drinker must suck the soul from another being's mouth, leaving their victim an empty, yet obedient husk." He took one of my hands in his. "Which is why, Miss Monroe, I implore you, please be careful should a vampire—*any* vampire—try to kiss you."

I closed my mouth, which I only now realised had been hanging open.

"Is Ivan a Soul Sucker?" I asked, recalling the ease with which he'd lifted me by the arm.

Madigan flashed a rare smirk. "Does he look like he can glamour?"

I thought about Ivan's appearance, his broad features and hulking frame. He was a sight to behold, but beautiful? No. "Fair point. And you promise you aren't a Soul Sucker?"

"Do I look like I can glamour?"

I looked into his grey eyes, noting his prominent brow, thin nose, hollow cheeks... and inviting lips. He wasn't exactly *beautiful*. And yet...

"To me? *Yes*." He was still holding one of my hands. I closed my fingers around his tightly. "But if you promise that you're not a Soul Sucker, and never will be, I believe you." I slid closer towards him, my leg now against his. His eyes were looking directly into mine.

His chest was heaving, lips parted, like he was feeling exactly as I was. "You trust me?"

My heart felt as though it were about to burst. I nodded, leaning closer; so close we shared a breath.

A smile tugged at the corner of his mouth. "You barely know me," he said, his voice husky as he mirrored me, our noses almost touching.

"I'd like to know you better."

"What would you like to know?"

I swallowed. "I want to know..." Did I dare say it out loud? His sweet aroma infiltrated my senses, and the words slipped out before I could stop them. "I want to know what your lips feel like."

"Miss Monroe," he whispered, but before he could continue, I closed the millimetres between us, pressing my lips to his, kissing him softly. His lips were smooth, without a trace of stubble around his chin. But his body went rigid, sharply inhaling through his nose like I'd stolen the air from him.

"I'm sorry," I said, pulling away, blood aflame in my cheeks. "I should have asked."

For a moment, we just looked at each other, my heart hammering, breath almost failing me completely as I waited for him to say something. Madigan's widening eyes burned into mine before flicking down to my mouth, transfixed. He swallowed. Then brushed my hair from my face, and slid one finger across my cheek to my chin, gently tilting my face up to his. His teeth grazed his lower lip, and I could practically hear his mind battling with itself.

The next thing I knew, his fingers were tight in my hair, and his lips crashed against mine, nipping, biting, drinking me in. I swallowed his moan as his lips parted mine, allowing his tongue to invade my mouth and dance against my own. Heat raged through my body, across my lips, down my throat, down my chest, down, down... down...

His hands were now on my waist, pulling me onto his lap with such ease I could have weighed nothing, then slid down to clasp my hips, pinching my flesh with such intensity, it was more than simple desire. It was *need*. Like years of suppression had finally overpowered him.

My mind was a blur, hardly daring to believe what was happening. Wrapping my arms around his neck, I kissed him as hungrily as he was kissing me, a wave of electricity pulsing through my body, grinding my hips against his and had to suppress a moan as his erection pressed against the growing wetness between my legs. I let out a shuddering gasp against his mouth, gripping him like he was the only thing keeping me tethered to reality, until—

He pulled back, panting. "This is wrong..."

"What?" My insides lurched, like when missing a step in the dark.

"We shouldn't do this. It isn't right. It isn't professional." He lifted me off his lap, his grip pinching painfully.

"What are you talking about?"

"I'm your master. This would be... an abuse of power."

"No, it wouldn't!" I sounded desperate, but I didn't care. "I'm a consenting adult. I want this."

"I'm sorry, Miss Monroe." He tugged his cuff, turning his head away from me. "We can't do this... I... I mustn't take advantage."

"Take advantage? What are you talking about?"

"You're likely looking for escapism from your torment, and as much as I want to... No. My decision is final." He got to his feet, brushed himself down, and started to extinguish the fire. I stood too, watching him work, rubbing my arms against the chill of winter.

"Is it because you're self-conscious?" I asked, throwing caution to the wind.

He stopped, snapping his head around to look at me, glaring.

"Excuse me?"

"I just thought maybe... you were shy... about..."

He took a few steps towards me, looking down his nose at me like he'd done during our first meeting, the moonlight reflecting off his cold, flinty eyes.

"About what?" His tone was dangerous, like he was daring me to finish my sentence. Unfortunately, I'd never known when to refuse a dare.

"About the scars you got during some war."

"Some war?" He pinched the bridge of his nose, exhaling. "Miss Monroe..." His tone was now frostier than the night. "It wasn't *some* war. It was *the* war. The Great War. For your information, I got these scars whilst I, and my dearest friend, emerged over the top, heading into No Man's Land. Shrapnel from a German shell. My companion was not as lucky as I. He took it to the face, shredding him. Didn't kill him, though."

He leant down, his face close, eyes locked on mine. "His screams still echo in my mind when I sleep. And that's not all. I've seen a man with dysentery drown in a trench of his own faeces. Waking to find rats eating me alive. The feeling of taking off my boot to find one of my toes has ripped clean off my foot. Clearing a slurry of corpses in the trenches, tripping over one and falling into his body. Not on top of it. *Into* it. A soup of bone and organs. I couldn't wash the putrid stench off for weeks."

My mouth was hanging open. The butterflies in my stomach had long since died, replaced by a wave of nausea that threatened to overpower me. "I... I'm sorry... I didn't know..."

"No, you didn't. We're from different worlds, and that is why we're not compatible."

"Maybe I could help you?"

"Really? You think you could erase a trauma of over a hundred years?" He shook his head. "That just confirms your naivety. Compared to me, you're still but a child."

"I'm... sorry."

"Forget it," he said, stamping out the remaining embers with a huff.

He didn't make eye contact when he asked if I'd need help through the dark woodland, and when I said yes, he held my wrist instead of my hand. When I tried to speak, the words died on my lips before I could summon the courage to spit them out.

Once we'd reached the showmen's yard, Madigan released my wrist and walked ahead, and all I could do was follow, looking at the marks in the gravel he'd left behind. I cleared my throat for attention as he reached the door to his caravan.

"Would you like me to ask Latisha if I should stay with her for today?" I gritted my teeth, trying to stop my voice from cracking.

Madigan looked through me, before hanging his head and sighing. "Perhaps that would be best."

Without looking back, he headed into his caravan and closed the door behind him.

EIGHTEEN

I didn't go to Latisha, but instead, stared into the heart of the campfire as thoughts chased themselves through my mind. The party was over. All that remained were a few discarded beer cans that had evaded clean up.

What have I done? I'm such an idiot...

I was too close to the fire. Thanks to the rips in my jeans, my exposed skin burnt sweetly. Even my face was flushed. It wasn't painful, but blissfully hot, irritating, itching.

I'm a fucking idiot!

I grabbed a nearby beer can, crushed it in my fist, and hurled it into the fire, sending a spray of embers into the air.

The scene replayed itself inside my head. His smile. His *laugh*. His perfect lips on mine. And then, the coldness in his eyes. The bitterness in his voice.

'That just confirms your naivety. Compared to me, you're still but a child.'

He's right though, isn't he? Here I am, about to lose either my life or my humanity, and what's my priority? Dating. Like a stupid child with a crush.

I clenched and unclenched my fists, my fingernails biting into my palms as another overwhelming urge to throw something took hold of me.

Greg was right about me... Too clingy, too intense, too desperate.

"Aggghhh!" I grabbed the nearest thing to me, a stone, and chucked it into the fire after the beer can.

"Blondie!"

My heart jumped up into my throat. "Billy, I didn't hear you coming."

"Too busy screaming, I suspect," he said, laughing, taking a seat opposite. "Might want to sit back, though. You're pretty close to the fire."

I did as he advised, not in the mood for an argument.

"I was worried when you didn't come back from Ivan's," he said. "How's your first night of freedom?"

"Fine."

"Aye, right." He nodded slowly, eyes narrowed with scepticism.

The truth bubbled inside me, longing to burst free. I shouldn't have tried lying in the first place. "It's just a stupid crush. It's nothing."

Whatever Billy had been expecting, this wasn't it. "I see." He looked away, rubbing the back of his head, eyes settling on the fire. "To be blunt, matters of the heart are not my forte. Now, if you need someone to catch flies, I am your guy, but otherwise..." He shrugged, pulling a face. Despite my tetchiness, I snickered; I couldn't imagine his fly catching abilities were often sought after. "I can find Tish if you like? She's better at this."

"No, please—"

But he'd already rushed off to the campers. I groaned, burying my face in my hands. I wasn't looking for sympathy and was already regretting my confession. Billy soon returned with Latisha, who seated herself beside me, pulling me into a one-armed hug.

"Billy said you were a bit upset," she said, giving me a squeeze. "You can tell me about it. Billy is a bit rubbish, isn't he?"

We shared a laugh at Billy's expense, who played up his offence with great gusto, pouting and flailing his arms, reminiscent of a teenager having a strop, and soon enough, I felt able to confide in them both.

"Latisha, during our first meeting you said you would have taken me as your familiar if you had the chance."

"Yeah?" Her eyes narrowed as she leant forward, leaning her elbows on her knees, hands clasped together.

"Is it too late to accept that offer?"

She and Billy shared a look.

"Oh, boy..." she said with a sigh, not making eye contact as she scrunched the curls at the back of her head. "I wasn't being entirely serious. I told you that witch's familiars become shifters, right?"

"Shifting looks cool," Billy said, "but you *feel* everything: your bones breaking and organs moving." He wrinkled his nose. "You get used to it, but the first few times are horrific. It only takes a second to shift, but it seems like time slows down."

He shook his head, turning his gaze from me to the floor.

"Yeah, because becoming a vampire will be sooo much better," I said, unable to hide my irritation. "Never able to walk in sunlight. A week-long transformation. Blood sickness. Addiction. Sounds great! Sign me the fuck up."

Latisha pressed her lips together into a wry smile. "Both are equally shit. But Len will look after—"

"I don't think he will. We kinda had a falling out."

"Oh, really?" Latisha raised her eyebrows.

But Billy squinted at me as the realisation hit him. "Wait," he said, his calculating expression now replaced with a smirk. "It's *Len* you have a crush on?"

"Fuck off, Billy," I said, glaring, but that only encouraged him.

"That miserable old git with a stick up his butt?" He was now howling with laughter.

I stood, clenching my fists, adrenaline pumping through me. "Seriously, Billy, shut the fuck up."

Billy, still sniggering, raised his hands defensively. "Calm your tits, Scrappy-Doo. I'm only messing with you."

Latisha put a calming hand on my shoulder and guided me back down to my seat, giving Billy a filthy look that shut him up immediately.

"Ava," she said, her voice calm but filled with a natural authority, "I understand you're going through a tough time. But think rationally. If Ivan *really* wants you to become a vampire, then there's no point fighting it. Len won't abandon you. He just likes to keep things professional. Trust me on this."

Professional... that's the exact word he used....

"You're probably better off without a relationship anyway," Billy said. He wasn't teasing anymore. "Aye, Len is a supernatural, unlike my Anna. But if Ivan found out that you two were an item, do you think he'd give you his blessing and you'd live happily ever after? Or do you think he'd weaponize it against you?"

I chewed my lip, looking from Billy to Latisha, before sighing and said dryly, "Don't suppose either of you fancy challenging Ivan for leadership of the coven, do you? I'm sure it would be easy."

"Naw, not tonight. I've got a wee headache," Billy said, feigning a casual air. "Besides I'm not leadership material. What about you, Tish?"

"Sure," she said, rolling her eyes. "Leadership worked out so well for me last time."

"You led a coven?" I asked, dropping the joke. "When? What happened?"

"The Hallows happened. But you don't want to hear about that," she said stiffly.

"Yes, I do!" I said, and to my surprise, so did Billy.

"Maybe another time."

"But—"

"*Maybe another time*," she said, clenching her jaw. "It's getting early. I need my bed."

"Any chance I could sleep at yours?"

"Sure." She got to her feet. "You coming?"

"In a bit," I said. "Just give me ten minutes alone and I'll be right there."

"I'm off to bed, too," said Billy. "See you later, Ava. Don't let the bastards get you down." He hurried to walk with Latisha back to the campers. "Latisha, tell me how you were a leader of a coven…"

His voice trailed off as they walked together, and though I didn't give them a backward glance, I was sure I heard him yelp in pain, as though Latisha had thumped him.

Our talk had helped. Despite a hollow feeling in the pit of my stomach, I knew I had to resolve things with Madigan. Crush or no crush, I needed his help to endure the nightmare of transforming into a vampire, and then get the hell out of here.

I was so consumed by my thoughts that I didn't notice the sound of someone approaching until they were right behind me.

A hand seized the back of my head, shoving me to the ground. Gravel scratched the side of my face as the weight of my attacker crushed me.

"If you're going to talk about overthrowing our master, keep your voice down," hissed a nasally voice. Randall's.

"Get off me," I gasped, his weight pressing down so hard I could barely draw breath. His grip was as tenacious as Dominic's had been. Fingers traced over my neck, sending a shiver through my body.

"Remember our first fight?" His voice was light, conversational, but with a hint of mockery. "We were pretty evenly matched."

"I'd have wiped the floor with you."

His grip tightened, but he continued as though I'd not spoken. "But not anymore. Now you're completely at my mercy." His lips brushed my ear, his breath on my skin. "I could do *anything* to you."

My heart stopped. I didn't want to beg. But what he was suggesting made my stomach turn. A sour taste in my mouth. Even my bladder felt weak.

"Don't." I wanted it to sound commanding but came out a whimper.

To my surprise, his grip slackened, and the weight pressing me down lifted. Immediately, I scrambled away, attempting to maintain what little dignity I had. My heart pounded so violently it reverberated through every cell of my body.

"I wouldn't do *that* to you, Ava," Randall said, and though his lips were still twisted into his usual smirk, he spoke sincerely. "I'm not a monster. In fact, I'm quite the opposite."

"I'm sure," I said, rubbing my cheek from where the gravel had scratched it.

"For real. I actually came to apologise for attacking you while suffering from blood sickness. I don't remember much, but after Master Dominic told me, I thought I should say sorry."

"You going to apologise for pinning me on the ground, too?" I said, curling my hands into fists. I knew I was no match for him, but I wasn't letting my guard down.

"Don't be so salty. Fine, I'm sorry for that, too. I was listening to your conversation with the witch and the shifter and gathered you don't want to become a vampire. I was trying to show you it's not all bad. The transformation was rough, but I'm *so* much stronger. It's the best thing that's ever happened to me. And probably for you, too."

"Deep joy."

"For real. And to show there are no hard feelings, I'll keep what you said about overthrowing Master Ivan just between us."

My stomach lurched. The whole situation whiffed of blackmail. "What's the catch?"

"No catch. We're even now." Randall folded his arms, tilting his head and looked me up and down. He was smiling, but his eyes were hungry. "But I meant what I said. I think becoming a vampire will be the best thing to happen to you. Unrivalled speed, strength, and senses. The other vampires will respect you. Even Len might *change his mind*, if you know what I mean."

My face burned as his smile widened. I guess he'd heard the *whole* conversation.

"My advice," he continued, "is to get your blood supply up. The cravings are"—he inhaled deeply, leering at me—"*insatiable.*"

A cold bead of sweat trickled down the back of my neck.

He hummed a laugh through closed lips. "I'll leave you to think about what I've said. See you later, friend."

And with one last suggestive look over my body, he left towards Dominic's camper. I had a sudden urge to add several more layers of clothes.

I awoke shivering on the floor of Latisha's motorhome. I'd used the largest of her knitted throws as a blanket, but it was nothing compared to the thick duvet from Madigan's caravan. Slowly kneeling, my back made a horrible clicking noise. I stretched, tilting my neck from side to side, working out the stiffness.

Latisha and Hetti were asleep, or at least ignored me as I let myself out. The sun was setting, and as I stepped outside, my breath appeared as mist before me. It would probably be another hour until Madigan was awake. I headed over to his caravan and let myself in to get showered, dressed, and make some tea.

When he finally emerged, he spoke with forced politeness. It was like attending a society meeting.

"Are you going out tonight?" he asked.

There was no point in fighting it. He was my master; I was his familiar. This was my life now.

"Yeah. I'd better harvest blood for myself, Master Len."

Madigan frowned slightly, as if my words had hurt. "You don't have to call me that."

"I think I do. Y'know, to be professional. It was your suggestion in the first place."

"Yes, but that was before..."

"Before what?"

"Before we became friends."

"Friends? Is that what we are?"

"Miss Monroe," he said in a low voice, "I appreciate you are deeply troubled right now, but there is no need to take your ill mood out on me. I am trying to help you."

"Help me?!" I leant in close, and said in a whispered shout, "If you really want to help me, get my blood from Ivan so that I don't have to become a monster like Randall or..."

His eyes widened as he blinked at me, pained. "Or, like me?"

I instantly regretted my harsh words.

"I'm sorry," I said, my temper dying almost as quickly as it had risen. "I didn't mean that."

But Madigan turned away, not looking at me, remaining silent, ignoring my ongoing apologies and excuses. He showered and dressed, and without asking me to accompany him, left the caravan.

"Damn it! You can't keep your fucking mouth shut can you?" Mustering my strength, I kicked one of the little cupboard doors. This achieved nothing but a throbbing sensation in my big toe. The force of my kick overpowered the magnet that usually kept the door closed and it pinged open.

I rubbed my toe, seating myself at the foot of Madigan's bed. In his rush to leave, he hadn't turned it back into sofas. I glowered at the little cupboard, as though it had been *its* fault for hurting me. Once the throbbing had faded, I went to close the door when the sight of a half-empty liquor bottle inside stopped me. I couldn't tell what it was, so squinted at the old, faded label.

"What the bloody hell is cog-nac?"

Its fragrance burnt my nostrils but did nothing to deter me. I swigged it. It scorched my throat, making me cough, tears streaming down my face as my body shuddered in involuntary spasms. The effect was immediate. A warm, tingling sensation ran through my body and I grinned.

That's better...

My bag of harvesting equipment sat on my bed opposite me. As I stared at it, I felt as though it was staring back, taunting me.

"Just another obstacle to overcome..."

And with a sigh, I picked up my bag and headed out.

Perhaps it was my determination, or perhaps it was the alcohol, but as I made my way through the park and into town, I was surprised to find my heart wasn't thumping against my ribs. Nor was my throat constricting with nerves.

Rather than wandering the streets, I went from pub to pub, seeking potential targets whilst having a drink at the bar. On one occasion, a guy who I recognised from my course approached me. Though we'd never spoken before, he offered to buy me a drink. Flattered, the carefree university student inside me flared into life, wanting to accept his offer. I imagined having a drink with him, going to the next pub, then back to his apartment. But then, the reality of what I needed to do reared its ugly head. My fantasy ended with me puncturing his arm with a needle and a fall down a flight of stairs during a scuffle.

No. Not him...

Instead, I thanked him for his offer and invented some excuse about getting up early in the morning.

The next nearest pub was the Black Dragon. The big, bearded guy was at the bar again. But to my disappointment, his was the only face I recognised. It would have been a stretch for the theatre society to visit the rocker's pub twice. They were probably at Club Clique again. I'd never get in with a bag full of needles. But then again, I didn't need to *enter* the club. Just find people leaving.

I necked the last of my drink and got ready to move on. By now, my lips were numb, and the cold no longer bothered me. It took a while to reach the club, giving me time to mentally prepare myself, with a little help of Dutch courage.

The smoking area at the front of the club was packed full of people, reminding me of farm animals in a pen, standing in their own filth. The usual smell of sweat and vomit that engulfed the club spilled outside, only now it was mixed with the stench of stale cigarettes. I looked for someone I could convince to leave with me. One girl leant against a wall, her face pale, occasionally spitting on the ground like she was trying not to be sick. I was about to ask if she wanted me to call a cab when I identified a familiar face.

"Greg?" I called.

He whirled around and waved when he saw me, beaming.

"What are you doing?" I asked. "You don't smoke."

"Ava!" he shouted over the noise. "Stay there! I need to speak to you!"

I shook myself, baffled. What did he need to talk about? He pushed his way through the crowd and up to the metal barrier that separated us.

"What are you doing in the smoking area?" I asked him again. It was so unlike him—he'd tried to get me to quit the habit throughout our entire relationship.

"I can explain that later," he dismissed with a wave of his hand. "Are you busy? I need to have a serious chat with you."

"No, I'm not busy. But I'd rather not shout through *this*." The barrier clanged as I gave it a little shake.

He nodded in agreement. "Give me five minutes. I'll meet you by the entrance."

I waited, fully expecting him to bail, but to my amazement, he came stumbling out of the club to join me.

"Let's walk," he said, wrapping his coat around himself and heading off.

We walked for about five minutes in silence. I kept my head down, my hands in my pockets, though I noted he was having difficulty walking in a straight line, just as I was.

"So, what is this all about?" I prompted, growing impatient.

After a deep breath, Greg said, "I wondered if you would consider coming back to the society."

I rolled my eyes. "Sorry. I can't. Not until the end of the month."

"Come on, Ava. I know I hurt you, and I'm sorry."

"I *can't*. I need some more time. But you're right about one thing. You hurt me. I don't think I can forgive that."

"I'm not asking for forgiveness." He halted, seizing me by the arm, but I swatted his hand away, fed up with being handled by men who thought they owned me.

"Watch the threads," I said, wiping the spot he'd grabbed, like I was brushing away dirt, but Greg ignored my comment.

"I'm asking you to return because I know the society means the world to you. I bullied you away, and that was wrong of me, and I'm sorry."

I raised an eyebrow at him, snorting with mocking laughter. "Sure you are."

"I mean it. I really do. Don't get me wrong, I still stand by my decision to breakup. But I still care about you, even if you were clingy during the relationship."

"Gee. Thanks."

"Come on Ava, you know you were. You called me at all hours of the night, convinced I was sleeping around."

"Yeah, but—"

"Or the time you called every ten minutes while my sister was in labour?"

"Yeah, but—"

"Or the time you texted me saying you were going to kill yourself if I didn't immediately come and find you?"

I swallowed. I remembered that night vividly; finding the photograph of my grandma, the comfort of a bottle of vodka, neat. The loneliness. The stupidity. It was no excuse...

"I'm twenty-one years old, Ava," Greg said, eyes pleading with me to see things from his perspective. "It was too much, and I handled it badly, and for that I'm sorry. I never meant to drive you away from your society. I was just scared. The truth is, I was in that smoking area looking for you. It's been eating me up inside."

"You really want me to come back *that* much? It's only a couple of weeks."

"Yes. I think after the burglary ordeal you need your friends around you right now. And I don't want you to isolate yourself because of me."

I licked my lips, thinking. I'd told no one of those instances with Greg, and I knew why: shame. But then, the image of his smug smile as he sat across the table from me burned into my mind.

"How about we discuss this properly over a cuppa?" I said.

NINETEEN

G reg had rearranged his bedroom furniture, so despite the hours
I'd spent there, it felt like I was stepping into a parallel world.
The only sign that we'd been friends was a group photograph of the
theatre society he'd pinned to his corkboard. My cheerful face looked
back at me, full of life and hope. Perhaps a trick of the light, my skin
looked peachier and cheeks fuller. I scanned the corkboard, admiring
the doodles, flyers, and photos of his friends; some from the society,
others from his course, or from home. I smiled at one of him holding
a fat, little baby, his sister beside him, beaming with pride.

"One sugar?" Greg poked his head around the door frame.

"Two please." At least he remembered I took sugar at all.

Greg ducked into the kitchen while I dumped my bag on the office
chair sitting out of place in the centre of the room, then wheeled it
under his desk. Best to keep it to hand, but out of sight. I picked up
a pair of socks and crumpled jeans from the floor and dumped them
into a pile of dirty clothes at the foot of his bed. Old habits die hard.

"What are you doing?"

I whirled around. Greg stood in the doorway, a mug in each hand.

"Just tidying up. You haven't changed at all."

"You have." He handed me the mug of tea before seating himself
on his bed and patting the space beside him, indicating for me to sit.

I perched next to him, recognising the navy-blue bedsheets his mum had bought him.

"I guess I have. A lot has happened recently."

"Would you like to talk about it?" He blinked at me, sincerity etched on his face, an expression I'd forgotten he was capable of.

"I'm just focusing on my studies. It's my last year, after all."

I sipped my tea. It was still too hot, but I persevered, giving myself the excuse to drop the subject. Greg set his own mug down without trying it and watched me, waiting. I avoided making eye contact, but his eyes burned into me.

"I know you're keeping something from me. After all we've been through, I'm not surprised you want to keep secrets. But if you need someone to talk to, I am here."

I squinted at him over the rim of my mug. *If only you'd showed me this kindness a fortnight ago. Perhaps I'd never have danced with Austin...* "A lot has changed for me. It's put things into perspective."

"I bumped into your housemate, Charlie, yesterday. He said you've still not gone back to your house."

My insides fizzed. "It didn't feel safe. I'll go back when I'm ready."

"Would you like to stay here tonight?"

"Cheers. I can kip on the sofa."

"You don't have to sleep on the sofa." His blue eyes lit up, shining with warmth.

I laughed through my nose. Once, I'd longed for him to look at me this way. Now it left me deflated.

He lay back on his bed, an arm spread out, inviting me to join him.

"You're drunk," I said, raising an eyebrow.

"We can just cuddle."

I bit my lip. "Alright, but no funny business. Just sleeping."

I set my mug down and lay beside him. He wrapped his arm around me, his hand on my waist. Once this would have lit a fire inside me. Not anymore. I laid my head down upon his chest and returned the embrace, as if by holding him, I'd hold on to my humanity, too. His body was warm, yet it felt like I was holding a dead man; the ghost of boyfriends past.

I lay as still as possible, eyes wide open, terrified that I *would* fall asleep, but I needn't have worried. The adrenaline coursing through me would ensure that wouldn't happen. After one of the longest hours of my life, snores erupted from Greg, but I waited until I was confident I could untangle myself from his grip without disturbing him.

I watched him for a second, his chest slowly rising and falling with each breath, expression peaceful. I'd imagined this moment multiple times: a dark satisfaction as I drew his blood, the feeling of justice. But the reality was very different. Instead, there was just an emptiness inside my heart as I readied my equipment. I attached the tourniquet and a fat, blue vein bulged outwards. The needle hovered, ready to pierce him.

I swallowed, my thoughts consuming me. Austin's final moments flashed before my eyes. *Do it, Ava. Just do it.*

I pictured Ivan's sadistic grin as he crushed Austin—no—as he crushed *me* for not fulfilling my duty. Latisha's and Billy's crestfallen expressions. Madigan's disappointment.

Randall's words echoed in my ears. '*Becoming a vampire will be the best thing to happen to you... Even Len might change his mind...*'

I inserted the needle and connected the vial, watching as his blood pissed into the small plastic tube. It was only when a metallic flavour coated the tip of my tongue I realised I'd been chewing my lip.

I cleared my equipment away and gave the vial of blood one last examination before putting it in my bag. As silently as possible, I crept from the room, not wanting to disturb Greg's housemates, which could lead to unwanted questions. I left by the front door, closing it behind me with a soft *click*, applying minimal pressure. It wouldn't lock automatically, and the guilt that weighed on me grew heavier.

Stepping out onto the empty street, I inhaled the frosty night air, eyes closed, then sighed, clearing my mind. *Thank fuck that's over...*

"Ava," a voice whispered in my ear. I spun on the spot and found myself nose to nose with a pale, pointed face.

"Dominic!" I said, plastering a smile on my face, though my voice almost disappeared inside my throat. "How did you get there?" Though I tried to sound casual, the wicked glint in his eyes suggested he knew he'd caught me doing something I shouldn't have been.

"Didn't you hear me? Humans have such ineffective ears. I was just checking up on our newest addition to the coven." His unblinking gaze made his wide smile even creepier, reminding me of the night he had first tracked me down.

"I am doing great, thanks."

"Just harvested?" he asked.

"Yes, actually. I'm getting pretty good at it if I say so myse—"

"From a friend of yours?" His smile widened even further.

"Not a friend, no." I coerced the words out, though my mouth had gone dry. "Just someone I met tonight."

"Is that right? Well, in that case, perhaps I'll feed from them, too."

"Go ahead. You just need a mouthful. Right? That's what Madigan said."

"I'm not sure about that. I get ever so thirsty."

He grabbed me by the wrist and yanked me towards the front door, forcing my hand onto the handle. I'd almost forgotten his impossible strength. "I think it is about time you saw how a *real* vampire feeds." He closed a white hand over mine and pressed the door handle downward. The door clicked open and squeaked on its hinges as it swung open. "Not even locked. Tut tut. Students are so careless."

How does he know Greg's a student? My muscles tensed and stomach tightened, but I focused on my breathing to remain calm, knowing he would sense my fear if I let it overpower me.

"After you," he said, as he nudged me over the threshold. "Lead the way."

For a moment, I considered taking him to a different room, but he would smell the blood that had leaked during harvesting. He knew which room to go to; this was all part of his game. I opened Greg's door and found him still sleeping on his bed, blissfully unaware of what was going on.

Dominic pushed me inside and followed behind.

"You have to pity students," he said, taking in the drab surroundings. "Such high rents for such tiny rooms."

"What makes you think he is a student?"

"Well, there is this." He pointed towards the corkboard. My heart skipped a beat, thinking that he was gesturing towards the group photograph, but then noticed his long, bony finger was pressed to a flyer that read, '*Join Kinwich University's Student Union*'.

"Oh, yeah, I hadn't noticed that," I said, stifling a sigh of relief. "Well, if he is a student, he will probably have housemates. We should be quick."

"I will be, don't worry." He wet his lips, placing a hand in his pocket and withdrawing a small pocketknife, flicking it open. "Let's hope he isn't a screamer, eh? Keeping him quiet is your job."

"What?!" Before I could protest, Dominic had seized my ex-boyfriend, jerking him into a seated position.

Greg's head lolled forward and his eyes snapped open. "What the—Get off me!"

Dominic dragged him away from the bed with one hand without breaking a sweat. "Don't worry," he hissed against Greg's ear. "It will all be over soon." He flashed the blade in front of Greg's pale, clammy face.

Greg's wide eyes were glued to the knife, his lips trembling. "W-what are you going to do? Please let me go. I won't tell anyone you were here!" His eyes darted from the blade, to *me*. "Ava, I'm sorry! I didn't mean to hurt you! Stop this! Please!"

Words failed me as acid rose into my throat.

Dominic laughed, a sinister cackle that penetrated my soul. One-handed, he lifted Greg by the neck into the air, before slamming him down into the floor with a sickening crunch. I clasped my hands to my mouth, momentarily paralysed. With one last flourish of the blade, he slowly slid it a few inches into Greg's neck before clamping his mouth over the wound and drank. Greg let out a shriek that cut right through me.

My body acted on its own. I grabbed the socks I'd dumped on the pile of clothes and jammed it into his mouth. I summoned my strength, pressing his lower jaw upwards, silencing him. But his pleading, hurt eyes remained focused on mine. Tears soaked my face as I wrestled with him, keeping him quiet. Soon, the light behind his eyes started fading.

I chanced a glimpse of Dominic. I couldn't see his face. He was bent over the struggling boy, his lips sealed tightly over the wound, a disgusting gulping sound emanating low in his throat.

Greg's resistance slackened and muffled screams died down.

"That's better." Dominic tilted his head back, taking in a gasp of air, crimson blood dribbling down his chin and onto his chest. Greg was still awake, but his eyes were unfocused and breathing was shallow.

"Are you finished?" I asked, but Dominic laughed in response.

"I think not." He flashed me a horrible smile, resembling a monster more than ever. His canines were sharper, ears pointed, and white skin now shiny, leathery. His irises had turned a pearly-white, pupils two tiny pin pricks. He opened his mouth wider than was humanly possible, like a python about to swallow its prey, before clamping his jaws down onto Greg's neck once more.

No longer needing to keep Greg quiet, I stood, stepping back, wishing I could run away. Greg's eyes were glassy, but they remained on me. Betrayed.

I'm sorry. I'm sorry. I'm sorry... I repeated the words inside my head, hoping that somehow Greg would hear them. Though they'd be of no comfort.

Dominic came back up for air again. A long, red tongue snaked out of his mouth, licking his lips clean. Getting to his feet, he pulled Greg's now limp body into a standing position.

"Watch this," he said with a snigger, before letting go. Greg's corpse slumped face first, smashing into the bed frame before landing in a heap on the floor. "You look a little upset?"

I wiped my sodden face with both hands. "I... I..." My useless brain refused to function, unable to string words together.

"Never assisted in the murder of one of your friends before?" Dominic asked, the glee in his voice unmistakable.

"I didn't! I wouldn't!"

"You did. You assisted in the *murder* of your *friend,*" he repeated.

"He's not my friend," I croaked. Dominic laughed a cold, cruel cackle that cut me to my core. He suddenly sprang forward, pouncing on top of me, pinning me to the floor as he'd done with Greg. One of his burning hands on my neck.

"Do not lie to me!" His lips brushed my cheek, his foul breath filling my nostrils. "Do you think after your miraculous first harvest, Master Ivan wouldn't ask me to tail you?"

My blood turned to ice. *Ivan scolded him in front of me after I'd passed my trial. How had I forgotten?* My mouth opened and closed as I wracked my brain for some sort of explanation, but none came. "He is not my friend." My voice was barely audible, the hand on my throat restricting my airway.

"Stupid girl. Don't you remember? The night you ran away, you came knocking here. I know, because you left a nice bloody mark on their front door before dripping blood all the way home."

All I could do was stare at his monstrous face. I couldn't lie my way out of this one...

"What's wrong? Nothing to say?" His lips twisted into a smirk, getting up and pulling me to my feet with ease. "I can't wait to see how Master Ivan deals with you. Perhaps he might even let me..." His long tongue darted out of his mouth and traced from the bottom of my chin and up my face, the unmistakable scent of blood on his putrid breath. "And don't worry, I won't make it quick, like I did for your little friend here. I will take it slow, so that you can feel each drop drained from you until you are too weak to move before finishing you off. Assuming Master Ivan doesn't play with you first, of course."

TWENTY

The streets were deserted as Dominic marched me back to the showmen's yard, his burning hand at the nape of my neck. His grip pinched, his long fingernails cutting into my skin. My heart hammered against my ribs so violently that I was sure it would burst out of my chest, and my throat was so tight I could only take quick, shallow breaths. Despite the winter's frost, sweat soaked my shirt, making it stick to my back.

"Not long to go now," Dominic's cruel voice hissed in my ear as we entered the park, passing the hedgerow that had frequently become my hiding spot. "Not that it will be of any comfort to you, I suppose."

I clambered over the metal gates into the yard, praying that this would be the one occasion a policeman would spot us, mistaking us for trespassers, but no such luck. Dominic climbed after me, giving me a boot to the head as he descended, sniggering to himself. The pain hardly registered. All I could focus on was how close the campfire looked, its red, ominous glow leading me to my doom.

As we drew closer, I searched for a friendly face—Billy, Latisha, or Madigan—but found no one.

"You know which one is Master Ivan's, don't you?" Dominic asked, gripping me by the neck again and steering me toward the largest vehicle in the row of caravans. He wrapped his knuckles on the door.

The entire camper quaked as the silhouette of the giant appeared in the window.

The door swung open and Ivan's colossal frame blocked the light streaming from inside, casting his great shadow over the pair of us, followed by a huge, foul-smelling plume of smoke. He had a tape measure draped around his neck, and had his shirtsleeves rolled to his elbows, the tattoo of a figure shrouded in flames visible on his forearm.

"Dominic," he said, his voice low and soft. "That was fast. I guess she didn't need much persuasion from Randall to go out harvesting. Bring her inside."

I stumbled up the steps that led into his home, my legs having turned to jelly.

"Sit." He gestured to the sofa beside the wooden coffee table, strewn with sewing patterns and a single ash tray cradling a half-smoked cigar.

I did as I was bid. There was no point in refusing.

"So, what happened?" he asked his henchman.

"It was as you suspected," Dominic said. "She was harvesting from her friends from the university. Quite a clever idea. It might have worked if she hadn't returned to the house that she'd fled to previously."

"I knew Leonard Madigan was full of shit..." Ivan said, cracking his neck from side to side. "You may leave us now."

"But Master, I was hoping—"

"I said, leave us. Round up the coven and have them meet us at the campfire. Including that worm, Leonard Madigan."

Ivan didn't need to raise his voice, the danger in his tone was enough. Dominic bowed his head, shoulders slumping, and turned to leave.

"Oh, one last thing."

Dominic turned his face to his master, eyebrows raised expectantly, but Ivan's lips were curled in disgust.

"Leave it a couple of nights before you feed again. You look dreadful."

"Yes, Master." Even an arse-licker like Dominic couldn't hide his displeasure at having been dressed down, but still managed a nasty grin at me as he closed the door, flashing pointed canines.

"So, Ava Monroe," Ivan said, "can I get you a drink?"

"Excuse me?" I must have misheard him.

"A drink." He headed towards a cabinet and opened the double doors, revealing his stash of liquor bottles. "What would you like?"

"Uh..." I ran my fingers through my hair that I only now realised was slick with perspiration, totally perplexed. "Vodka?"

What was he up to? Poison? It was probably the best I could hope for.

He brought two tumblers, tinkling ice cubes submerged in the colourless liquid, handing one to me.

"Cheers," he said and clinked his glass against mine before I drained it in one.

Chuckling as he watched me, he seated himself at my side, the sofa squeaking in protest at his weight as he leant forward to set down his full glass and pick up his cigar. The smell from it was already making me feel sick.

"I knew it wouldn't be long until we had this discussion," he said.

"What do you mean?"

"I mean, I knew you hadn't passed your trial, and that you couldn't harvest following my rules." He chewed the end of his cigar before puffing smoke into my face. "I can instantly discern who is capable, and who isn't. You need a certain"—he rotated his hand at the wrist as he searched for the words—"*enjoyment* of the sport. I am sure you have noticed that Dominic Chase takes great pleasure from his feedings."

"A little too much pleasure, if you ask me." The words spilled out before I could stop them. My stomach clenched as I fixed my sights on his face for any signs of anger. His eyes flicked downward to my forearm, then back up to my face, smirking. The burn he'd given me, though healing, seemed to blaze, as though fresh.

"There is some truth to that," Ivan said with a chortle, enjoying my discomfort. "But even the cowardly Leonard Madigan doesn't resist the call to feed when he needs to. Had you noticed that at all during your training?"

I thought back to the occasion I'd watched Madigan harvest from the young woman by the cathedral. He didn't look as though he enjoyed it to me. But the more I thought about it—how easily he'd drawn blood, the speed of his hands as he handled the equipment—the more I doubted. Perhaps he didn't enjoy what he was doing, but he certainly didn't show signs of hating it, as I did.

"It's not your fault," Ivan said in a tone disguised as kindness. "I wouldn't have recruited you myself. And you achieved more than Austin Blaine. That's something to be proud of. He was another mistake made by Leonard Madigan, who convinced me to let him live after discovering the coven. He needs to learn that humans are, mostly, identical. Unworthy of their mortal life, let alone an immortal one."

"Humans hurt you, didn't they." It wasn't a question. It was a statement. Ivan raised a thick eyebrow at me, drawing his lips together. For a moment, I thought he was about to lose his temper, but he remained calm.

"Why would you assume that?" he asked. Just as he had spoken to Dominic, there was a danger in his tone. If I thought it would save me, I'd have dropped the subject, but I knew my fate was sealed.

"The way you speak about them. It's the same way I spoke about my ex. There is a bitterness that no matter how hard you try, you cannot hide it. You only hold a grudge this long after being hurt."

Ivan sniffed, his face contorting into a tight expression. "Humans have always hunted supernaturals—"

"No." I shifted in my seat to face him properly. If these were my last moments, I wouldn't simper and beg. I'd confront Ivan for the bully that he was. "I am not asking what humans do to supernaturals. I am asking what they did to *you*."

Ivan shifted his weight, mirroring me, and leant his face closer to mine, his tombstone-like teeth gripping his cigar.

"Ever wonder how I came to run a funfair?" he asked.

This wasn't the response I'd expected, but curiosity got the better of me and I shook my head.

"I inherited it from my master. But that was a long time ago. He led a travelling freak show and I was a main attraction. The Giant. I'm sure that's not surprising.

"We put on brilliant performances for the locals, charged very little, and on rare occasions, we'd harvest from patrons after they had drunk themselves into a stupor and passed out in their own vomit. After years of hard graft, sleepless nights, and abuse at the hands of our observers, my master made enough money to buy land for us to spend our winters. This land. The locals didn't like that; the fact we *freaks* owned land didn't sit right with them. One night, they attacked the campsite, raped our women, killed many of our performers. They found our leader, and with their combined strength, overpowered him, tied his limbs to the horses that pulled our caravans and ripped him apart. And it wasn't as swift an execution as you might imagine. After three failed attempts, they resorted to cutting away some of his flesh to make it easier."

Ivan rolled his shoulders and cracked his neck again before continuing, "I was too late to save him. The humans fled when I arrived. Still, I managed to pull the head off one. Another, I picked up and broke in half." With his sausage-like fingers and thumb, he snapped what remained of his cigar. "Those of us who survived the mob rallied together to form a new coven under my leadership. We had to leave the yard. But times were different back then, and it was easy for me to forge some papers and take my master's name, becoming the owner of this land. So, tell me, Ava Monroe, does that answer your question?"

I closed my gaping mouth as his story came to an abrupt halt, then reached out to the table, grabbed his drink and necked it. If he wanted to stop me, he could have, but he simply watched me, wearing an expression of slight amusement.

"Yes, that answers my question," I said, wiping my mouth on the back of my sleeve.

"Good. Now then, we should go." He removed the tape measure from around his neck and pulled on a jacket. "The rest of the coven will be waiting for us. I'm sure you'd like to see them again. After all, this is your last chance. The real question is the manner in which you leave us." The smile on his face now wasn't forced, but one of genuine pleasure. He grabbed me by the upper arm, yanked me to my feet, and pushed me towards the door. It was only a light tap but sent me flying so that I nearly fell to the floor before regaining my balance.

As we exited his motorhome, I took a deep breath of fresh air, in part because the smoke-filled camper had irritated my throat, but also because I knew I should make the most of it. I didn't have many breaths left to enjoy.

I took in my surroundings, as though seeing them for the first time. The black trees that encompassed the yard. The sound of gravel beneath my boots. The dark-blue, starless sky, teasing the dawn.

A crowd had gathered around the campfire. I could make out the distinct groups of witches, shifters, werewolves, and vampires. Madigan's tall silhouette was unmistakable, held on either side by Jacob and Sebastian. My stomach lurched horribly. What would they do to him?

"Why is Madigan being held like that?" I asked Ivan, but he simply laughed.

"Didn't Dominic tell you? He fed me some cock-and-bull-story about Hallows and tried to sneak into my camper. I'm not sure what sort of game he was playing, but I've grown tired of his insubordination."

My stomach dropped as my heart felt like it cracked down the middle. *He did what?!*

With another push, Ivan sent me hurtling forward as we approached the campfire. He didn't hold me as Dominic had—he didn't need to. I couldn't outrun any of them, and if I tried, it might only inspire Ivan to make my death more drawn-out and painful. The best I could do was comply and hope for a swift end.

"Coven," Ivan's deep voice echoed throughout the showmen's yard, "I'm afraid we have yet another traitor among us. Ava Monroe has been flouting our rules, endangering all of us. We all know what happens to traitors, don't we?"

Billy looked confused and hurt, his eyebrows knitted together in disbelief. Latisha was shaking her head, rapidly blinking as though trying to suppress tears, looking from me to Ivan, and back again. I looked at Madigan last, his expression worst of all. He looked *disappointed*, head bowed, eyes fixed on a spot near my feet, frowning.

"Unfortunately," Ivan continued, "on this occasion, I think it would be appropriate to punish both familiar and master." There was a sudden intake of breath from the entire coven. "Leonard Madigan, you have disobeyed me, talked back to me, let your familiars break our rules and tonight, you tried to break into my home. After witnessing your familiar's demise, I'll see to it that you are suitably punished. And as for Ava Monroe"—Ivan turned to me with the same sadistic expression he'd worn while sentencing Austin—"I think the best method of execution for you will be..." He tilted his head to one side, rubbing his chin, before muttering to himself, "Burning might attract unwanted attention. Perhaps drowning? No, too quick..."

"What about flaying?" said Dominic.

Ivan laughed, shaking his head. "A favourite of mine, but not what I'm looking for." He rubbed his chin before his eyes lit up with inspiration. "Stoning..."

My stomach flipped, my last meal creeping up my throat. I knew of stoning: buried up to the neck, unable to move, as rocks were thrown until the poor bastard—or rather, *I*—died.

"Allow me to do it," Dominic said, rubbing his hands together.

Ivan chuckled low in his throat. "*Everyone* will do it. Each and every member of this coven will have their turn." He stepped forward, towards Madigan. "Starting with *you*."

Madigan, whose eyes had remained on the floor, lifted his head, scowling at Ivan in a display of burning rage.

"I won't," he said, lips pulled back into a savage snarl.

"You will, or you'll be joining her. Or perhaps I'll kill you the same way the Hallows killed your former master. You remember that, don't you?" Ivan snapped back, his own temper bleeding through his casual facade. "The crunch of his bones. The pulp of his remains."

"You bastard!" Madigan lurched forward, still restrained, teeth bared, but Ivan just laughed, delighted at Madigan's reaction.

"Ha! Now, now, don't say something you'll regret. I'll allow your little indiscretion this time. You can dwell on it while casting the first stone that will end your familiar's life." Ivan turned on the spot, heading towards me, towering above.

"Wait!" Madigan shouted. "Ivan! I formally challenge you for leadership of the coven. A fight to the death."

"Excuse me?" Ivan asked, raising an eyebrow, clearly as dumbfounded as the rest of us. "Ha! You know that would be a death sentence for you."

"I formally challenge you," Madigan repeated.

"You can't do that," Dominic said. "Master Ivan is—"

"Actually, he can." Latisha flicked her curls, stepping forward to square up to Dominic. "A formal challenge can happen anytime, anywhere, and takes precedence over everything else."

Ivan raised his palm, and for a moment I thought he was going to strike Latisha, but clenched his fist, cracking his knuckles.

"Master?" Dominic looked at Ivan, awaiting an answer.

Ivan looked from his most loyal henchman, to me, and then to Madigan. I could almost hear the cogs in his brain whirring. Finally, he looked up at the sky, and his lips bulged outward as he ran his tongue across his teeth.

"It is nearly dawn," Ivan said, clenching his jaw. "Confine the scum to their caravan. The witches will take it in shifts to keep them from escaping. After nightfall, I shall take on Leonard Madigan's formal challenge. A fight to the death, followed by the execution of his treacherous familiar."

TWENTY-ONE

Dominic's hand was like a battering ram as he shoved me into the caravan. I collided with the bathroom door, smashing my face into its plastic handle as I tumbled to the floor.

"Keep your filthy hands off me," Madigan said from behind, his face twisted into a grimace as he slapped Dominic's hand away. He glided up the steps, and Dominic slammed the door behind him.

Madigan stood over me, one of his eyes twitching, a tight expression on his face. I looked at the floor, his judgemental stare hurting far more than the welt now forming on my cheek. "Oh, Miss Monroe..."

I chanced a look at him through my eyelashes, to see he was pinching the bridge of his nose, eyes shut, head bowed.

"I'm sorry." My lips mimed the words, but my voice had disappeared. I turned my face downward again, unable to look at him. But he pulled me to my feet by my forearm, gentler than Ivan had ever been, but strong enough that I couldn't resist.

"What did you do?" he asked, voice breaking as his perpetual frown deepened.

"I... I..." How could I possibly put into words what I had done?

I helped Dominic kill Greg. I broke the rules. I lied to you. I betrayed you...

My lower lip quivered as I clutched at my chest. "I've killed us." Saying the words out loud made my head spin. As my knees gave way, I grabbed the front of his tailcoat to stop myself from falling and he seized my arms in return. I peered up into his face. He was still frowning, but now his eyes glistened. "I've killed us!" My face contorted and a stream of tears cascaded down my cheeks. Madigan pulled me into his chest and within seconds, I'd drenched the front of his shirt.

Still supporting my weight, Madigan assisted me towards his end of the caravan and sat me down on the edge of his bed. He sat reclined, arms outstretched, inviting me to sit between his legs. I accepted, curling myself into as small a ball as possible, my shoulders shuddering with my sobs as I rested my head on his chest, held within his embrace.

"Take deep breaths," his low voice said in my ear. I complied, closing my eyes, trying to match his own steady breathing, focusing on the rise and fall of his chest. "Tell me what happened."

Though the tears still trickled down my face, I told him of how I'd harvested from Chloe and Greg, how Dominic had tracked me down, and how I'd assisted in Greg's death. His *murder*. By the end of my story, I'd stopped crying, but my heart was heavy, each dull thud aching within my ribcage.

I hid my face in my hands. "All of this is my fault. The only reason I harvested from Chloe was because she was an easier target. I'd originally been going after Greg. And then when the opportunity to harvest from him arose, I took it." I emerged from behind my hands, sitting up to face Madigan, though his arms remained locked around me. "That's how I got into this whole situation. I danced with Austin to make Greg jealous, and then had a one-night stand because I stupidly thought that getting with someone meant I was *winning* the breakup, like it was a game. I was too bitter to see that the way to win is to be happy." I looked down at my hands, feeling Madigan's pained expression bore into me. "Perhaps if I'd grasped that a bit sooner, I wouldn't have taken your rejection so badly and got us into this mess."

Madigan brushed a few stray strands of hair from my face. "I didn't want to reject you." He paused, pressed his lips together for an instant, then sighed. "I did—no—I *do* have feelings for you. That's why I tried to retrieve your blood sample tonight. To spare you from the transformation. I cared too much."

Even now, during my last hours, butterflies fluttered in my stomach at these words. "I shouldn't have asked you. I didn't mean it—my temper was doing the talking."

He took a breath, briefly looking away, steeling himself, then returned his gaze to mine. "Do not think everything is entirely your fault. Given that we have such little time left, it only seems fair that I give you an explanation.

"The night I rescued you from Dominic, it was because I knew I shared some blame for your situation. I hadn't mentored Austin as well as I should have, causing him to take drastic action. The truth is, I was afraid. Afraid of growing attached to him, only to witness his eventual execution, like every other familiar I've had while part of this wretched coven. So, I distanced myself from him." A pink tinge appeared in his pale cheeks. "In the end, I couldn't help but grow attached. But it wasn't to Austin. It was you. And it was more than mere fondness." His blush deepened. "I guess even those of us in our hundreds can still have a crush." He snorted a humourless laugh. "How childish..."

My stomach squirmed. "Oh, Madigan, I'm so sorry."

"For what?"

"You're going to die because of me."

"No. I am going to die on my own terms. I knew the risks of getting caught." The flush in his cheeks had vanished, replaced with a glare of defiance. "I told you there were two methods of escape; to retrieve the vials, or to kill Dominic. But there is a third option." He looked into my eyes to see if I'd understood. I didn't need it spelled out for me. "Supernaturals join a coven for safety, for a sense of belonging and family. What I'm a part of, right now, is enslavement, and I'm choosing freedom."

I smiled in admiration. I wasn't about to ask him to bring up his painful memories, but I knew this wasn't the first time he'd faced death. Perhaps, to him, this was another storming of No Man's Land.

"Miss Monroe, can I ask you something?" He rubbed the back of his neck, eyes now averted, but I reached out, tilting his face to look at me, brushing my thumb across his cheek.

"You can ask me anything. I've nothing to lose," I said, my voice a whisper.

"Well, given that these will be our last hours"—his breath was hot against my skin as he leant closer—"might I be so bold as to ask... to kiss you?"

My insides melted, heat radiating up through my body, to my heart. I looked deep into his grey eyes and could sense the emotions trapped behind them. His hurt. His desire.

"Yes."

I brushed his lips with mine, closing my eyes. They were as perfect as I remembered.

I breathed him in, devouring his vanilla scent, revelling in every sensation. One hand was in my hair, caressing with a tenderness I didn't think possible from a creature with such strength. The other was at my back, pulling me against his firm body. I clutched the front of his coat, like I was afraid to let go as I deepened the kiss, slipping my tongue into his mouth, tasting him. He mirrored me, his tongue sweeping against mine, the hand at my back sliding to my thigh as

I straddled him, grinding my hips into his. Even through the kiss, Madigan couldn't stifle the soft moan that escaped his lips as I felt him stiffen between his legs. An electric excitement pulsed through my body. I wanted more.

"Can I do more than just kiss you?" Madigan whispered against my mouth, his grip on my thigh tightening with need.

"Oh God, *yes*."

His hands found my hips, pulling me tight against him, rolling with each of my grinding movements. There was no mistaking the bulge in his trousers now, bigger than before. He watched my reaction, eyes wide and unblinking, as blood rushed up my neck, into my face. God, I wanted him. I wanted to *see* him. *All* of him.

He traced his hands up my back, beneath my shirt, the heat of his fingertips making my skin tingle on contact. He helped me pull my top over my head, then sat back, his eyes roaming my body, gliding his fingers over my arms, shoulders and then my stomach, setting my skin aflame, his tongue darting out to wet his lips. I shivered, my skin prickling from the way he looked at me, like he didn't know if he wanted to fuck me, or eat me. And then, where to start? He licked his lips again as his eyes settled on the soft flesh of my breasts.

I placed my hands over his, guiding him upward until they reached my bra.

He tore his gaze from my cleavage long enough to catch my eye, as though asking permission. I nodded. My body shook as he unclasped my bra and cast it aside, his eyes widening as he hungrily inspected my exposed breasts.

My surroundings fell away as in a movement too swift for my mind to follow, he seized me and lay me back on the bed, palming one breast and planting hot, wet kisses across the other. Slow at first, but then faster, more desperate, as though ravenous, and only my flesh could sustain him. My nipples stood erect, begging for attention, and like he could read my mind, his tongue flicked over one, while his fingers plucked the other. *Once.* A soft moan escaped my lips, my pussy aching with need—and he *knew* it. A vibration coursed through me as he pressed his lips to the plump flesh of my breasts again, letting out a low chuckle at how I melted at his touch.

"You're a tease," I gasped.

His lip curled. "I'm just admiring you. Your body. How it reacts to me." He rolled his thumb over a nipple as he pressed his hips against mine, his cock longing to be freed.

"I want to see you too..." I reached up to pull off his tailcoat, but he took hold of my hands and escorted them down to his hips as he straddled me. Even hidden beneath his clothes, his body was gorgeous. Lean. Firm. The front of his trousers was straining, unable to conceal his erection. My heart skipped a beat as my mouth filled with moisture, imagining what it looked like. How it would *feel.* Either at the tip of my tongue or buried within me; it didn't matter.

"Allow me." He pulled off his tailcoat, painfully slowly, before getting to work on the rest of his layers: removing his waistcoat; sliding down his braces, one at a time; unbuttoning his shirt. All the while, his eyes darted from my face, to my breasts, and back again, his expression starving with lust. He finally shrugged off his shirt, revealing the bone-white skin of his bare chest.

I brushed a hand up his stomach to his pectorals, sliding my fingers between the grooves of his modest, but toned muscles. Save for his scars and the dark hair beneath his bellybutton, his skin was silky soft, searing with heat. Begging to be touched; to be kissed; to be licked.

But before I could, he was bearing down on top of me, the warmth from his chest almost burning against the coldness of mine as he nuzzled at my neck.

"You're so beautiful," he whispered in my ear, with more emotion in his voice than I'd ever heard before.

"So are you." I wrapped a leg around his hips, drawing him closer, the bulge in his trousers pressed against my inner thigh. I dragged my nails down his back, making him shudder, before exploring lower, sweeping over the curve of his firm arse.

"You're making it difficult to take it slowly," he said, his voice a low growl, nipping at my ear.

"Then don't." I squeezed his ass, making him jump and pull back.

His eyes bored into mine as a smirk split his lips. "As you wish," he said, in a voice so low it reverberated through me.

He leant back, unfastened his belt, and slid out of his trousers, now down to his pants. I couldn't keep my eyes off the curve of his cock straining against the thin fabric. He chuckled when he caught me staring, his eyes alight with devilish mischief. Then his hands were at the front of my jeans, unfastening them and pulling them—and my knickers—off with a flourish.

I felt his eyes on my naked body. And I wanted it. I wanted him to see me. Just as much as I wanted to see him. I'd waited long enough.

I reached forward to pull his pants away, but he'd already guessed what I was about to do. His hand a speedy blur, he tapped my hand away and leant down, first trailing kisses down my neck, my collarbone, between my breasts.

Lower.

Lower.

Down my stomach. Across my hips, that bucked at his touch.

Burning hands spread my legs, squeezing my thighs as his warm breath caressed my sex.

I trembled. Waiting. Waiting. And then he parted me.

"Madigan!" I gasped as his hot tongue brushed my clit.

"Shhh. Unless you want everyone to hear," he said, looking up at me from between my legs, amusement in his voice. I clasped a hand over my mouth, biting my lip as his tongue swirled around my most sensitive spot. Slowly at first, but his pace quickened. Faster. Faster. Building to an impossible speed, his tongue did things to me I'd never experienced before. A pressure built inside me, and I bit down on my lower lip, clutching the bed sheets like they were the only thing keeping me grounded.

"M-Madigan... what are you... doing to me?" My back arched, hips bucking as the buzz intensified to such a peak that my body quivered, out of my control. My muscles contracted, wave after wave of pleasure throbbing through my pussy, and radiated through my entire body, causing me to thrash among the bedding. But Madigan's hands gripped my thighs tighter. Caught in ecstasy, time fell away.

I caught my breath, panting, as I awoke from my orgasmic hypnosis, face flushed, sweat coating my prickled skin. Madigan was smiling, and my eyes homed in on his perfect mouth.

"I want you inside me. Now." The words erupted from me, a primal growl, and before he could argue, I pulled his pants down, his erection springing forward. I eyed the length of him, as big and beautiful as I had always imagined.

"Are you sure?" he asked.

"I'm certain."

He leant down, leaning on his forearm, so that his body pressed to mine, and as he did so, I became hyperaware of how his cock slid up my thigh, then brushed against my aching pussy.

"How would you like it?" he whispered.

Hard. Fast. I don't care how you give it to me, but I need it now. I just want your cock. I need your cock.

But no. If these were, indeed, our final moments, I was going to make it last.

"Slow. But firm." I put a hand to his face, tracing my thumb over his lower lip, and said in a whisper, "I want *every* inch of you."

He smiled. "Of course." He ran his fingers through my hair, eyes locked on mine, and with a smooth movement, he entered me. I gasped, warmth penetrating through me from within as I took him, inch by inch, until I could take no more, and let out a soft moan. It didn't matter if someone heard me.

Let them hear. Let them know what we are doing.

He slid out gently, until his absence was almost devastating, before gliding in again, extracting another moan from me as I basked in pleasure. The feeling of fullness, before it was teased away... and then returned.

His pace quickened, rhythmically gliding in and out, his skin slapping on mine with each thrust. His breath became ragged through parted lips, as he too, let out a low groan beyond his control, a blush spreading across his cheeks. I could have sworn he stiffened even further.

I tilted my hips upward, allowing him deeper, until he pressed against a spot that sent a spasm through my body. I gripped his shoulders, unable to keep myself from gasping as my chest grew tight. His blush intensified as another moan escaped his lips—louder than the first. He bowed his head, planting hot, wet, frenzied kisses across my neck, like being inside me wasn't enough. He needed more. He needed *me*.

We made love until with one last thrust, he let out a long, shuddering gasp as his cock twitched deep inside me. I clung to him as tightly as he was holding me, my face buried in his neck as his body quaked with involuntary convulsions, his fevered breath burning my skin.

His grip slackened, and he pulled back to look at my face. His hair was slick with sweat, his chest rising and falling with laboured breathing.

"Sorry about that," he said, cheeks now crimson.

I took his face in my hands. "You don't need to apologise. I haven't..." I swallowed, my own face burning. "I haven't *enjoyed* myself like that before. Never."

"Really?" He raised an eyebrow, not sure if I was teasing him or not.

"Well, not with anyone else. Just on my own. How did you do that thing?"

"What thing?"

I smirked. "That thing, with your mouth."

He grinned, half-laughing, and shrugged, feigning modesty. "Vampire speed."

I giggled, brushing his wet hair from his forehead. "It was kind of you to let me go first."

I didn't think it was possible, but his smile widened. "I have manners, Miss Monroe."

He laid back, and I snuggled alongside him, resting my head on his chest, listening to his rapid heartbeat, my skin soaking in the warmth emitting from his.

"I wondered—just for a second—when you asked if you could kiss me, if you were after my soul. I thought maybe that was your plan all along. To seduce me, take my soul and then be powerful enough to kill Ivan."

"Then why did you let me?"

I turned my face to his, staring into his eyes. "Because I trust you. And besides, is losing my soul any worse than being stoned to death?"

Madigan's grip on me tightened, pulling me even closer against his body, burying his face in my hair. "Don't talk about that. Just savour this moment."

I don't know how long we laid intertwined, but it would never be long enough.

"You need to rest up before your fight," I said after a while, sitting up and stretching, though doing so pained me. I wanted to spend every second I had holding him, but if he was going to survive, he'd need every drop of his strength. "Get some sleep."

"I don't think I can."

"In that case," I said, pulling on my shirt, "we should do what all British people do in times of crisis. Cuppa tea?"

TWENTY-TWO

Madigan's tea was lukewarm, the remaining half covered in a scummy film. I tipped it down the sink. Though unlikely someone would drink it, it would be safer disposed of. I cleaned down the kitchen, chucking the tea bags that had accumulated on a dish into the bin, hiding the now empty, tiny, blue bottle with the red gem lid that I'd thrown away fifteen minutes ago without Madigan noticing.

He didn't snore, but from his slow, steady breathing, I knew he was sound asleep. Hopefully, he'd get enough rest before his fight with Ivan. He needed it, and there was little chance he'd have managed without my intervention.

I watched him sleep, taking in every detail of his relaxed, peaceful face, aware that this was likely the last chance I'd have to do so.

Brushing a strand of hair from his face, I said, "I hope this isn't goodbye, but I think it probably is. Thank you for everything." I planted one last kiss on his forehead before tearing my stinging eyes away.

I crept to the opposite end of the caravan, where I peeled back the duct tape that encircled the blind on my window. Last time I'd escaped the tape had been brittle with age, whereas this was freshly placed. Fortunately, the sleeping draught kept Madigan snoozing, even through the ripping noises as I tugged at the tape. I peered through the small gap I'd made. Only a small beam of light streamed inside, but Madigan stirred with a sudden intake of breath. I wrenched my curtain closed around my bed, praying I'd been quick enough. After a few seconds of silence, the soft sounds of Madigan's breathing emanated from him once more as he settled.

I peeked through the gap again. One of the twins had her back to me. It was 9.50 in the morning. Hopefully the witches were changing shifts every hour, though it wasn't guaranteed that Latisha's shift was next. To my dismay, it was Alex who relieved the blonde from her duty, leaving me to wait until the next changeover. It was a struggle to keep myself from clock watching, with my heart hammering inside my chest and stomach writhing.

11 a.m. came and went, and Alex remained at her post.

Shit. I guess they aren't changing hourly.

At midday, my heart leapt into my throat as Latisha approached the caravan. This was my first time seeing her during the day, a golden shimmer of sunlight shrouding her curls like a halo. Once Alex had retired to her caravan, I peeled back the remaining tape and, careful not to let the hinges squeak, opened the window.

"Latisha!" I tried to call in a whispered shout, but either she ignored me or had not heard. "Latisha!" She turned her head, jumping when she saw me leaning out the window.

"What are you doing?" she asked, her eyes widening.

"I need to speak to you." I gestured for her to come closer.

Wrinkling her brow, she scanned the showmen's yard before approaching.

"You need to be careful about letting light in there."

I dismissed her warning with a wave of my hand, getting straight to the point. "I need your help. I have an idea that might save Madigan."

"Just Madigan?"

I shrugged noncommittally; I might survive, but it wasn't exactly my idea of *saving* myself.

Latisha's eyes narrowed, tilting her head to one side, unable to hide her intrigue. "Go on."

"Am I right in thinking that Madigan has to kill Ivan himself? No one else can do it?"

"If you are thinking about killing Ivan now, before the fight, forget it. His minions guard him at all hours."

"No, that's not what I meant. I mean, *during* the fight, no one else can get involved?"

"Correct, and no one will *want* to. We're no match for Ivan, assuming we could reach him without Dominic or the other vampires killing us first." She looked at the ground, shaking her head. "Besides, if one person gets involved, then others will, too, and we wouldn't know whose side they'd choose. It would be a bloodbath."

"That's what I thought." I nodded slowly, rubbing my chin, my mind racing as thoughts tumbled over each other. "We need to handicap Ivan without anyone noticing."

"Yeah? How?"

"We'd need a shifter's help. Someone who could become something tiny, crawl onto Ivan, and give him a bite; something painful enough to distract him and give Madigan the upper hand."

Latisha studied my face, frowning, perhaps trying to work out if I'd lost my mind. I stared into her eyes, silently pleading, though the doubt on her face didn't fill me with optimism. She scrunched the curls at the back of her head, running her tongue over her upper lip.

"Get back inside and I'll try to convince Billy. He's the only one who might give this some consideration. But I wouldn't get your hopes up."

"Thank you."

"Don't thank me just yet," she said, turning to leave. "I don't think he'll help, but I'm willing to do this to give you and Len a fighting chance."

I closed the window and patted down a corner of duct tape, keeping the light out for now, but could open it again with minimal noise. Though I tried to keep myself distracted while waiting for the knock at the window, time dragged, the clock hands ticking in time with the blood rushing in my ears.

An hour passed and still nothing. I glanced through the window. Latisha stood with her back to me, completely alone.

Another half an hour passed and my palms started sweating. How long would the sleeping potion last? Would Madigan wake soon? Had Billy refused to come? Had Latisha contacted him at all? Had she even tried?

After another fifteen minutes, my stomach felt as though it was trying to push itself up my throat. Latisha's shift would be over soon. What would I do then?

My heart leapt as a soft tapping noise of long fingernails on plastic interrupted my thoughts. I opened the window to find Latisha and Billy wearing grim expressions.

"Thank you for coming," I said to Billy, opening the window.

"I'm only here to say sorry," he said, not meeting my eye. "Tish has filled me in, but I'm sorry, Ava. I like you and Len, but I can't risk my life and the lives of the shifters to help you. I'm the only venomous shifter in the coven, but my venom isn't strong enough to—"

"Stop." I held up a hand, aware of the ticking clock. "That's not what I need. I want you to steal something from Trevor's menagerie that would be suitable. Another spider, perhaps. Can you do it?"

"Ayyye," he said in a slow, drawn-out voice, eyes narrowed in confusion. "But how would that help?"

"Here's my idea: I'll escape the caravan and you'll get the creature. We'll all meet up somewhere and carry out the ritual for me to become a shifter."

"What?!" they said in unison, but before they could stop my train of thought, I continued.

"I'll attach myself to one of you and wait until nightfall. When Ivan comes to collect me and Madigan, it will appear like I've run away again. I'll wait until you get close enough to Ivan for me to crawl onto him, and when the fight begins, I'll give him a quick nip."

"Aye, right," Billy said, rolling his eyes. "And how would we explain your escape while under constant watch?"

I opened my mouth to answer, but no words came. *Shit. I hadn't thought of that.*

"The next person on watch is Cassandra, a familiar," Latisha said, running a thumb over her lower lip, squinting. "I could temporarily knock her out, no problem. We could say that Ava gave her the slip after using one of Madigan's potions—the Slumber Smoke. If we leave the bottle lying around, Ivan will draw his own conclusions."

Billy nodded slowly, still unconvinced. "And how would you stop Dominic from finding you like last time?"

"Last time he could smell me. Would he be able to smell me if I was a creepy-crawlie?"

Latisha and Billy blinked at each other for the answer, Billy's sceptical frown subsiding. "I don't think so. Shifter's blood is different to a human's—even while in human form," he said, rubbing his temple with a finger.

"If we're doing this, we need to decide fast," Latisha said. "Cassandra will be here soon to take over my shift. I'll play my part if we're committed. Ava, have you got the Slumber Smoke?"

"I'll grab it," I said, ducking back into the caravan to retrieve the bottle from my bag.

"I'll wait until she's been there a while, then knock her out." Latisha took the bottle from me, giving it a little shake, listening to the liquid sloshing inside. "I'll tap on the window once the coast is clear, then take you to the Sacred Ground. Billy, will you find the creature and meet us there?"

We both looked at Billy, awaiting his answer, putting him on the spot. He opened and closed his mouth as he internally argued with himself before answering. "Fine, I will do this for you." He shook his head, ruffling his copper hair before murmuring to himself, "Eejit... you're a bloody eejit..."

I reached out and clasped his hand. "Thank you so much. Both of you. I know you're putting your lives on the line doing this."

"You won't thank me later," Billy said, unable to hide his grumpiness. "You don't know what you are getting yourself into."

"I know the consequences of doing this," I said, swallowing the lump in my throat. "I also know the consequences if I *don't* do it. If I do nothing, Madigan will die."

"True," Billy said, cocking his head, but remaining surly. "Pity about the demons that will hound you for eternity, but you can cope with that, right?" And before he turned to leave, he momentarily shifted so that instead of his usual, kind eyes blinking at me, I was met with eight, jet-black, beady ones.

Waiting for Latisha's knock at my window—it was only twenty minutes, but felt more like an hour. That time was spent internally arguing with myself.

Billy said, 'Shifter's blood is different to a human's—even while in human form'. That means I could escape after the ritual and Dominic wouldn't be able find me. But of course, that leaves Madigan to fight Ivan... alone...

That wasn't an option, not after he'd tried to steal my blood to spare me from becoming a vampire. He was willing to face death as means of escape... and so was I.

I jumped when my thoughts were interrupted by the sound of Latisha's knuckles on the plastic windowpane. As I opened the window, Latisha jerked her head to signal the coast was clear.

I stuck my head out, looking around for any signs of movement. The only person besides Latisha was Cassandra, lying face down on the gravel floor, the blue bottle patterned with moons and stars beside her. I wanted to ask if she would be ok, but I dared not speak.

As I'd done before, I squeezed through the window. Latisha put a finger to her lips, before twitching her head again, toward the containers. We slipped through the showmen's yard in silence; the only sounds were our feet crunching on the gravel and the song of birds—a sound that I'd almost forgotten—but they sounded like screaming sirens, warning of my escape.

Latisha led me to the farthest container, identical to the rest. Catching her eye, I squinted and shrugged with raised hands, as if to ask, 'What are you doing?'

Latisha pointed to herself, then me, and finally at the container's door, telling me we were going inside. I held my breath as she unfastened the bolts and prised the door open. The door screeched, making me wince. It was pitch-black, but I didn't hesitate to dart inside, glad to be hidden from the outside world. She followed, closing the door behind her and plunging us into darkness.

I could hear her fumbling around. With a scraping sound, the smallest glimmer of light appeared, a lit match at the end of Latisha's fingers, and she set about lighting candles that littered the container. As each of the candles flickered into life, they filled the container with a soft, orange glow that didn't quite reach the shadowy corners.

"Why are we here?" I asked in a low voice, saying aloud the question I'd wanted to ask outside.

"This is the Sacred Ground. The spot were a coven's witches can perform their rituals."

"Doesn't look so sacred to me." Besides the candles and a huge wooden chest carved with intricate patterns, it appeared identical to the other containers that held the funfair's equipment.

"Yes, well, Ivan doesn't like rituals. It was hard enough getting this container. But I'll take what I can."

She waved out the flame on the match after lighting the last candle and bent down, unlocking the chest with a chunky, old-fashioned key. Inside was a vast array of materials. More candles, dried herbs, bottles containing different coloured liquids, and scrolls of parchment. I could have spent hours looking at the different objects, but the nerves that twisted my stomach dampened my curiosity; I was looking, but not really seeing. Latisha gathered the supplies she needed from the trunk before pulling more items from a bag that she'd brought with her. Whatever ritual we were about to carry out, it involved a lot of materials.

I wasn't sure how long we were there for, but neither of us spoke as she began her preparations.

The screeching of the container door broke the silence. My heart leapt, and for a moment, I was sure it was Ivan, but sighed in relief as Billy entered holding an ice bucket, an ominous scuttling sound echoing from inside.

"Are you ready, Tish?" he asked, closing the container door and stepping into the glow of the candlelight.

"I have everything I need. I'll finish setting up while you explain everything Ava needs to know."

"Have a look, Ava." He held up the bucket. I didn't want to look inside, but taking a steadying breath, I peered over the rim. Inside was a tiny, yellow scorpion. My breath hitched in my throat.

I'd never seen a scorpion in the flesh. The sight of it made my skin crawl.

"Are you alright?" Billy asked, sensing my fear.

I nodded in response, though I was anything but alright. The scorpion was about two inches long, its pincers slender like a pair of scissors, not like the broad ones I'd seen on TV. Its tail was thick, curled to one side, the stinger just visible. I counted its eight legs that clicked against the metal as it scurried around. My plan to shift into something small and creepy wasn't scary whilst conjuring my plan, but now, seeing the creature before me, the horror of what I'd signed up for hit me like a sledgehammer.

"This," Billy said, holding the bucket out towards me, "is the most venomous creature Trevor has in his collection. It's called a death-stalker."

He waited for me to take the bucket from him, but my hands remained firmly at my sides.

"Obviously it's not native to this country and would usually hibernate during the winter but given the short time it—or should I say, *you*—will be exposed to the cold, I think you'll be alright. It will probably be uncomfortable, but we have known scorpions to survive being frozen."

"Great," I said, the single word sticking in my mouth like glue.

"Though deadly, someone like Ivan will survive being stung. But it's extremely painful and will certainly give him a shock. Aim for the face if possible—somewhere sensitive—for maximum effect." Billy tried handing me the bucket again, but I still couldn't bring myself to take it. "If you're too afraid to take the scorpion, how do you plan on becoming one?" he snapped impatiently. "This isn't temporary. Once you have bonded with the scorpion, you and it are one. Forever."

I held out trembling hands, and Billy thrust the bucket into them. I couldn't take my eyes off the creature at the bottom, staring at my fate.

"Will it hurt?" I asked, knowing the answer.

"Aye," Billy said, folding his arms. "The more you transform back and forth, the more you get used to it. But the first few times are agonising." He gripped my shoulders and gave me a little shake. I prised my eyes away from the scorpion, returning Billy's gaze, his face full of a fierce determination. "But as painful as it is, once it is over, you'll adjust quickly. And if you are still afraid, ask yourself this: is it worse than stoning? Or what if Ivan changes his mind and decides flaying *is* a good idea. I've seen him do it once before. You want to know the worst part? After the poor bastard had his skin sliced and ripped away, it took him *days* to die. It was the middle of winter, and Ivan locked him away in a container, with nothing but his own flayed skin for warmth."

"Alright, I get the point!"

"Good." Billy licked his lips, then tightened his grip on me. "This was your idea, remember? You got this." He forced a smile.

"Are you two finished?" Latisha asked.

I turned to look at her. She was done setting up. I hadn't even noticed that the container was brighter now, as eight black candles encircled a white ring that Latisha had painted on the floor. Within the ring were patterns that reminded me of crop circles.

"I'm ready when you are, Ava." She gestured to me to step into the circle, seating herself on the floor in front of me beside a large, open book, so old that the pages had turned yellow.

"Take the scorpion with you," Billy said. "Tip it out and throw the bucket to me. Latisha will begin the ritual, and neither you nor the scorpion will leave the circle until it's complete. Just stay calm."

I closed my eyes, took a deep breath, and stepped into the circle. I glanced into the bucket one last time, squinting at the scorpion. For a second, I thought about dropping the bucket and running from the container. But then I thought of Madigan. Was I really that fond of him I was prepared to become a shifter? I pictured his face. The way his lip twitched when he was trying to suppress a smile, the perpetual furrow of his brow, the sadness behind his eyes. My decision was an easy one.

"Let's do it." I tipped the bucket upside down so the scorpion dropped to the floor, then threw the bucket to Billy. As soon as I had done so, Latisha spoke.

"Astra, lend me your light." She held her hands peculiarly, the tips of her thumb and forefinger pressed together, the rest of her fingers interlocked. The paint on the floor changed from white to luminous-green, and the scorpion scuttling on the floor froze.

Latisha continued, chanting words I couldn't understand, "Cono Simul, Tighin Comla, Enono, Yukta..."

Her hands were almost a blur, switching from one hand sign to the next before I could get a proper look at what they were. I shook as adrenaline pumped through me, gritting my teeth to stop them from chattering, clenching and unclenching my fists. At first I felt no different. But then, I was compelled to do the unthinkable: touch the scorpion.

I knelt down as the scorpion inched closer towards me, then glanced at Billy, who nodded in encouragement, a slight smile on his face. With one finger, I reached out, and the scorpion mirrored me, extending one of its tiny pincers. We connected.

One second of calm, before the chaos.

What started as a burning at the end of my fingertip became a tidal wave of pain that pulsed through my body, turning a gasp into a feral scream. The bones in my legs vibrated before cracking, distorting, tearing through my flesh as I crumpled beneath the weight of my upper body. I reached out to stop myself from hitting my head on the floor, but the movement only caused my arm bones to snap. I collapsed, shapeless, as my bones crushed into dust. The screams that had issued from my mouth silenced, but still rang in my ears—in my mind. I was suffocating beneath the weight of my... whatever had piled on top of my lungs. The bones shifted inside my flesh, organs slipped and slid inside me, gliding over each other, finding their new positions, or melted into nothing. I was no longer suffocating, and yet I wasn't breathing.

Bones reformed, pushing up to the surface, pulling my skin taut until I was sure it would rip. My skin hardened, itching as what felt like fine hairs sprouted over me.

A crunching noise reverberated through me, as what I believed to be my hands split down the middle, a tear that reach my mid forearms, as they morphed into pincers. What had once been my spine stretched behind me. I couldn't see what was happening; even if I'd had a neck to turn, I was totally blind as my eyes split in half, then halved again. Six more appendages burst from my sides.

A compressing sensation followed, my body becoming hotter and hotter until I was certain I was on fire.

My mind was blank, save for the silent screams that still echoed inside my head.

Then it stopped, as suddenly as it had started.

I laid still. Exhausted. Terrified. Vulnerable.

I opened my eyes, or at least, that's what I thought I'd done. Nothing but darkness. The hairs that now covered my body prickled, sensing. Was I in a cave? The walls were soft and covered in tiny holes that looked strangely familiar—like something I'd seen before, but magnified beyond recognition.

I scuttled down a tunnel, towards warmth and light. My hairs prickled again, and slowly I sensed more. My vision was terrible, but I could build a picture in my mind of my surroundings. Latisha and Billy towered above me. To call them giants was doing them a disservice. If I hadn't known who they were, I would have considered them monsters. That was when I realised, despite my scorpion body and senses, I still had my mind.

"Ava? Are you ok?" Latisha asked, her voice a vibration on the air that I could translate. I waved a hand—or rather, a pincer—to show that I'd understood. Moving my appendages felt wrong, like when I'd had too much to drink, unable to control my limbs.

Billy had been right about the cold. The temperature was unpleasant while human. Now, it was almost painful. And I longed for someone to huddle beside and sleep.

Billy knelt down. "If you want to return to your human form, wish it."

Wish it? What does he mean? Of course I want to be human!

As soon as the thought crossed my mind, the world beneath me seemed to fall away, Billy and Latisha raced toward me. Bones reformed, organs shifted, muscles knitted together. My eyes merged and the container that once seemed so dark flooded with light. Someone was screaming. It was me! I had a mouth, with teeth, and a tongue, and a voice. I was kneeling on the floor, panting, drinking in air with aching lungs. I raised my head to find Latisha giving me stiff sideways glances, while Billy had turned away from me completely.

"What's wrong?" I asked through ragged breaths. I looked down to see I was completely naked. "My clothes!"

"Over there," Latisha said, pointing to the pile of clothes I'd lost during my transformation.

I scrabbled to pick them up and cover myself.

"Don't be shy. That will happen every time you shift. You'll get used to it. Some covens don't bother with clothes at all."

"I thought it would never end," I said. I was shivering, but it had nothing to do with the cold and everything to do with my transformation.

"From our perspective, it only took a second."

"Forget all that," Billy waved his hand impatiently. "We have more pressing matters at hand." He stepped towards me, making forced eye contact before taking me by the shoulders again. "Ava, there are two important things you should know."

I nodded, staring at his lips in concentration, but my transformation back and forth dominated my mind.

"First, shifting consumes energy. Do it too frequently and you will tire out and find you can't shift again until you've rested."

I nodded again to show I understood.

"And the second—" Billy began but was interrupted by a sound that made my heart stop.

The container door screeched open.

TWENTY-THREE

I plunged back into darkness and agony as I shifted, not knowing if the screams were issuing from my mouth or inside my head.

"What the hell are you two doing?" asked the intruder, their tone dripping with a fiery rage.

"We were... We were..." Billy's voice said from high above me.

I scuttled behind his trainer, hiding from the intruder, before climbing up the back of his heel and nestling myself into the upturned cuff of his jeans. I vaguely registered that climbing vertically was not only possible, but easy.

"Billy was helping me clean up," Latisha's voice joined in.

I peered over the edge of the cuff of Billy's jeans, not that my eyesight was of much use. As my hairs prickled, I sensed the intruder was male.

"Do you think I'm stupid?" he asked, his deep voice raised, a voice I could finally translate as Trevor's. "Helping you clean up that heap of clothes, was he? Helping you clean up that paint off the floor? For fuck's sake, Tish, I'm the shifter's rep! You think I don't recognise this ritual? So come on then, where is she?"

Neither Billy nor Latisha gave an inch.

"Do you know what?" said Trevor. "Don't tell me. I don't want to know. Whatever you two—I mean, you *three*—are doing, keep me out of it. I only came looking for you because Cassandra is unconscious. You want Ivan to kill you, too, Tish?"

He ran his fingers through his thinning tuft of brown hair, the lines on his face more pronounced as he scowled at my friends. He marched towards us and seized Billy by the front of his shirt. Billy might have been bigger and stronger than Trevor, but I felt him flinch.

"Dammit Billy, I can't control what the witches do, but I'm responsible for you."

"Sorry, Trevor." Billy's voice wavered in a way I'd not heard before.

"You bloody will be. Is that the bonded animal? Over there?"

I shrank back, terrified he'd seen me.

"Aye, it's under the bucket."

It was then I sensed the upturned bucket, still within the circle, a tapping noise coming from within. Trevor strode past us, picked up the bucket, gingerly flinging the scorpion inside.

"The deathstalker? You've got to be shitting me. If you *ever* steal from me again Billy, so help me... I'll..." He growled as he searched for the words. "I'll tell Anna how old you *really* are."

"You wouldn't!"

"Don't tell me what I would or wouldn't do, you little gobshite!" Trevor's voice echoed around the container, overwhelming my senses. "You're bloody lucky I don't hand you both over to Ivan right now! And if I find Ava, don't expect me to cover for her!" And with that, he stomped outside, slamming the door behind him.

Both Billy and Latisha breathed sighs of relief.

"That was too close," Latisha said, a hand on her chest. "You alright, Billy?"

Billy said nothing, head bowed, a drop of perspiration dropping from above and splattering on the ground.

"Where is Ava?" Latisha asked, and I gave Billy a little nudge with one of my pincered hands. He looked down.

"Stay where you are for now," he said, smiling, though his eyes were frosty. "Do your best to stay alert to what is happening around you. You'll need to attach yourself to Ivan before the fight. Preferably before we reach the clearing. Give me a wave to show you have understood."

I waved a pincer, finding it easier than before, slowly gaining better control of my body. The images inside my head were becoming sharper, like I really was *seeing*.

"Until then, rest as best you can," he said. "You'll adjust to your new senses and soon won't even notice a difference between these and your human senses."

I waved again. Though exhausted, I'd struggle to rest, my mind still racing, and though I no longer felt a hammering heart inside a rib cage, I felt a surge of an adrenaline-like instinct. The instinct to protect myself. An instinct to kill.

Billy seated himself near the campfire, legs crossed below the knee so that I'd benefit from the heat radiating towards us but keeping me a safe distance. Others sat with him. One I sensed as Trevor, another as Marcus, but the rest were too far to identify. My sense of smell was stronger than my sight, so I'd worked out that they were werewolves, but nothing more than that. I had adjusted well to my new senses, and could build vivid pictures in my mind of my surroundings. It was only when I moved my limbs or tried to move my head that I was reminded of my new form, otherwise I'd have forgotten.

Billy and the others were talking. When I chose, I could easily translate the vibrations, but equally, I could ignore them. Billy had been making small talk in his usual upbeat tone. If I hadn't known the plan, I wouldn't have guessed anything was amiss.

His giant fingers reached down towards me as he pretended to adjust the cuff of his jeans, giving me a gentle prod. I peeked over the cuff. I couldn't see the caravans but heard a powerful scream from their direction. A scream I recognised as Ivan's.

"Oh, God, what now?" Marcus's small voice whined.

"I think I can probably guess," Trevor said, though so quietly the vibrations of his voice barely reached me.

"We had better check it out." Billy got to his feet, brushing himself down from the ash and dirt from the fire.

"Do we have to?" Marcus asked. "I'd rather avoid Master Ivan if he's pissed off."

"I'm afraid so. Ivan is worse to those he knows are afraid of him." Billy pulled the young man to his feet.

"Which is everyone," said Marcus.

"Stop your moaning. Just be grateful it's not *you* he's angry with. And let's try to keep it that way."

The shifters ran toward Madigan's caravan. Even when running, I could grip onto Billy's jeans easily, aware of the motion but not bothered by it, similar to driving a car with the window open.

Ivan's booming voice grew louder and louder until he came into view.

"Where is she?" he seized a smaller man roughly, knocking him to the ground.

Madigan...

My stinger twitched instinctively.

"I don't know." Madigan spat blood onto the ground, getting back to his feet and brushing himself down, resuming his usual stance, head held high. "She spiked my drink. I've not seen her since. Why don't you get your mad dog to sniff her out?" His tone might have been mistaken for normal, but there was an underlying hurt that penetrated my soul.

Dominic emerged from Madigan's caravan and I noted that though he'd resumed some of his usual appearance—his skin was no longer leathery, nor his irises white—his ears remained pointed, as were his canines, on full display as he flashed a wicked smile.

"Oh, I'll find her," he said, unable to hide his excitement.

"Not yet." Ivan cracked his neck. "She won't get far. We have important business to attend to, and the entire coven must be present. Latisha!"

She stepped forward from the group of onlookers that had gathered. "Yes, Master Ivan?"

Ivan backhanded her across the face with a sickening smack, drawing a cry from the witch as he knocked her to the ground. "It was your job to guard the caravan. I'll deal with you and your lot once this is all over."

He turned to look at his coven.

I shrank back into the fold of Billy's jeans.

"What a pathetic bunch you are." Ivan's eyes were wild, lips peeled back as he bared his teeth, his false pleasantness nothing but a distant memory. "You should think yourselves lucky that you have me protecting you, and you're about to see what happens to those who don't count their blessings." He grabbed Madigan by the back of his collar and shoved him forward. "Walk, scum."

Ivan barged past the onlookers too quickly for me to crawl forward and attach myself to him. Both he and Madigan led the crowd towards the woodland. Billy quickened his pace to get closer, but another kept getting in his way—Dominic.

"Back off, William," Dominic said. "Trying to get near the front? Want a good look, do you?"

"Wind your neck in, pal," Billy snarled in response. "I've done nothing wrong. What's your problem?" He came to an abrupt halt as Dominic blocked his path.

"Know your fucking place, ratbag. Vampires near the front, vermin at the back. Got it?"

Unable to get to Ivan, attaching to Dominic was my best chance. I made a break for it. As fast as my eight legs would carry me, I scuttled out of the fold in Billy's jeans and bolted towards Dominic.

"Aye, sir," Billy said with a one-fingered salute. Though I could only hear him through the vibrations, I could still sense his sarcasm.

"Lose the attitude, or I'll see that Ivan culls you from the ranks next." Dominic's last taunt bought me enough time to crawl up onto his boot. I clung to the back, hoping he wouldn't notice me. I'd a tougher time gripping onto leather but clasped onto a strap as best I could. Dominic turned and hurried to re-join his master.

"Are the preparations complete?" Ivan asked him.

"Jacob and Sebastian headed to the woodland about an hour ago. They should have finished by now if they value their lives." Dominic bounced alongside his master to keep up with the giant's long strides.

"Perfect."

"It's the little touches that make these events so exciting. Randall is collecting the stragglers. We don't want anyone to miss such a spectacle!"

Once again, I felt my singer twitching. It would've been easy to crawl up the leg of Dominic's trousers and find a sensitive spot. Perhaps the back of the knee? Perhaps higher... The image of him

draining the blood—*the life*—from Greg flashed before me and my
stinger raised in an arc behind me. The bastard deserved it. I'd have
him writhing in pain. Maybe he'd even die. The scrawny bag of bones
couldn't be that resistant to my venom, could he? A small drop of
venom oozed from the tip of my barb.

No.

I composed myself. Dominic might deserve a good sting, but my
venom took time to replenish. Better save it for when I needed it.
Besides, I didn't want to be detected and stomped on before I'd completed my task.

Instead, I turned my thoughts to Madigan. He must have thought
I'd abandoned him and fled. A shiver ran through my body.

I hope you can forgive me one day...

We reached the clearing in the woodland, and something immediately overwhelmed me with a powerful, chemical stench. It was
emitting from the centre of the clearing, so strong but I couldn't
identify it. If I'd been human, I was sure my eyes would have watered.
My every instinct told me to let go of Dominic and run, but I pushed
these thoughts aside and held on tighter. Madigan and Ivan went on
ahead, while Dominic turned.

"You maggots stay back," he commanded the coven. "Enjoy the
show."

He then walked on, following his master. The darkness didn't hin-
der my senses. As we grew closer to the centre of the clearing, I sensed
Jacob and Sebastian.

The ground differed from when I'd last been here. Once where
there'd been only grass and mud, was a vast ring dug into the ground
filled with branches, issuing the potent aroma.

"After you," Ivan gestured for Madigan to enter the ring.

Madigan took one last glance towards the coven, like he was looking for someone. With a sigh, he returned his sights to Ivan, his eyes cold, a muscle working in his jaw. He removed his tailcoat, tossed it aside, and entered the ring. As lanky as his legs were, he had to hitch his knees up over the tangle of branches. Ivan followed, stepping over them easily. Those same branches towered above me, a forest in their own right. I hadn't been able to attach myself to Ivan and now they'd entered the ring, Dominic wouldn't get any closer. I'd have to run for it.

I let go of Dominic's boot and dropped into the grass, scuttling as fast as possible towards Ivan. In reality, I was close, only a few feet's distance, but in my tiny form, the fighters appeared miles away.

"Ah, Randall, you caught us up. Is everyone accounted for?" asked Dominic.

"Everyone is here." Randall's nasally whine came from somewhere within the crowd.

"Good." Dominic cleared his throat. "We have gathered to witness the formal challenge between Ivan Terrell and Leonard Madigan for leadership of the coven."

The glee in Dominic's voice made my stinger spasm, but I pressed on, pushing past the blades of grass, using my pincers to force them aside and let my eight legs carry me closer.

"The challenge: a fight to the death. Ivan, do you accept Leonard's challenge?"

"Yes." Ivan's booming voice echoed around the clearing, the vibrations issuing from him acting like a beacon, drawing me closer. The chemical scent was almost overpowering me, but I kept going. Closer and closer. The branches were inches from me. All I had to do was navigate them and I'd be within the makeshift arena.

"Then let the challenge begin!"

I heard a scraping sound above me, followed by an orange glow, like a UFO flying through the sky. But this UFO was on a collision course, crashing down to Earth. I watched helplessly as it flew down towards me. Had I been discovered? Was this Dominic's way of disposing of me? I realised with horror that it was a lit match, and at last, identified the chemical scent. *Petrol...*

CRASH!

The light collided with the branches, erupting into a towering wall of flames that caused me to scurry back as the intense heat washed over me. I was sure it had hit me, certain that my body was aflame. I took cover in the grass, examining myself. I had not caught fire, but the flames still irritated my skin, making it tight and itchy.

The fighters were illuminated by the flames that encircled them, whilst I was trapped on the other side, unable to reach them.

TWENTY-FOUR

The wall of fire blocked every path through the twisting forest of branches. I scurried from left to right, searching for an opening, but found nothing, until I discovered the narrowest of gaps between the branches and the trench they burned in. I pressed myself to the dirt, flattening my tail, then inched forward. About to squeeze myself into the opening, the small hairs that covered my body singed, sending scorching pulses through me, blinding me with an all-consuming agony. I darted back into the blades of grass for cover, though they, too, were now blackened and smoking.

The burns to my hair impaired my senses, but with all the focus I could muster, I watched the fighters.

Madigan moved like a dragonfly darting through the air, evading Ivan's lunges before jabbing at the giant. But Ivan took the pummels without even flinching, a fortress within a storm. They played the game of cat and mouse, Madigan a blur as he eluded Ivan's swinging fists, until the behemoth caught his retaliating strike and wrenched him in close. Ivan seized him by the back of his hair and drove him, face first, into the ground.

Madigan was no longer visible beyond the flames, but I heard him grunt as Ivan's hammer fist plummeted. Again. And again.

A white-hot rage that burned more brightly than the circle of flames engulfed me, my stinger involuntarily curving into an arc, ready to strike. I *had* to reach them, and there was only one way: to become human. The pain was a mere inconvenience as I burst free of the scorpion's restraints, hurtling upward as the chaos before me became crisp and clear, my screams a battle cry.

I was kneeling, lungs filled with smoke, too close to the ring of fire. I scrambled back, coughing, my bare skin raw as the flames licked me with a scalding tongue.

I rose to the sounds of indistinguishable voices, yelling, gasping, swearing.

"Ava! Watch out!"

I whirled on the spot. Dominic charged towards me, his eyes lit by the embers of hell and a demonic grin spread his lips. He pounced. I raised my arms, bracing for the impact, but from nowhere, a gargantuan spider bulled into him, knocking him down. They wrestled in the mud, Dominic grappling with the spider's front pair of legs as its snapping jaws oozed a clear, sticky liquid into his face.

"Get her!" Dominic's command was just audible over the commotion. Jacob and Sebastian raced towards me. It was now or never. Protecting my head with my arms and clamping my mouth shut, I propelled myself through the fire. For a second, my body was aflame, incinerated as I passed through the barrier, then hit the hard ground on the other side. My nostrils filled with the stench of burning hair. Torched, I dropped to the dirt, rolling, slapping at my head and a shower of sparks rained down.

Once I'd extinguished my head, I hauled myself to my feet, searching for Madigan, but that one second of distraction was all Ivan needed to bull rush me, sending me flying, the ground shredding the skin from my back clean away.

The back of my head smashed into the ground. The world spun sickeningly. Lights burst in front of my eyes.

A hand clenched around my neck, yanking me upward. I blinked, and through foggy vision, I made out Ivan's jeering face, his warm, stinking breath washing over my face.

"How nice of you to join us," he said through bared teeth, his eyes wide with fury, the orange glow of the fire dancing in his pupils.

He lifted me off my feet as I clawed at his hand, but my strength dwindled as he squeezed the life from me. Blood pounded in my ears as the skin on my face grew taut and lips swelled. Even my eyes threatened to burst from their sockets.

And then he dropped me.

My legs gave way as I crumpled to the ground, gasping in thin air, the darkness that shrouded my vision fading.

Ivan was kneeling, fighting with the arm now locked around his neck. Madigan's arm. Madigan's already bloodied and swollen face contorted with the strain of holding the giant in place, teeth grit, eyes screwed shut. Without thinking, I staggered to my feet and lurched forward.

Madigan opened one eye, fixing it on me, pleading with me to act. Ivan too had his gaze locked on me as he pried the weaker arm loose, a smile creeping across his face. I trembled, the only idea I had twisting my innards.

I grabbed Ivan's head and plunged my thumbs into his eyeballs. He tossed his head from side to side, growling in pain, but I gripped onto him harder. And harder. Screaming, I summoned my strength and forced my thumbs in deep, penetrating through the squishy globes with a *pop*, blood and goo erupting from his sockets. Ivan shrieked, a noise that shook me to my core. With one of his mammoth fists, he lashed out, sending me hurtling. Then, gripping onto Madigan's arm, he threw himself backward, slamming Madigan into the ground, pinning him beneath his colossal weight. A splatter of blood issued from Madigan's mouth.

Ivan stood, raising a quivering hand to his eyes, before turning his head in my direction, blind, but still sensing me. He then turned to Madigan, who lay at his feet, groggily stirring.

He's deciding who to kill first.

"Come on then, you big ugly fucker!" I called, though my voice was raspy from where Ivan had choked me. "Not so tough now, are you? Blinded by a *girl*!"

With a growl, Ivan advanced, towering above me, his face a horrifying mess as crimson dripped down his cheeks. I took what I believed to be my final breath, saying a silent prayer that I'd bought Madigan enough time to get up.

Ivan grabbed the side of my head in his monstrous hand, and before I could even utter a noise, he hurled me into the ground with a crack that echoed in my ears, something hot and wet pooling beneath the side of my face, the taste of metal and dirt coating my tongue.

Darkness.

I've died...

"*Ava!*"

Weird... That sounds like Madigan... Is he dead, too?

"Ava! Move! Now!" It was definitely Madigan's voice. I prised my eyes open. Madigan was still on the ground, propped on his elbows, his face just recognisable. "MOVE!"

I rolled to one side, flopping onto my back as a fist crashed down, right where my head had been, leaving a crater in its wake. I looked up at Ivan, who drew his arm back for a second blow.

He formed a knife hand, then drove it into my stomach, penetrating through my body as a torrent of blood burst from me.

I stared, unable to register what had happened. Ivan's fist had disappeared. Buried in my navel. Inside me. Up to his wrist. I coughed, a stream of blood dousing my chest.

"I'll admit it, Ava Monroe," Ivan said, leaning down so that his lips brushed my ear, "you've got *guts*."

Ivan wrenched his hand out of me, sending my entrails splattering across the ground, glistening in the firelight.

I laid back, turning to look at Madigan. He was barely visible as the world grew dark. His blood-soaked face tracked with tears, a hand reaching out towards me. I mirrored him, only for Ivan's boot to come hurtling down onto my arm, shattering the bones. All that remained was a bloody pulp, like a squashed bug.

I failed...

"Ava..." Madigan's lips were moving, though I couldn't hear him.

Ivan's boot was now on my chest, pressing with the slightest force. My ribs bowed, creaking, about to snap. But I just looked at Madigan, determined he'd be the last person I'd see.

I wish I could have saved you... I wish I could try again...

My remaining bones disintegrated, reformed, and pushed themselves to the surface. My surroundings fell away, and I was plunged into darkness. The pain of the transformation merged with my wounds until there was nothing. I had pincers, eight legs, and a stinger, but most importantly, I was *whole*.

Ivan raised his foot. "What the...?"

He reached down, feeling for a body that was no longer there. He bowed his head, listening, smelling, but unable to detect me. Rising, he turned his head to Madigan. "Where is she?"

Madigan was kneeling, one hand pressed to his ribs, blood soaking through his white shirt, but shakily got to his feet.

"I don't know," he said, nose wrinkled into an expression of revulsion as he surveyed his former master. "And if you think I'd tell you, you're more deranged than Dominic."

That was all the time I needed. I pounced, attaching myself to Ivan's boot with my hook-like feet, and charged, climbing up his leg.

Ivan strode up to Madigan, grabbing him by the collar and drew him in close. Madigan bit back a snarl of pain as Ivan jerked him about, and now I sensed that one of his ribs was protruding through a rip in his shirt.

I scrambled up Ivan's torso.

"I said, where the fuck is she, Leonard!" Ivan shook the smaller man, whose composure finally slipped as he roared in agony.

"Go... fuck... yourself..." Madigan spat blood into Ivan's face.

I was on Ivan's neck, and at last, he felt my presence. He released Madigan, and with the back of his fingers, swatted me away. I fell but clung onto the fabric of his shirt before I could drop to the ground.

A bead of sweat rolled down the giant's neck. "What's that?" Even through the vibrations of his voice, I could sense his panic.

I charged once more.

"No! Get off!" His fingernails barely scraped my back as I reached his chin. I had to act now. My stinger arched, barb struck, and connected between his upper lip and his nose, pumping venom.

He screamed. For a horrifying moment, I thought I'd fall into his gaping mouth, but he smacked me away, sending me flying into the abyss below. The fall felt like an eternity. I was certain I'd die on impact as the ground raced up to meet me...

I plopped on the ground, and with ease, scrabbled to my feet, feeling no more pain than some slight bruising.

Ivan staggered, his feet moving erratically as I dodged them, his roars of anguish overwhelming my senses, his thundering feet making

the ground quake. He'd trample me if I wasn't careful. It wasn't safe
for me to remain in this state. I wished to become human again, but
unlike the previous attempts, nothing happened.

Shit!

Ivan lumbered closer, his enormous foot inches from me. I scuttled
away, by no matter how fast I moved, the distance I put between myself
and the monster was negligible.

Ivan's foot was about to come crashing down on top of me. I *had*
to shift!

Please, let me be human! Please!

My body sluggishly responded, quivering for a microsecond before
transforming, and I found myself squatting on the floor, limbs aching,
head pounding, panting for breath.

Ivan, clutching at his ruined, tortured face, tripped over me, barely
missing the ring of fire that still raged around us. Meanwhile, Madigan
was still holding the wound to his ribs, but lumbered to my side,
standing over Ivan. Steeling himself, he released his hold on his side,
seized the monster's collar with bloody hands, and with a frenzied
outcry, dragged Ivan, head first, into the fire, pinning his writhing
body to the ground.

I clambered onto Ivan's legs, not giving him a single chance to make
an escape. Ivan screamed, sealing his fate.

I scrunched up my eyes, clinging to his legs as they grew weaker, the
scent of burning flesh making me wretch, acid blistering my throat,
and it was only now I realised hot, salty tears soaked my face. And still,
I clung on, until finally, Ivan twitched, and stopped moving. I raised
my head, squinting through the flames, bracing myself for the likes of
Dominic or Jacob to come to their master's aid.

My mouth fell open at the sight of all out carnage. Bodies lying
in pools of blood, their limbs spread out at awkward angles, bones

protruding out of gaping wounds. Screams filled the air, some shrieks of pain, others the unmistakable wails of loss. A figure ran past, blood-soaked and dirty, almost unrecognisable, her hair matted, lacerations across her face, and the usual glimmer that surrounded her had vanished. *Latisha.*

"Ivan is dead!" she said in a raised, authoritative voice over the din. "It's over! Ivan is dead!"

TWENTY-FIVE

My brain shut down as I tried to make sense of what I was seeing. The body beneath me that wasn't moving, and the half-human figures beyond the flames. They seemed far away, like I was watching through a TV screen. But the scent of burning flesh and bodily fluids anchored me in reality. My legs were as heavy as lead and unresponsive. Though my battle wounds had healed, I ached with an all-consuming exhaustion.

The surrounding flames vanished in an instant with a loud hiss, and in their place, huge plumes of smoke billowed from the trench and wafted into the sky.

Hands seized me, hauling me to my feet, but as soon as their grip eased, my legs gave way and I slumped on top of Ivan's corpse.

"Come on, you," said a gruff voice as they grabbed me a second time.

I squinted into their face through watering eyes, the smoke making it hard to identify them. Short, messy, hair and a lined, scarred face. Trevor.

"Here, cover yourself up," he said, draping his tatty, bloodstained coat over my shoulders once he was sure I could support my own weight.

"I want Madigan," I said, slurring my words. My lips, like my legs, didn't want to cooperate.

"He's being seen to."

A large, bearded man with a long ponytail helped Madigan to stand. It appeared he was having just as much difficulty getting up as I was. Trevor assisted me over the trench still hissing smoke, and into the hellscape. A combination of muck and blood seeped between my toes as I set my foot down with a squelch.

"What are you waiting for?!" screeched a voice, sending a shiver down my spine.

Filled with a burst of adrenaline, I spun, eyes peeled for Dominic. He was lying on the ground, pinned beneath Aurora, who sat on his chest, blonde bangs tangled and dripping The familiars Alex and Cassandra restrained each arm.

"Get these bitches off me!" he snarled.

"It's over, sir." Sebastian was cradling his right arm. From the way he held it, I suspected it was broken. "Ivan is dead. Leonard is coven leader now."

"It's not over!" Dominic thrashed, but Aurora and the familiars held him fast. "He cheated. Get Jacob. We can still avenge our master."

"Jacob's dead, too." Aurora said, slapping Dominic around the top of his bald head, to which Dominic responded with a growl, lips peeled back to reveal pointed canines.

Latisha approached the heap of people and shook her head. "Take him to the Sacred Ground and subdue him by whatever means necessary. We'll decide what to do with him later." She then turned her attention to Sebastian. "Can I assume you'll not put up a fight?"

"You will have no fight from me, or my familiar, if he has survived. Ivan is dead. I take orders from Leonard now."

"Very good." Latisha assisted her witches to stand whilst keeping Dominic captive. The small group led him away but came to an abrupt halt.

Aurora let out a bloodcurdling scream. "Luna!" She released Dominic and ran, dropping to her knees a few feet away.

"Grab him!" Latisha shouted as Dominic took the opportunity to make an escape. Two werewolves seized him and dragged him away, writhing in their strong hands.

"Luna..." Aurora cradled the body of a creature that made my already squirming stomach twist. Its arms were bent backwards at awkward angles, white, bloodstained feathers sprouting from them. Black, shrunken legs looked incapable of supporting the body they were attached to. Limp, mousey-brown hair framed a pointed face, its nose and lips protruding outward, more like a beak than a face, but the wide, glassy, green eyes staring at nothing were undoubtedly human.

"We look different without our glamour, don't we?" Latisha said, low enough that Aurora wouldn't hear.

"That thing... is it...?"

"Yeah, that's Luna." A single tear tracked down Latisha's face. "She won't be the only fatality. Most are wounded and many won't make it."

I cast my eyes around, looking for faces I recognised. Randall was lying in a pool of blood, his neck bent at a strange angle. No one cared. One werewolf assisted their injured companion to walk, and as he did so, stepped over Randall's body as if it were nothing more than a fallen tree branch.

A short, stocky body with wild, tangled, dark hair was lying face down nearby. Jacob. No one cared about him, either. Though, the way he lay seemed *wrong*. His back arched upward, as though he were lying on top of something. Or someone. Curled around his body was something flesh coloured, long, thick and hairy, that at first I couldn't identify, but then my stomach dropped as I worked out what it was.

"Where's Billy?" I asked Latisha, praying that she would tell me he was accounted for, probably patching up Marcus, teasing him about how useless he'd been.

"I don't know," Latisha said, grunting as she assisted another body—Hetti—to her feet. Hetti was swimming in and out of consciousness, losing blood from a gouge in her thigh. "I last saw him wrestling with Dominic, and then some other shifters got involved and I lost him."

"You take care of Hetti. I'll find Billy."

Urging myself to put one foot in front of the other, I approached Jacob's body, hoping my suspicions were wrong.

"A-Ava..." Billy coughed, blood dribbling out of a corner of his mouth.

"Billy!" I tried to roll Jacob's body off him, but the strength in my arms failed me. Instead, I sat on the sodden ground, planted my feet against Jacob's carcass, and pushed with my legs. The body rolled off of Billy, landing with a splat in the mud.

Billy smiled weakly at me. "This is why I didn't want to get involved," he said, forcing a laugh that turned into a cough. Now viewing him properly, I saw that the right side of his body remained shifted, and the spider's leg that had been curled around Jacob's corpse was, in fact, Billy's right arm. Four beady eyes blinked at me on the right side of his face, his smile lopsided, the maw of the spider dripping clear goo. I put a hand to my mouth, gasping as my eyes lowered to his torso. Someone had ripped away the left side, five distinct claw marks of their hand visible in his flesh. Blood pooled beneath him among muscle and fat.

I put a trembling hand to his wound, as though I could stop the blood flow. "Billy, you need to shift."

He took hold of my bloody hand in his. "I can't. I overdid it during my fight."

He coughed again, spraying blood.

"You can! Just once. You're going to be fine." My eyes burned, lower lip quivering as I tightened my grip on his hand.

"I can't." He shook his head, his human eye welling up to mirror mine. "I've tried. I think... I think it's over for me."

"No, Billy, you're going to be fine." The tears spilled as I brushed his copper hair from his face. His appearance might have scared me once, but instead of a half-human half-monster, I saw nothing but the broken form of my friend. "I never meant for this to happen. Least of all to you."

"Ahh, stop with all that sentimental crap. I knew what I was getting into. Better to die free than live in captivity. Aye?"

"Aye," I said, forcing a tight-lipped smile. "I will get Latisha. She can help." I was about to rise, but Billy grabbed my wrist, pulling me back down with a wince of pain.

"I'm beyond repair. But I wanted to say... I'm sorry... for teasing you..." His human eye flickered.

"Don't be stupid." The words barely escaped my lips, caught inside my throat. I pressed my forehead to his chest. "This is all my fault."

I felt his fingers on my head.

"Shhh. It's ok... just do one thing for me?"

"Anything."

"Tell Anna, I'm sorry..." His voice cracked, "And help her... with Rosie..."

"I will," I said, finally breaking as my shoulders heaved with shuddering sobs. Though I didn't fully understand his last request, I was determined to fulfil it. "I promise I will."

I wrapped an arm around him, weeping, counting each of his shallow breaths, until finally, his chest stopped moving. But I remained where I was, breathing in his familiar scent, clutching at him, until I, too, was swallowed by darkness.

My temples throbbed. I tried to open my eyes but the spinning, blurred images before me made my stomach lurch and I snapped them shut again. Noises surrounded me, but I couldn't make out what they were. The only comfort was a vanilla scent on the soft surface I lay on. Could this be a bed? The sounds that hummed in my ears began to make sense; they were words.

"... surprised you survived at all." A female's voice.

"That was not my intention." A male's. A low yet soothing voice that warmed me to my centre.

Madigan...

I tried to open my eyes again, and this time, I made out the fuzzy outline of a body lying beside me. I realised I was lying on my side, a cold pool of dribble on my pillow.

"Madigan." I raised a heavy arm to wipe away the drool on my chin. The figure beside me turned their head to face me. Gradually, my focus sharpened, and I saw Madigan's faint smile.

"Hello, Miss Monroe."

"I'm... sorry..." I said through ragged breaths.

"Don't try to talk," he said firmly, but reached out towards me, his warm fingers brushed my cheek. "Take your time. You're safe."

I moved a weighty hand out to him to return the gesture, but my depth perception was off, and brushed the empty air.

"Don't move either," said the female's voice. This time I could identify it as Latisha's. In defiance, I turned my head slightly to look up at her. She smirked, shaking her head in disapproval. For a while she and Madigan talked, and I allowed my mind to wander, simply looking at Madigan as the details of his face became crisp and my focus was near perfect.

Summoning all of my strength, I shuffled closer to him, nestling my head against his chest and closed my eyes again, listening to his heartbeat, drinking in the warmth radiating from his body.

"What happened?" I asked, bracing myself for the answers that I didn't want to hear, gripping onto Madigan tightly, as though he could protect me from the bad news. "Is Hetti... is she... alright?"

"She died," Latisha said, her voice almost breaking. "She fought valiantly. But she lost too much blood."

"What about everyone else?"

"Besides Len, Sebastian is the only surviving vampire. The moment Billy attacked Dominic, there was chaos between the vampires and shifters."

The sound of Billy's name made my eyes sting. I didn't even try to hold the tears back, I just let them flow silently.

"The vampires dominated but were overpowered when my girls and I joined. Only the werewolves held back, joining last minute." I could sense the tension in her voice, but she added, "We can hardly blame them. They swore allegiance to Ivan, after all."

"I didn't ask you to get involved," Madigan said, a distinct huffiness in his voice.

"No, but Ava did. To save you. And you were willing to give your life for your freedom. That's what I was fighting for. And Billy."

Madigan gave me a tight squeeze.

"I'm leaving you both to rest," Latisha said. "I've done what I can with my healing remedies and I'm sure you will both make a full recovery in time for the funeral tomorrow night. But you must take it easy."

She drummed her fingers on the kitchen counter, causing the four empty blood vials and two small, glass jars sitting upon it to tinkle.

"We will," Madigan assured her.

"I mean it. I know vampires have basic regeneration, but without my intervention, you probably wouldn't have survived." She pulled another vial of blood from the fridge. "Hmmm, last one..." she muttered, then handed the vial to Madigan. "Take this now, and I'll raid Ivan's stash for more. But this should be enough to replenish your strength without giving you cravings, I'd hope."

"Yes, Mother," he said, the corner of his mouth twitching before knocking back the blood and adding the empty vial to the collection on the kitchen counter. Despite his weakness, Madigan appeared to be in good spirits.

Latisha turned her attention to me. "Ava, it's going to take time for your strength to return. You've been unconscious for about twenty-four hours, but I think another night's rest will do you good. I don't want to return to find you've passed out from overexertion."

"Don't worry, there's no chance of that," I said.

Latisha tidied away the vials and jars before leaving, forcing a farewell smile as she did so.

"I thought you'd abandoned me," Madigan said once we were alone, his voice shaking, though his expression remained composed.

"I thought you'd try to stop me if I told you what I was planning."

"I probably would have. During the fight, there was a moment when..." he brushed his fingers through my hair and he frowned, his grey eyes glistening. "I thought you would die."

"Me, too. I didn't know shifters healed between their transformations."

"Reckless." Madigan shook his head, lips twitching. "Did you know you'd lose your clothes?"

"Yes," I said through gritted teeth as my face flushed with heat.

"What about your hair dye?"

"My what?"

"Your hair dye," he repeated, unable to hide his smirk now.

I touched my hair, only now registering that it had re-grown after my leap through the fire. I pulled at a tuft near the front of my head, bringing it into my line of vision.

White.

I then tugged at the sides, viewing it through my peripheral vision.

Brown.

"Uh... no... I didn't," I said, my cheeks growing redder. "Guess there's no point in re-dyeing it."

Madigan ran his fingers through it once more. "Not that it's any of my business, but I think your natural hair suits you."

I grinned.

TWENTY-SIX

The last funeral I'd attended was my grandma's. Full of strangers, people from her past I could no longer ask her about. The longer I talked to them, the worse I felt, realising there were entire parts of her life that I'd never known. This funeral was no different.

For the first time since I'd arrived, the showmen's yard gates opened, and throughout the night, people I'd never met flowed inside. A group of men and women approached, dressed in black, patterned with silver stars and symbols. They were so beautiful they had to be warlocks and witches.

"We're here to say goodbye to Luna," a warlock said, shaking me by the hand as I pointed him toward entrance to the woodland, the pyres hidden within.

"Aurora will be pleased to see you," I said, pressing my lips together into a dim smile that slipped the instant the group moved on.

After the witches, Latisha introduced me to a group of vampires who appeared friendlier than the man they were saying farewell to—Jacob. Latisha seemed to know everyone. But then, after living nearly a thousand years, it was hardly surprising.

Latisha stiffened as another figure passed through the gates. At first, I thought he must be a warlock, his skin glowing with an ethereal beauty, but as he drew closer, I quickly realised that he was another being entirely. Witches and warlocks were alluring, but he was on another level. He was as tall as Madigan, but heavily muscled, his skin a flawless, golden colour that shimmered as I looked closer. His eyes were the deepest, darkest blue, almost purple, that twinkled when he smiled, causing my heart to flutter.

"Evening's Greetings, Latisha," he said, in a breathy voice that made the witch shiver.

"Lascivious," she said with a bow of her head. My mouth fell open, remembering the name. *A demon.*

"I was most saddened to sense Luna's passing," Lascivious said, though his smooth lips spread into a pleasant smile as he traced his thumb over his square jawline to his dimpled chin. "And Hetti, too. I was hoping to make her one of my own. But alas, it wasn't meant to be."

Latisha nodded, avoiding eye contact with the demon, though I found it impossible to pry my sights away.

"And who is this delightful young lady?" he asked, turning his near-purple eyes to me. I found myself momentarily stunned, unable to speak, hypnotised.

"This is Ava."

"It's a pleasure." He took my hand, brought it to his lips and kissed my knuckles, sending a shiver through me I couldn't identify as fear or arousal. "I smell the scorpion on you, Ava. Still fresh. Don't worry, I'll be in contact with you soon. Perhaps"—he leant in close, sniffing me, making the hairs on the back of my neck stand on end—"in about a year, I'd wager. Mischievous might pay you a visit, too. And"—he smelt me again—"yes... with wrath like yours, Pernicious should also be interested." He traced a finger across my cheek. "But please, save yourself for me."

He winked, then turned his attention back to Latisha.

"I must speak with you before I leave," he said. "I have news regarding the Hallows that you'll be interested in."

He flashed me one last, dazzling smile before leaving to join the other guests.

The warmth that had been creeping up my chest turned to ice. I shuddered as a clammy sweat coated my skin. "What the fuck just happened?"

Latisha winced. "He has that effect on everyone."

But before I could question her further, the next couple of guests arrived.

She looked to be in her late twenties or early thirties and was holding a baby girl who, I guessed, was perhaps a year old, with curly, ginger hair.

"Welcome, Anna." Latisha wrapped an awkward arm around the young woman. My heart stopped.

"Thank you." Anna's eyes were bloodshot and her makeup smeared. "Is there somewhere I can clean myself up before... before..." A fresh wave of tears cut her sentence short.

"Of course." Latisha nodded toward her camper. "You and the little one can use it as you please."

"Anna?" I asked. The young lady looked at me. "Is this Rosie?" I gestured to the baby.

She nodded. My guts wrenched, the realisation of who she was crashing down on me.

I hesitated, wondering if it was the right time to relay Billy's last message. Would there ever be a *right* time? "Billy said he is sorry. He loves you both, and if you need any help, just ask." I looked at the baby, whose blank expression blinked back at me.

Anna's face crumpled, lips miming, "Thank you", before heading towards Latisha's motorhome.

I pinched the tears from my eyes. "This is so fucking shit," I hissed through my teeth. "Why didn't anyone tell me he had a baby?"

Latisha's hand was on my shoulder, squeezing. "For the same reason he kept Anna a secret: to keep her safe. But with Ivan gone, we can offer them both support."

"When Billy said I didn't know what I was getting into, I assumed he was talking about shifting. But it's all of this, isn't it?" I swept my hand. "Demons, and death, and loss, and probably worse."

"Yeah, pretty much." Latisha wrapped her arm around my shoulder, pinning me to her side. "But hey, it will be better with Len as leader, won't it? And I'll look after you, too."

I forced a weak smile as she pulled me into a hug. For a second, I was almost at peace, but it was short-lived with the next set of strangers passing through the gates.

I sat near the back during the service, unable to meet the eyes of the guests, feeling—*knowing*—that if it hadn't been for me, their loved ones would still be alive. As the new leader of the coven, Madigan gave a quick speech, welcoming the guests and thanking them for coming. Speeches from Latisha, Trevor, and Alfred followed, speaking on behalf of the supernaturals they represented. And finally, the pyres were lit.

I watched the smoke billow into the sky, hoping to make out a shadowy form of Billy ascending into the heavens, but I saw nothing.

Once it was over, the guests departed, and the coven cleared the remains. I tried to slink away, longing for isolation, and was about to climb the steps to Madigan's caravan when a warm hand on my shoulder stopped me.

"I'm afraid not, Miss Monroe."

"Busted." I turned my head to smile feebly at Madigan.

"I am holding a meeting with the representatives of the coven. I'd like you to attend."

"But I'm not a rep."

"I am well aware. But I'd like you to attend all the same. Would you be so kind as to light the campfire?"

With a mock salute, I said, "No problem."

I sat farther from the campfire than I usually would have; I'd had enough contact with fire to last a lifetime. Madigan, Latisha, Trevor, and Alfred encircled the campfire, and though Madigan requested my attendance, I felt like an intruder.

"I'd like to start proceedings with a thank you for your help," Madigan said, leaning forward, resting his elbows on his knees. "Everyone present broke the rules of our coven, but in doing so saved my life, and my familiar's, for which we are grateful."

Latisha smiled at me, and even Trevor looked a little abashed, though Alfred remained composed, arms folded, a serious expression upon his face.

"The way I see it," Madigan continued, "there are three items of business. Decide if we should remain a coven or disband? What to do with Dominic Chase? And what to do with Miss Monroe?"

"What?!" Latisha and I said in unison.

"What do you mean, '*what to do with*' me?" I asked, growing hot as I felt all eyes on me.

"I mean," Madigan said, raising a hand for calm, looking directly at me, "you're now a shifter. It would be inappropriate to remain my familiar. I couldn't guide you through your transition from shifter to witch if that became your desire. I've met demons, but I'm not as well acquainted as others. For this reason, I believe you'd be better in the service of Trevor or Latisha."

"I'll take her," Latisha cut in. "It would be my pleasure to take her as my familiar."

"Would that be agreeable to you, Miss Monroe?" Madigan asked.

I blinked at him. It was all happening so fast. I didn't know how to respond. What he said made sense, and really, I should have seen it coming. But a foolishly optimistic part of me that bubbled with childish romance had fantasised about us leaving the coven... together...

I looked down with a bitter smile and nodded, accepting reality.

"Yeah," I said. "It's agreeable. After all, Latisha is now without Hetti. And it was too cramped in that tiny caravan anyway."

"Then that's settled. You are now Latisha's familiar. Be sure to listen to her instructions."

"What are we doing with Dominic?" Trevor asked, cracking his knuckles as a vein bulged in his neck. "That sack of shite killed my people. I want his head, and will rip it off myself if you'll let me."

"He was doing what was right by his master," Alfred said with a shrug. "Strictly speaking, we should have done the same."

Latisha let out a humourless laugh. "Dominic is near enough rabid. By our own rules, he shouldn't have progressed this far. If we free him, he'll become a Brain Eater. You mark my words."

"Miss Monroe?"

"Oh, I, uh..." I hadn't expected to have my opinion asked. The image of Dominic draining blood from Greg flashed before my eyes. My muscles tensed, pulse rising, balling my hands into fists. I wanted to insist upon his execution. But then, I recalled my last conversation with Ivan, and the tightness in my muscles relaxed. I sighed.

"I hate him and I want him dead," I said, examining my hands as I uncurled my fingers. "But that's how this all started. Hatred drove Ivan to become a killer. If we become killers, too, we are no better than him."

The corner of Madigan's mouth twitched. "There is another option. I can escort him to the Vampires' Nest to be tried and judged by our people."

"The journey to the Vampires' Nest is long," said Trevor, shaking his head. "You'll be gone weeks. Maybe months. Coven leaders can't leave for that long."

"And that brings us to our last order of business," said Madigan. "Should we disband? If we remain a coven, you'll need to elect a new leader, as I will stand down as soon as we conclude this meeting."

"You can't do that!" Trevor said with a frown.

"Actually, I can. All coven leaders can resign. Many don't, as they enjoy the power trip, but I never wanted that. I simply wanted to dethrone Ivan."

"But then, who would we elect as our leader?" Latisha asked.

"I was going to nominate you, Latisha, if you would accept the position."

"Me?" She looked around at us, mouth agape, dumbfounded. "Len, you know I can't."

"You can't? For what reason?"

Latisha wrinkled her nose, her eyes flicking in my direction for the briefest of seconds, before glaring at Madigan and saying through a clenched jaw, "*You know why.*"

"Because of your history as a coven leader?" Madigan raised an eyebrow. "It is *because* of your experience that I think you would be ideal."

"*All* of my experience?"

The two stared at each other.

I had no idea what they were talking about. But as I recalled how she'd commanded the survivors after the fight and nursed us back to health, I knew she would make an excellent leader.

"Yes, all of it. All those in favour?"

Both Madigan and I raised our hands, and upon seeing us do so, Trevor raised his own. Alfred hesitated, but then sighed.

"I suppose I have no objections," he said, and he, too, raised his hand.

"Do you accept?" Madigan asked.

Latisha blinked at him, then dropped her gaze to the floor. I overheard her mutter to herself, "I suppose the timing can't be a coincidence…" She raised her head, now frowning with determination. "Very well, I accept. And you should know I spoke with Lascivious today. He's confirmed the rumours: the Hallows have returned to Kinwich. Their numbers are small, but they are recruiting, and right now we are vulnerable."

"Then what do we do?" Trevor asked, leaning forward, fixing Latisha with an intense stare.

"We must do the same; start recruiting. While Len is at the Vampires' Nest, he will inform them of the Hallows return. Right, Len?"

"Yes, ma'am," he said. "The timing couldn't be more perfect. This year they hold the election of Liege Lord or Lady of the Nest. Vampires from all over the country will flock there to cast their vote. I'm sure I can persuade several of them to return with me for aid."

"Excellent." Latisha clasped her hands together. "Alfred, is there someone you can trust to go to the Wolf's Den?"

"I can go myself—"

"No. Unlike Ivan, I've not forgotten that *some of us* are hiding from our own kind," she said with a smile, and I recalled the first time

I'd met Alfred, and his hushed conversation with Latisha. "Besides, I need you to run the funfair. It's fallen into disrepair, and only you and your pack tried to restore it. We need a source of income and blend into the human world."

Though difficult to see behind his thick beard, I was sure Alfred was giving Latisha a rare smile. "It would be an honour. I can send my mate. She is the most loyal within the pack."

"And what about me?" asked Trevor.

"You and I can recruit from within Kinwich. Shifters are easier to recruit within the human world, and we should avoid Havoc while our numbers are so dangerously low. It might be an option once the others return. But not yet."

"Sound," Trevor said with a nod, and despite his usual stern appearance, I was sure I'd picked up a trace of relief in his voice. Whatever *Havoc* was, it sounded dangerous.

"Does anyone have any questions?" Latisha looked at us. "No? Then I think that's meeting adjourned."

After giving their new leader a small nod, Trevor and Alfred made their way back to their campers, but Latisha pulled Madigan aside. "Len, how long do you need to prepare for your trip?"

"If I begin now, I would hope to be ready within a week, Mistress Latisha."

"Then go ahead. And don't bother with the formalities. Just *Latisha* will do. And one last thing. I know the Vampires' Nest holds a lot of memories for you. While I want you to take your mission of recruitment seriously, I'll understand if you do not wish to return."

For a moment, Madigan's eyes hovered over me, then returned to Latisha.

"I shall give it some thought." Madigan brushed himself down, bowed his head, and took his leave. I watched him glide to his caravan and my stomach dropped.

"The same goes for you, Ava," said Latisha. We were alone now. "With care, shifters can blend into the human world. It would be challenging, and I would recommend remaining with me until you have grown accustomed to your developing abilities. But should you wish to leave, I will not stop you."

"I could go back?" I instantly thought of Hayley, of having a phone, and even going to lectures. But then Greg's unmoving body flashed before my eyes. Then, the homeless man crumpled at the bottom of the steps. I *couldn't* go back. It hadn't been Ivan's rules that had trapped me within the supernatural world. It hadn't even been my transformation into a shifter. I had sealed my own fate.

"I'll let you know," I said.

"Of course. Take all the time you need. Until then, I have laundry for you."

I let myself into Madigan's camper. He jumped as he heard the door open, clutching something to his chest. The shoebox he'd had up on the shelf was now on the table, the dust-lined lid to one side. I saw now it contained photographs, letters, and trinkets.

"Miss Monroe!" Madigan's shoulders relaxed as he lowered his hand from his chest, returning a pendant on a silver chain to the box. "You startled me."

"Sorry. I only came here to move my stuff over to Latisha's." We both looked at my bag of belongings sat next to my bed, then back to each other. "I'll need help. Might take a couple of days."

Madigan laughed, a sound I'd miss. He rubbed the back of his neck, cheeks tinged pink as he said, "I'll miss your company. I hope you realise I wasn't trying to kick you out."

"Nah, I understand. It's the right thing to do."

An awkward silence followed as we both looked about the camper, unsure of what to say to the other.

"Will you be staying at the Vampires' Nest?" I asked, fishing for information, but tried to fool myself into believing it was just small talk.

Madigan tugged at his cuff. "I'm... I'm not sure." He seemed to be internally wrestling with himself. "There is an old friend there who believes I'm dead," he blurted out, just as I was about to give up on receiving an answer. "I've been dreaming of seeing him again for over twenty years, but now that the time has come, I find myself somewhat... nervous."

"I'm not surprised! Twenty years is a long time for someone to think you're dead. That's going to be one hell of a reunion!"

He laughed again, filling me with warmth that I'd eased his nerves, if only for a second, before he resumed tugging at his cuff, so hard now I was sure he'd rip it off.

"Miss Monroe, if I were to return to the coven... would you still be here?" His cheeks reddened.

"Yes, I'll be here."

He took a step towards me, closing the gap between us, and said in a breathy voice, "Then I will come back for you... if that is what you would like?"

"Yes!" I said too quickly, before forcing a cough as I tried to say with a casual tone, "Yes, that would be nice."

The warmth that had been ignited by his laughter now spread throughout my body. My eyes locked onto his lips, desperate to kiss them. He seemed to want it, too, as he leant in close, then whispered against my mouth, "Miss Monroe... would you... would you..." Nerves taking hold of him again, he drew back slightly, but I put a hand to his cheek.

"Go on, ask me."

"Would you like to begin a courtship?"

"Yes." I kissed him softly. "Yes."

He returned the kiss, driving fingers through my hair, pulling my body into his.

"Wait," I said, pulling back, already slightly breathless. "You're not bothered by the age gap anymore?"

He blushed. "Well, you're a supernatural now, and since you won't age anymore, I just wondered—"

"Wait. I don't age anymore?"

He made eye contact with me, though his blush remained. "My understanding is that each time you shift, your body heals itself. Including the effects of aging."

His eyes burned into me as I processed everything he'd said.

"I don't age," I said, repeating the words out loud to make sense of them.

"No."

A smile crept across my lips. "And you just asked me out?"

He laughed again. A low chuckle deep in his throat. Music to my ears. "Yes."

"So, you would be... my boyfriend?"

He traced the back of his fingers over my cheek, down to my chin, and tilted my face up to his. "I am yours."

He pressed his lips to mine once more. My insides dissolved. I closed my eyes as I returned his kiss, wrapping my arms around his neck as one of his hands slid down my back and over the curve of my ass, pulling my hips into his. A ripple of arousal pulsed through me.

"Perhaps my preparations can wait," he said. "Just for a while... my..."—he looked away, nose wrinkled as he forced the words—"my darling?"

"Oof, that was painful," I said with a dry laugh. "You don't have to do that."

"No? What would you like me to call you?"

"Ava is fine," I said, smirking as I looked up at him through my eyelashes. "Although, in the bedroom, you could call me Miss Monroe."

End of Book One

The story continues in:
Book Two of the Blood and Venom Saga: *The Vampire's Crown*

More From The Author

Want to know how Madigan joined Ivan's coven?
Get the **FREE Prequel *Out For Blood*** by signing up to my newsletter.

Book Two: *The Vampire's Crown* will soon be ready for pre order.

For updates on future instalments, and other projects, follow me on social media and sign up to my newsletter!

linktr.ee/k.e.beale

About the Author

Hello. My name is Kat, and I'm an alcoholic. (I'm joking. But not really. Now you will never know for sure.)

I live in the UK with my husband and two children. When I'm not writing, I'm looking after my kids, who inspire me (and test me) every single day. I'm also an avid reader (quelle surprise), intermediate crocheter and mediocre gamer.

Acknowledgements

Thank you to my husband, Brendan, for supporting our family while I spent my free hours locked away in another world, and thank you to my children, Freya and Stan, for sharing me with my imaginary friends.

Thank you to my alpha and beta readers, Kyf, Lyn, Charlotte, Charlie, Nicola, and Becca, for the time you spent reading my early drafts and the feedback you provided, and thank you to my editor, for helping this newbie realise her dreams.

Thank you to my sister, Charlotte, for your beautiful artwork.

Thank you to my writing bestie, Chachi, for all the wonderful support (and hours of your time) you have given me.

Thank you to my parents and in-laws for your support, and help with the kids.

And finally, a special thank you to baby Charlie. I never would have started this journey without you.